W9-CGU-762

Book

In Blacker Moments

In Blacker Moments

A KATE AND RAY FREDRICK MYSTERY

S. E. Schenkel

aka
SEATTLE

An imprint of Accord Communications Ltd.

SEATTLE, WASHINGTON

To my parents,
Raymond and Kathleen,
in whose honor I have created
Ray and Kate

In Blacker Moments

akaSEATTLE March 1994

ISBN 0-945265-43-3

akaSEATTLE

is an imprint of Accord Communications Ltd.
18002 15th Ave. NE, Suite B, Seattle WA 98155-3838
(206) 368-8157

HC 10 9 8 7 6 5 4 3 2 1

"…these flashes of light that enable us to see and understand. … Get them down on paper … It is then that little by little the cast our Lord seeks to give to our soul gradually takes shape. In blacker moments we hold on to (these) words …"
Teilhard de Chardin

One

"Want me to trim the hair in your ears?" Jim picked up a pair of tiny scissors and snipped twice at the air. He waited. The man in the chair turned from the window with its drab view of a damp summer day. He squinted at the small man beside him. "Hair in my ears?" he queried.

Jim's large, mud-brown eyes blinked nervously. An edge of tongue slithered out, darted back in. He scratched his thinly bearded cheek with one blade of his scissors. "They are getting pretty long, Ray. I just thought you might like them cut."

Ray Fredrick swiveled the chair half a circle. Leaning sideways, he examined his profile in the large polished mirror. He fingered the contours and cavities of an ear as though sight needed the confirmation of touch.

"I'm starting to sprout some there, myself," said the barber. He propelled himself between Ray and the mirror, pulled pointedly at an earlobe, and withdrew.

Ray followed the man with his gaze, his green-gray eyes beaming amusement. "No kidding," he said.

"A lot of men grow hair in their ears when they get older," offered Jim enthusiastically. "I have an eighty-year-old client who has more hair there than on his—" Jim fell silent. He fixed his eyes on the ceiling as though to consider the course of the conversation.

Abruptly, the barber dropped the scissors onto his work-table. He picked up a comb. "I'll be glad when they finish the repairs on our street," he chattered. "Business is bad enough without that obstacle course." Jim prodded the hairs at the back of Ray's head. "Do you have the day off?"

"All day."

"Do you want your usual cut?"

"What's with the twenty questions?"

"It's just that the longer cut is in style."

"Styles interest me almost as much as commercials about toilet paper." Ray swiveled the chair another short distance and studied the outline of his other ear. A sudden movement caught his eye. An image in the mirror. A green car crossing the road outside the shop. Accelerating. A scream and a great screech of tires. Then the crunch of metal and the shatter of glass.

Ray tore the striped sheeting from his neck and tossed it, toppling a can of hair spray. He sprang from the chair and collided with Jim. He grabbed the barber's arm, steadied him. "Call nine-one-one. Tell them we need medics and police ," he ordered.

Ray bolted out the door, catching just a glimpse of the green car as it disappeared down a side street. He felt the urge to give chase, yet knew he hadn't a chance. Not with his car parked behind the building. He turned and ran across the street.

A lone car stood at the curb, a blue Chevy with its left rear fender tangled and twisted like a modern sculpture. A woman lay behind the car, sprawled partly in the street and partly over the curb with her head smack against a light post. Beside the victim knelt a stout woman wearing an apron and smelling of freshly baked bread. Tears filled her eyes as she picked bits of glass from the injured woman's gray hair.

From a distance came the sound of sirens. A small crowd began to gather: a woman in a waitress's uniform and two men wearing coveralls with a service-station logo embroidered on the pocket.

"I'm a police officer. Please stay back, folks." Ray crouched, felt for and found a pulse. He eyed the gash on the left side of the victim's face. It ran from cheekbone to chin. A dribble of blood had found its way to the collar of her blouse, pooling at the side of a small silver cross.

The sirens grew louder—shrill, biting, welcome sounds.

Ray noticed a small black purse near the rear wheel of the Chevy. He reached for it. A driver's license was tucked neatly into a side pocket. He pulled it out and read the name: Theresa Loomis. Sister Theresa Loomis.

Kate Fredrick looked up as her husband entered the kitchen. "I thought you were going to get your hair cut," she said, marking the page of her book with a paper napkin.

Ray took a mug out of the cupboard, poured himself some coffee and sat opposite his wife. "Didn't you deliver Meals on Wheels with a Sister Theresa from Saint Luke's?"

"Yes. About a year ago. Why?"

"Someone just tried to run her down."

Kate studied her husband's face. "Are you serious?"

"Very serious. Happened across from the barbershop. In front of the Burns Bakery."

"Is she all right?"

"She has a broken arm and a bad cut on her face. She could have internal injuries as well, but she was at least conscious by the time the ambulance arrived at Tanglewood General."

Kate stood and untied her apron.

"Where are you going?"

"To the hospital to see Theresa."

"You won't get in. I put a guard on her door."

Kate sat back down. "Guard? Why?"

"It wasn't a simple hit-and-run, Kate. From all appearances, it was both deliberate and premeditated."

An amused smile spread across Kate's face.

"I'm not kidding."

"It wouldn't be the first time you've muddied up some sorry accident so it required the attention of a homicide detective. I swear, Ray, I think you could find intrigue in a classroom full of first graders."

"Yeah, well, I didn't need to muddy up anything in this case. That woman was deliberately run down. And probably would have been killed if it hadn't been for Carol Burns screaming the way she did.

"Maybe the driver had some kind of attack and lost control. I can't imagine anyone deliberately running down a nun. And especially not Theresa."

"Well, mark your calendar. 'Cause it happened."

"I don't understand how you can be so sure. Did you catch the man?"

"No. I do have a description of the car, though."

Again, Kate stood. "Well, regardless, Theresa's in the hospital, and I'd like to go see her. You *can* get me in, can't you?"

"I could. But I'd have to go with you, and the doctor doesn't want me to question her before tomorrow. Besides, I did have other plans for my day off."

"Yes, and one of them should be to visit your uncle. When was the last time you went to see him?"

"After the operation."

"That was a week ago." She reached for the collar of his shirt and straightened it. "You're all the family he's got," she said quietly.

Ray drank some coffee.

"Come on, we'll go see him together. Then you can distract the guard while I sneak in to see Theresa." Kate took her husband's mug and emptied it in the sink. "I'll buy you a fresh cup at Millie's."

Kate crossed to the patio door and locked it. She called to the dog, a tall Irish setter with sad eyes. "Are you ready, Thumper?" She held out a piece of rawhide shaped like a cigarillo. The dog took one end in his teeth, worked the rawhide to the side of his mouth and wagged his long red tail in anticipation.

Ray stepped ceremoniously over to the dog, struck an imaginary match, and affected a light. The dog held still for another moment, then began chomping happily on his treat.

"Do you really believe it was deliberate?" asked Kate, passing into the hall.

"I'm afraid I do." Ray followed Kate out the front door and locked it. He joined her at the bottom of a short flight of steps. "I saw the car five minutes before the fact. The engine was running, and it was parked at the curb across the street from the bakery, just out of view of the barbershop."

"Did you see the driver?"

"Just his profile. He had a newspaper propped up against the steering wheel. Reading, I thought. He couldn't have been very tall. Actually, I thought it might have been a kid, till I caught a glimpse of whiskers. Older man, too. A lot of gray."

They reached the brown Volkswagen parked in front of the house. Ray opened the door for Kate, then circled to the driver's side.

A quarter of an hour later they were waiting for the elevator in the hospital lobby.

"Do you want to visit your uncle first?" asked Kate.

"Let's check on your friend." The elevator nearest them opened. They got in, moving toward the rear as others followed, quickly filling the small space. Two men toted giant potted plants. A third man, younger, clean-shaven and visibly distraught, gripped the strings of two pink balloons with black lettering that together spelled out "HAPPINESS IS—NOT HAVING TO MAKE YOUR BED."

At the fourth floor, the Fredricks and the man with the balloons stepped off. The balloon-bearer hurried down the corridor, dragging his charges like reluctant children. He turned right, into a room.

Forever curious, Kate glanced in as she passed. The

balloons were loose, drifting along the ceiling. The young man was leaning over the bed of a male patient. The two were holding hands.

Kate hurried to catch up with Ray. She took his arm as they headed down a connecting corridor.

Seated on a straight-backed chair with his legs crossed and his head resting against the wall was a uniformed officer. He turned at the sound of footsteps, and snapped immediately to attention when he spotted Ray. He was a thin man, and looked to Kate like he should still be in high school. His holstered revolver seemed to weigh heavily on his narrow hip.

"All quiet, Will?" Ray asked, shaking hands. Will nodded. Ray introduced Kate.

Quiet voices came from inside the room.

Ray tipped his head toward the door. "Who's there?"

"A couple of nuns. They just got here."

"Are they on the list?"

"Oh, yeah." Will picked up the clipboard propped against the leg of the chair. He gave it to Ray. A time—10:55 A.M.—was penciled in after two names: Seraphina Bergin and Gabrielle Peters. Ray pulled a pen from his pocket and added Kate to the authorization list.

"Seen anybody that looks suspicious?" asked Ray.

"Not that I noticed."

"Need a break?"

"Yeah, if you don't mind." He looked up and down the hall.

"Passed one coming," said Ray, nodding toward the elevators.

Will dashed off, hiking up his holster.

Kate moved toward the door and nonchalantly leaned an ear against it. Ray chuckled. "Go on in."

Kate moved away from the door. "I will. First we visit your uncle."

When Will returned, the Fredricks found their way down to the surgical ward on the second floor. They passed the nurses' station and several patients in the halls, some pushing wheeled poles with plastic sacks and tubing that connected to their arms.

Two-twenty-eight was at the end of the corridor. On the door was a metal slot with a card and a name, *Homer P. Fredrick,* printed in black.

Ray knocked on the open door and went in, ushering Kate before him. The room was rectangular and overheated, furnished with a single bed, a bedside stand, a wall-mounted television, and several comfortable chairs. It overlooked an empty field.

Seated in the chair near the window was a broad-shouldered man with a hawk nose and bushy eyebrows. His face was heavily freckled and spotted, but pale. He looked to be in his seventies.

Kate greeted him with a kiss. "Hello, Homer," she said, her tone affectionate.

Ray placed two more chairs by the window. He shook his uncle's hand and sat down. "How are you?"

"Frustrated." Homer shrugged. He seemed to want to say more; his mouth twitched as though strained by his silence. He forced a smile in Kate's direction. "You haven't missed a year at growing lovelier."

"One day I'll believe you."

"Don't wait too long." His words turned the room suddenly very quiet. Homer quickly broke the silence. "Is Ray being good to you?"

"Ever since you chewed him out thirty years ago."

The older man's head bobbed. He gestured toward the window. "The day could use a little sunshine," he said. His hands disappeared into the pockets of his robe.

A nurse appeared at the door with a wheelchair. "It's time for your treatment, Mr. Fredrick," she announced, wheeling the chair to where Homer sat.

"Ask for sunshine and what do I get?" murmured Homer with a wink at Ray. "I won't be gone long if you can wait," he said, his eyes hopeful.

"We'll wait," answered Kate.

"It usually takes about an hour."

Kate looked at her watch. "We'll meet you here in one hour."

Homer struggled to stand with the aid of the nurse and sank heavily into the lap of the wheelchair. Ray watched the old man laboring at the simple activity. His hand juggled coins in his pocket. Suddenly, Ray's attention fixed on his uncle's right ear. It was pale and freckled and flat, and cluttered with wiry white hairs poking out in all directions.

The nurse turned the wheelchair toward the door. Kate accompanied her. She squeezed Homer's shoulder; he patted her hand, sending a sad glance back into the room, to his nephew.

They moved on, patient and nurse.

Kate returned to find Ray at the window, his back to the room. She joined him. "I don't know if I want to wait around an hour," Ray said.

For some time, Kate said nothing. She watched the play of birds in a nearby tree. Then she whispered, "Homer needs us." Kate slipped an arm around her husband's waist. "They just renovated the cafeteria. We could go have lunch."

"You want to have lunch at a hospital?" Ray reached over and began massaging the back of Kate's neck.

"Why not? Lots of real people eat lunch here."

"Real people?" Ray turned toward his wife, his melancholy ebbing.

"Real people," Kate repeated, her tone emphatic. "Can you think of anything more real than dealing with pain?"

Two

At half past eight the following morning, Chief of Detectives Ray Fredrick and his partner, Detective Trevor Steward, left the Tanglewood Police Station through the rear door and headed toward one of two unmarked vehicles parked close to the building.

Trev tossed Ray the keys. "You drive."

Ray squeezed behind the wheel and adjusted the seat for additional leg room. His companion stretched the seat belt over his substantial belly, then pulled a Mars bar from his pocket and tore open the wrapper. "Are you so damned sure of what you saw?" he asked. "Still sounds to me like the guy lost control of his car."

Ray responded with a long look.

"Okay, so you're sure."

"He had the engine running, Trev. He was waiting."

"So what did you think he was waiting for when you first saw him?"

Ray shrugged. "Somebody in the barbershop. Who knows? I really didn't give it much thought."

Trev crunched the wrapper and dropped it on the floor mat. "Too bad you didn't get the license."

"I try not to memorize license plates on my way to get a haircut. It interferes with my concentration." Ray turned onto First Street and headed south with the traffic. "At least I know they were Michigan plates."

Trev finished the candy and licked a finger. He took a second bar from the same pocket.

"Having breakfast?" asked Ray.

"Just drive." Trev took a large bite. He shot Ray a sideways glance and ran a hand over his balding pate. His shoulders rose and fell with a sigh. They were moving east on Walnut when he asked, "Hear the latest?"

"About what?"

"About the chief."

"He's retiring. Yes, I heard."

"Yeah, but did you hear who's rumored to replace him when he does?" Trev watched his friend for a response.

Ray swerved to miss a cat. A few hundred yards further on, he pulled into the parking lot of Tanglewood General.

Trev struggled out, slammed the door and stepped around to the driver's side. "You didn't hear, did you?"

"What's with the quiz? You got a rumor to spread, be my guest."

Trev shrugged. He started for the entrance. They were in the lobby, passing the discharge desk when Trev mumbled, "They say it's going to be Sitarski."

Ray stopped. "Sitarski?"

"That's what I heard."

"Well, it's bullshit. This town would be better off with an inmate from the penitentiary." They were moving again.

"It isn't official," said Trev.

"Good, because the first piece of business to cross the jerk's desk would be my resignation." Ray's pace quickened. He stepped into an empty elevator and punched the button for the fourth floor. Trev rushed through the closing door. "If you want to go up by yourself, say so. I'll wait for you in the cafeteria."

"Sorry. It just gets my goat. Sitarski. He's the worst possible choice."

"A lot of guys don't see it your way."

"They don't know what I know."

"That's a lot of years ago, Ray."

"Some issues don't age."

"Well, you have to admit he's done a good job in Records and Administration."

The elevator stopped at the second floor. No one got on. Ray jabbed the *4* button with his thumb. "Damned stupid rumors. Where'd you hear it?"

"From Foler."

"Fred?"

"And Sam. He heard it over at the Mooring night before last."

"Figures. I suppose Sitarski was there, too, handing out free beer with pretzels and promises."

"Maybe he was. Sam didn't say."

Ray held the elevator door with a hard stare. As soon as it began to open, he pushed through and marched off.

"Are you serious about this resignation crap?" asked Trev, hurrying to catch up.

"You better believe it."

"Shit, Ray, you just made Chief of Detectives."

They caught up to a male attendant carrying an armful of plastic urinals.

"Hell. Wouldn't that be the thing to have for a stakeout," said Trev. "Trip him. I'll catch one and run with it."

Ray did not reply. They turned down the next corridor.

The officer on duty at the nun's door acknowledged the detectives with a nod and returned to his book.

Ray picked up the clipboard. It showed only the three visitors from the previous day: Seraphina Bergin, Gabrielle Peters and Kate. Ray set the clipboard down and rapped on the door. He waited for a short count of two, turned the knob and entered with Trev at his heels.

The room had two cubicles with the curtain between them pulled back to the wall. Both beds were empty and identically made, except for one having two pillows and the other none.

Sister Theresa Loomis sat in a chair by the window, outlined in light from the early morning sun. The left side of her face wore a bandage the width of a ruler, and her right arm was in a cast. She was dressed in a hospital-issue gown and robe; her slippers were blue, quilted and worn.

Trev closed the door.

"Good morning, Sister," said Ray.

Theresa responded in kind. She closed the notebook on her lap and set it on the bedside stand. She had the look of someone anticipating unwelcome news.

Ray stepped forward, introducing himself and Trev and showing Theresa his identification. The two men sat.

"How's your arm?" Ray asked.

"Sore." Theresa removed her glasses and folded them. She scratched lightly along the edge of the chalk-white dressing. "Fredrick," she said, her voice quiet. "Kate's husband?"

"The same." Ray settled back. "Do you feel well enough to answer some questions?"

"I suppose so. They tell me I'm going home tomorrow."

"You were lucky."

"So it seems." She set her glasses on top of the notebook.

"You're probably wondering why we're here."

"That, and why there's a guard at my door."

"I'm sure you realize that it has to do with yesterday's incident."

She smiled, amused. "That I had deduced on my own."

"Sister, did you see your assailant?"

There was a long pause. Theresa said, "You mean the driver?"

"All right, the driver. Did you see him?"

"I saw the car."

"You didn't see the driver?"

"No. And I probably wouldn't have seen the car if Carol hadn't screamed."

Ray took out a note pad and jotted a reminder. He glanced up to find the nun looking suddenly very tired. "Do you need a nurse?" he asked.

Theresa shook her head. "I need to know why I'm being guarded," she answered.

"For your protection."

"Do you guard every victim of a hit-and-run?"

"Sister, the man who ran you down did it deliberately. It was no accident."

Theresa took several deep breaths and let them out slowly, as though breathing were a task she set herself.

Ray thought of his uncle who, just the day before, had displayed this same absence of energy. Joy exiled.

Ray asked, "Are you all right?"

Theresa made no immediate response. When she did speak, it was in a whisper. "Why do you say it was deliberate?"

"Because I saw what happened."

"You were there?"

"I was across the street at the barbershop."

"Kate never mentioned that."

"I asked her not to. Not before we talked to you."

"I see." Theresa glanced toward the adjoining cubicle. "You're sure?"

"More sure than I am about most things."

She was silent, considering something carefully. Finally she looked directly at Ray and asked, "Did you see who was driving?"

"Not well enough to make a positive identification. But I know that he had a beard, and was probably around my age."

Color drained from the nun's face.

"And he was short," said Ray.

"A short man?" repeated Theresa.

"Short enough to have trouble seeing over the dash."

"Short." The nun smiled faintly.

There was a rap at the door. Ray and Trev turned. The

officer looked in. "Okay if I take a short break?"

"If you can be back in twenty minutes."

The door closed. When Ray turned back, Theresa was on her feet. She excused herself and went into the adjoining bathroom.

Ray stood and stretched. Trev yawned and crossed his legs. Neither spoke. Ray moved around the room, pausing to glance out the window. He shifted his attention to the bedside table and edged closer. It held the usual hospital trappings: a box of tissues, a plastic pitcher of water and a tumbler with a straw. There was also the black purse Ray had recovered at the scene the day before, the nun's glasses, and the loose-leaf notebook. The notebook was a little bigger than a paperback book. It looked old and well-used, its black cloth cover faded. Ray toyed with the idea of opening it. The toilet flushed. He stepped back to the window.

Theresa shuffled back into the room.

"I hope we're not tiring you," said Trev, uncrossing his legs.

"I'm fine."

Ray marveled at the change in the woman. As though a week had passed, instead of a few minutes.

"You seem to be feeling better," he said.

"I think I am," she answered. "What do you need to know?"

"I know this might sound like a strange question, but do you have any enemies, Sister?"

"Enemies?" Theresa's brown eyes showed a touch of mischief. Her lips pouted as if she were seriously pondering the matter. "Well, Sister Gabrielle and I are not really on the closest terms. But I would rather describe our relationship as 'periodically unpleasant'."

Ray responded with his own special smile. He said, "I was thinking more of an enemy outside the convent. Unless you think Sister Gabrielle parades around town disguised as a bearded man."

Theresa laughed. "She may don disguises, Mr. Fredrick, but only the kind we all occasionally wear for our own reasons."

Theresa fixed her gaze on the stout man on Ray's right. "You look familiar. Are you from Saint Luke's?"

Trev shifted his weight. "I suppose if you go back far enough, you could say so. Clear back to the graduating class of fifty-five."

"Fifty-five. I didn't start teaching at Saint Luke's until the mid-sixties."

Ray said, "No run-ins with parishioners, Sister?"

"No run-ins with parishioners, Mr. Fredrick."

"My wife tells me you oversee the mobile meals program in the area. Any problems turn up there?"

Theresa considered the question. "I did have a little trouble. About a year ago."

"Aha. Did the problem involve a man?" Theresa nodded. "Short?"

"I don't know. We only spoke on the phone."

"What was the problem?"

"He wanted meals delivered to his mother. I visited the woman, found her fully capable of making her own meals, and refused his request. He countered with some unpleasant phone calls and a slew of interesting words, half of which, I'm sure, would have shocked me if I had the background to interpret them." A smile lit her face. "I do think I understood more of them than most in my profession would have."

"Do you recall his name?" asked Trev.

"Not offhand. I could have it for you tomorrow, if you think it's important."

"I think it's worth our attention. When do you check out?"

"Mid-morning. Certainly by noon."

"Would it be all right if I stopped by around two?"

"That would be fine. And you can meet Gabrielle."

Ray grinned. "You won't tip my hand, let her know she's a possible suspect?"

"Absolutely not. That would take the fun out of watching you tell her."

Ray edged forward in his seat. "One last question and we'll let you get some rest. Do you mind running through your activities on the day of the incident?"

"Mass. Breakfast. Dishes. I left the house about twenty to eight, dropped Sister Yavonne at the community college and headed downtown. Once a week, I try to visit a few businesses, get them involved with the meals program—donations, food, cash. Sometimes I even recruit a volunteer driver."

"Weren't you early? Most places don't open till ten."

"Yavonne's class was at eight. Besides, I just stopped at the places I knew were open."

"So you drove to the college. Any sign that you were followed?"

"No, but I wouldn't know what to look for."

"Did you notice a green Pontiac?"

"Not really."

"Was the bakery your first stop after leaving the college?"

"No. That was my third stop. My first stop was at the Shell station at the corner of Main and Seventh. I'm trying to get some free gas for our volunteer drivers. After that, I stopped at the cleaners a block down. Then the Burns Bakery."

"And we know the story from there." Ray stood, pocketing his notebook. "Joking aside, Sister, you do understand why we've posted the guard?"

"I understand why you thought it was necessary. And I appreciate your concern. Really. But I'm sure this was only a freak accident. Things are not always what they seem."

Three

Thursday morning, Kate was out of bed and in the bathroom moments after the alarm rang. Ray stayed between the sheets and worked at keeping his eyes open for longer than a few seconds. When Kate came bouncing back into the bedroom to announce that the bathroom was all his, Ray grudgingly set his bare feet on the floor and stood.

"I called Homer last night," said Kate, rummaging in the closet for clothes. "He said that you were out to see him earlier in the day."

Ray shuffled his way to the bathroom.

"I didn't know you had gone to see him." Kate turned toward the bathroom door, a short-sleeved blouse in hand.

The tap water was running.

Kate approached the open door. "I didn't know you had gone to see him," she repeated.

"Trev and I were there to question Theresa. I just passed by to say hi before leaving." Ray hooked the door with his toe and closed it.

Kate pushed it open. She smiled and said, "I'm glad," and quietly closed it again.

Kate finished dressing. She flitted here and there, setting the room right. She straightened the bedspread and mused on how there was little of her life she didn't like. She loved the sound of the shower and the morning's quiet. She loved having the house to herself when Ray left, and the bustle and whir and talk at the supper hour on his return. She even liked the few nights he worked late.

Settling on the edge of the bed, Kate decided it was almost

sinful, the pleasure she took in her life. Then she laughed out loud, both at herself and at the fickleness of emotions. *Especially* guilt, she thought, *always ready to send the heart on a trip into self-loathing for the most innocent reasons. Whether I'm late, early, thrilled, depressed, or pleased with life, guilt will rush in like a zealot with a mission.*

"Well, today I'm not buying," Kate said aloud. She switched on the clock radio, found a station playing a waltz, raised the volume and hummed her way around the bed and into the bathroom.

A heavy spray pounded the walls of the shower. Kate pulled a towel from its rack, rolled it into a ball and tossed it over the top of the shower door.

"What the hell!" The door jerked open and Ray stuck out his head. Water dripped from his nose and ears and chin. Kate tweaked his cheek and danced out. She landed at the window overlooking the backyard. A predawn blush marked the eastern horizon. On the next street over, the figure of a man flashed past and disappeared behind a house. Kate set her gaze on the next opening and recognized a neighbor in a jogging suit and baseball cap pursuing his self-appointed task as though the world depended on him. Kate cheered him on in her heart.

The music stopped and a sonorous male voice began announcing the day's tragedies. Suddenly something large and squishy struck Kate in the small of the back. She whirled around. At her feet lay a mound of wet towel.

Ray stood in the doorway of the bathroom wiping an underarm. His gray hair was tousled and damp and he had a towel tied at his waist.

Kate swooped up the wet bundle and ran past Ray into the bathroom. She plunked it into the sink and proceeded to wring it out.

Ray picked up a comb from the counter. "What was so

interesting outside?"

"Keef Wagner must be feeling better. He's out jogging."

"Good for him."

"I bet he's close to eighty."

"Guy's got guts."

"Wouldn't do you any harm, a jog now and then."

Ray bowed his head and examined himself with exaggerated earnestness. "You want to improve on this?" he asked.

Kate frowned forcefully. "You know, dear, by the time a man pushes sixty, he's supposed to have lost some of his conceit."

"Can't be worse than a woman flaunting her charms after the age of fifty. That is, if you believe Uncle Homer."

Kate laughed freely. "All right. We'll both stay the way we are. What do you want for breakfast?"

"I thought I'd eat out."

"Are you meeting Trev?"

"No. He has the day off. Dentist appointment." Ray retrieved his watch and ring from the dresser. He eyed the clock. "I want to be at the community college by eight. Which gives me five minutes to dress and be out the door." He let the towel drop and pulled on his shorts.

"What's going on at the college?" asked Kate.

"It's one of the stops Theresa made on the morning of the incident. I want to follow the route she took, at approximately the same time. Who knows? I might get lucky and find a green Pontiac with a twisted front end."

Ray yanked a pair of slacks from a hanger. "How's your car running, Kate?" he asked.

"All right. Why?"

Ray hummed as he finished dressing.

By a few minutes before eight, Ray was parked in the lot facing the main building of Tanglewood Community College. He stayed in his car and watched the rush of the mostly young as they headed for class. After several minutes, he turned his car toward the main road. He took Washington Avenue back toward town, driving slowly and staying alert to any green car that came in sight.

At eight-twenty, he parked behind the Shell station at Sixth and Main, and surveyed the area with what he hoped was the mind of the perpetrator. Too much traffic. Too many witnesses.

Ray strolled over to the station. The pumps were busy. A stout young woman sat behind a Plexiglas wall, taking cash. Ray spotted a bearded man sipping coffee in a small office at the rear. Displaying his badge, he walked toward the man. "Always this busy?" he asked.

The man eyed the shield and answered, "Up till ten. Yeah. Why?"

"Were you here yesterday?"

"All day and part of the night."

"Remember a Sister Theresa stopping by?"

He smiled. "Sure. Soaked me for ten gallons of gas." He shrugged.

"You weren't by chance outside when she left, were you?"

"Yeah. I was talking to some guy about a deal on tires."

"Did you notice a green Pontiac parked anywhere in the area?"

He shook his head. His eyes sparkled with interest. "What's going on?"

"You're sure you didn't notice a green Pontiac? The driver was bearded, short."

"Sorry."

"Mind if I question the cashier?"

"Go ahead if you want. Only, she wasn't here yesterday."

"Who was?"

"Sue Darnell."

"Can you give me an address?"

The attendant fetched a card from a small box. He scribbled on the back of an envelope and handed it to Ray.

Ray's conversation with the couple who operated the cleaners at Main and Sixth gained him little more than a glowing account of Sister Theresa's good work. He left the shop, caught sight of the restaurant across the street, and jaywalked over to it.

The place was crowded. Ray searched for a seat near the windows on the street side, found one and headed for it, grabbing a menu as he passed the register. Waiting to place his order, he kept an eye on the cleaners across the street. There was a constant turnover of customers coming and going with armloads of clothes.

Ray ordered scrambled eggs, sausage and toast. He ate quickly and left. At Main and Fifth, he followed a detour for a block, turned left at Junction Street, and returned to Main by way of a shortcut down a narrow alley.

He arrived at the Burns Bakery a few minutes shy of half-past nine, the time of his appointment at the barbershop two days earlier. Glass crunched under his feet as he stepped out of the car. Ray scanned up and down his side of the street. The building to the right of the bakery was boarded up. On the other side was a fast-food place selling pizza and ribs with the posted hours of eleven A.M. to midnight.

On the north side of the street sat the barbershop, a small, square, flat-roofed structure painted the red of fired brick. Behind it stood the old frame house where the barber lived. Between the two buildings lay a gravel parking lot. Ray could make out the rear bumpers of two cars. One he knew to be Jim's.

A large vacant lot sat to the right of the barbershop. On the other side was an abandoned playground with only a teeter-totter still intact. Some distance back stood an old building that had served as a school in the thirties and forties and part of the fifties. A factory relocation and a school district revision had left the building empty, like too much of the neighborhood around it.

The Burns Bakery was an old brick building freshly painted. Ray entered to the sound of a bell overhead. Empty pedestal tables stood along the window wall, each with a pair of chairs and a plastic cover.

Carol Burns smiled at Ray from behind a glass case that filled the opposite wall. She glanced apologetically at the long trays with their scant display of cakes and pastries. "I hope we have what you want," she chirped. A look of recognition brightened her perspiring face. "You're the officer who was here the day of the accident, aren't you?"

Ray answered her question with a smile and a nod. He stepped up to the case and took a long whiff. "I have yet to find a perfume I prefer to this," he said.

Carol beamed a number of wrinkles into nonexistence. Her full smile bared a mouthful of crooked teeth. She asked, "Have you heard how Sister's doing?"

"I talked to her yesterday. She's doing fine. In fact, she's being discharged today."

"Oh, I'm so glad." Carol scratched at her flabby upper arm. "People drive cars like they're toys or something."

"I see you have coffee," said Ray. He eyed the donuts in the case. "How about a cheese Danish and a cup of coffee for here."

Carol busied herself as though the shop were full. Ray retired to one of the tables and sat down. Carol brought over a mug of steaming coffee and a doily-lined dish with a large cheese Danish. Hovering, she asked, "Can I get you anything else?"

"I could use some company. And to be truthful, I was hoping to ask you a few questions."

Needing no encouragement, she took a seat. Through an open window came the sound of a car approaching. Carol glanced up. The car passed. "These road repairs are going to put us in the poor house," she said.

"When are they supposed to finish?"

"Days ago."

"There really isn't much traffic, is there?"

"I can count on one hand the cars that pass in an hour." Carol sighed. "In the old days, it took three bakers and six counter girls to keep up with the business. Of course it's been quieter than that for years, but not like this."

"You're not here by yourself, are you?"

"No. My husband's in the back. He does the baking. I watch the shop. At least for now."

"My compliments to the chef. The pastry's really good." Ray swallowed another bite. "I hope you realize you saved Sister Theresa's life the other day."

She blushed a color that closely matched her dyed hair.

"Really," said Ray. "I was sitting in the barber's chair and saw it all. If you hadn't shouted, well—"

"I don't know what that driver was thinking," said Carol. "At first I thought he was going to make a U-turn. Then there he was, heading straight for Sister. Everything inside me just erupted. I was so scared for her."

"Well, you made the difference between life and death. That I can say without a doubt. By the way, the driver of the car wasn't anyone you knew, was it?"

"No."

"No, because you didn't recognize him or no, because you didn't see him?"

"A little of both, I guess. I saw very little of him and he didn't seem to be anyone familiar."

"Had you seen that car before?"

"I'm not big on cars."

Ray drank some coffee. "But you did see the car before it crossed the road."

"Oh, yes. Sister Theresa had just come into the shop when it stopped on the other side of the street. I thought it was someone going in for a haircut."

"Are you sure the green car wasn't there before Theresa arrived?"

"I'm very sure."

"And how long was Theresa here?"

"Maybe fifteen minutes. We had coffee together. We always do when she drops by. She's a real comfortable person to talk to, that Sister Theresa. I just don't get it. Why would anybody want to hurt her?"

Ray gulped the last of his coffee and pushed back his chair. "That is the question, isn't it?"

Four

Standing in full sun on the sidewalk in front of the bakery, Ray eyed his watch and considered returning to the station. He stepped into the shade of a large elm. The day was turning warm. Summer in full swing. *Kate will be wanting to take off for a couple of weeks,* he mused. Then maybe she wouldn't. Not with Uncle Homer in the hospital. Uncle Homer. And that jerk, Sitarski. It was going to be a long, hard summer. Ray ran a hand through his hair. To heck with the station. Too early for lunch. And he'd just demolished a Danish that would have given Trev Steward pause. Maybe Jim would have time to give him that haircut.

Ray walked across the street. Visible through the shop's window, Jim was snipping away at the long hair of a small boy. A dark-complexioned, intense-looking woman hovered at his elbow, towering over him by a good foot. Ray decided his haircut could wait. He moved on past the building. Near the spot where the green Pontiac had been parked, he stepped into the road. Dried leaves and debris hugged the curb. He began pacing the area, systematically moving at an ever-increasing distance from the curb. About five feet into the street, he stopped and turned back. He almost didn't see it, caught there in the fold of a tattered leaf. A toothpick. Snapped to form a lopsided V. Ray squatted to get a better look. One of the tapered ends was badly chewed and dirty. The remainder had the pristine, clean look of white birch. Ray wiggled the toothpick onto the tip of his pen. Balancing it at the break, he carried it gingerly back to his car, fished a paper bag from an evidence kit in the trunk, and dropped it in.

Carol Burns watched from the doorway of the bakery, puzzlement written across her broad face.

"Good luck," called Ray as he opened the car door. Carol waved her thanks and ducked back into the shop.

Settled in the driver's seat, Ray fished the gas station cashier's scribbled address from his pocket. Now that he had one bona fide possible clue, maybe he could conjure up a witness to go with it.

The address was for a fourth-floor flat on Junction Street. Ray found Ms. Darnell home, and occupied with a troupe of young children. Standing in the corridor, he questioned her about the green Pontiac. She half-listened, giving most of her attention to a towheaded tot engaged in tearing up the current issue of *TV Guide.* She denied seeing the green car, impatiently accepted Ray's card and request to call if something came to mind, and closed the door.

Back in his car, Ray followed Fifth Street north for three miles, veered left on Church Street, and slowed as he approached the Lodwick Oldsmobile and Cadillac Dealership. He knew Lodwick had bought the place just a few weeks before, and was surprised to see the changes the new owner had already made. The dealership now took up most of the block between Fourth and Fifth, and flew the Stars and Stripes from four enormous gold-painted poles placed at the corners of the property. Crews of workmen were repaving a large section of the west and east lots, and new and used cars stood, helter-skelter, in every remaining available space.

Ray left his car on the road, parked between a Bell Telephone truck and two vans belonging to Brown's Electronics. He wandered over to a spanking-new, sky-blue Calais. He was reading the window sticker when a salesman in a dark summer suit and bow tie approached. He shook Ray's hand and introduced himself as Ted Roebuck.

"Sorry you had to park out on the street. Things should be

back to normal in a day or two."

"Nice car," said Ray, nodding toward the Calais.

"Special edition. Climate control, tape deck, leather interior. Are you interested in something for yourself?"

"Actually, I'm here to see Mr. Lodwick."

"Oh. I hope it's not urgent. He's not here at the moment."

"When do you expect him back?"

"It's hard to say. Seems there's been some kind of tragedy in his family. He's been in and out at odd times. I heard he was here last night, after closing. The watchman said he looked rather ill. Family trouble can do that, can't it?" Roebuck's features tightened, as if pinched by a memory. He briefly massaged the sides of his jaw. "Is it something I could help you with? I'm representing Mr. Lodwick while he's away."

"Well, I'm not sure."

"Why don't we go inside." Roebuck led Ray through the showroom, down a narrow corridor and into an office. Ray took a seat and accepted a cup of coffee. He took a quick sip and set the cup near a gold holder filled with business cards.

Roebuck withdrew to the padded leather swivel chair behind the desk. "Now, what can I do for you?"

Ray removed a yellow carbonless copy from his back pocket and handed it to the salesman. "My uncle has a car on order. He's asked me to stop by and make some changes."

"Your uncle." Mr. Roebuck examined the document. "Homer Fredrick. The name sounds familiar." He read on. "Top of the line Cadillac. Looks like it has everything possible on it. What kind of changes did your uncle want?"

"Actually, he'd like to put the car in my wife's name. Problem is, she won't drive a Cadillac. So we're talking about changing the order to an Olds."

Roebuck pursed his lips. "Perhaps we should let Mr. Lodwick handle this when he gets back. If the order's already gone in…"

"I don't know how long this can wait," said Ray. "My uncle isn't well. He wanted the exchange made as soon as possible."

"Why don't I see if I can get in touch with Mr. Lodwick, then give you a call."

"All right." Ray stood. "If there's any problem and my uncle needs to be consulted, you can reach him at Tanglewood General. Room two-twenty-eight. Or call me," said Ray, handing him a business card, "but not at home. Uncle Homer wants to surprise her if we can pull it off."

Mr. Roebuck walked Ray to the door. "I'm curious. I know my wife would jump at a chance to own a car like this. What does your wife have against Cadillacs?"

"She says they make her feel uncomfortable."

"A Cadillac? There *is* no more comfortable car."

"Psychologically uncomfortable."

Roebuck shrugged. "They say the customer is always right."

Strolling the lot, Ray spent a good half-hour comparing the Oldsmobile models. At a quarter to one he left the dealership and went looking for lunch. He pulled into a McDonald's a few blocks away and parked to the right of a rusty pickup with a camper top and out-of-state plates. Ray glanced at the lone occupant as he passed: a withered old man, perched in the driver's seat, staring into space. He had a pen in his hand and an open checkbook balanced against the steering wheel.

Ray purchased a copy of the *Tanglewood Observer* from a vending machine near the door. He waited in line behind two raucous ten-year-olds with fistfuls of coins, ordered a Big Mac and coffee, paid and settled at a table by the window. He busied himself for the next hour with eating, reading and watching others, one of whom was the old man from the pickup. He had donned a cap and apron and was vigorously sweeping the parking lot.

Saint Luke's parish faced Church Street, two blocks down from the car dealership. It was one of the oldest parishes in the diocese. The buildings—church, rectory, convent and school—all dated back to the early part of the century.

Leaving his car in the shade of a towering oak, Ray walked to the convent and rang the bell. It was a few minutes past two. The door was answered by a stout woman with large smiling eyes. She wore a dark skirt and a simple white blouse with a cross pinned to the collar. Curly gray bangs peeked out from a sky-blue kerchief-like veil.

Ray identified himself and stepped into a paneled foyer with a polished hardwood floor. Responding in a soft, almost apologetic voice, the nun introduced herself as Sister Seraphina. She led Ray to a large parlor that looked like it had been furnished in the twenties.

"Sister Theresa did get home all right, didn't she?" asked Ray.

"She did."

"Perhaps she forgot that I was stopping by."

"Oh, no. And she certainly intended to receive you, Mr. Fredrick, only the trip from the hospital tired her terribly. I'm afraid Theresa is forever overestimating her strength. But don't worry. She asked me to see that you get the information you came for."

Ray settled at one end of an antique sofa.

Seraphina stepped back to the door. "First I'll go get Gabrielle. Theresa said you wanted to talk to her."

Before Ray could counter her proposal, the nun was gone, her footsteps echoing in the convent's silence. Shortly, a rather tall, broad-shouldered woman appeared at the door. She was dressed as Seraphina had been, and wore thick, wire-rimmed glasses that exaggerated the size of her eyes. A prominent nose hovered above a set mouth.

Gabrielle marched to a straight chair and commandeered the seat, her spine well away from the chair's back. "I'm not sure how you expect me to be of help," she said pointedly, bypassing any attempt at introductions.

"I'm not sure, myself," said Ray. He cleared his throat and tried to think of something to ask this woman. He imagined Theresa in her room, immensely amused at having created this little parlor scene.

"I'm investigating the hit-and-run in which Theresa was injured," Ray said.

"*Sister* Theresa informed me," Gabrielle answered. She might answer his questions, but she was not prepared to tolerate liberties.

Ray began to relax. Theresa would be right; this *was* funny. "By some quirk of luck, I was present when the incident happened." He crossed his legs. "Being in the crime-control business, and dealing daily with some very dastardly deeds, I am totally convinced that what happened outside the bakery was not an accident. Sister Theresa seems to think otherwise. Perhaps you have an opinion, since you know Theresa better than I do." He uncrossed his legs and leaned forward, making a show of earnest attention.

"I'm afraid I agree with you."

"You do? Oh. Well, can you tell me why?"

"Many people find our life style something of a threat, Mr. Fredrick."

"A threat? How do you mean?"

The nun's shoulders straightened. "To be blunt, Mr. Fredrick, we remind others of their erroneous ways. Some find such reminders uncomfortable. It threatens their status quo. Makes them question their actions."

"So you think Theresa was run down by someone who'd had it with such reminders?"

"With all the senseless violence in the world, nothing would surprise me."

"In other words, Theresa wasn't the target. Her style of life was."

"Christ was crucified because of the way he lived and what he said," instructed Gabrielle. "I doubt if his executioners were even sure of his name."

"Good point," said Ray. Clearing his throat, he stood. It was time to concede the field. "Thank you very much, Sister. And when you see Sister Theresa, be sure you tell her about our discussion. Tell her I found your theory very interesting."

"I certainly will." Gabrielle rose quickly and left Ray to sink gratefully into the antique plush upholstery.

Soon afterward, Seraphina returned, carrying a ring of keys. The information he needed was at the school; he could wait where he was or accompany her. "I could have Gabrielle bring you something to drink," she offered.

Ray was immediately on his feet. "The walk sounds good."

They followed a narrow, tree-lined, flagstone path that ran from the convent to a side entrance of Saint Luke's elementary school. Seraphina inserted a key, only to find the door unlocked. She clucked to herself as she pushed the door open.

A loud roar met them. Down the hall, a thin man dressed in khaki pushed a floor polisher in their direction. A few feet shy of the nun and her guest, he switched off the machine and doffed his cloth cap. "Afternoon, Sister," he said.

"Peter, I'm afraid the door was unlocked again."

"That so?" The custodian moved past Ray, opened the door a crack and cocked an eye at the face plate. "Probably needs some oil," he said. He shoved the latch in, let it out. "Yeah, that's the problem."

"This door has to be kept locked, Peter."

"No argument there, Sister. No, indeed, no argument

there. I'll get right on it." He slammed the door, made a show of making sure the latch had caught, and scampered jauntily off down a wide flight of stairs to the right of the entrance. Ray noticed an outline on his left hip pocket that looked suspiciously like a flask.

Seraphina and Ray stepped over the cord of the machine and headed down the corridor.

"I know your wife," said Seraphina. "She's been a great help with our meals program. Especially when a driver calls in sick and we need a substitute."

"I'll tell her you said so." Ray peeked into one of the classrooms. "So, the meals program is run from here."

"Yes, from the cafeteria downstairs. It takes a little juggling of schedules when school is in session, but we manage. Especially now that enrollment is down."

"Who's filling in for Theresa?"

"Nora Kelly. She's a volunteer who's been with the program for years. She's very good. She's replaced Theresa before. In fact she'll be taking over next week when we go on vacation."

They started down the stairs at the west end of the building. Ray said, "Sister Gabrielle seemed to think Theresa's attack had to do with your way of life."

"Yes. I heard. Gabrielle's voice tends to travel. I was surprised Theresa suggested you talk to her."

"I'm afraid Theresa isn't taking what happened very seriously."

Seraphina stopped on the mid-floor landing. She faced Ray. "I know. And I wish she would."

"You're concerned."

"I am. And not for the reason Gabrielle suggests."

"What reason, then?"

"I'm not really sure." Seraphina continued down the stairs. She stopped again when they had reached the lower floor. "I've known Theresa for over twenty-five years. She is a pure delight most of the time, but there are moments when she seems strangely preoccupied and distant. Almost... *possessed*. I know that's a terrible thing to say, but I don't know how else to describe it. When she has these attacks, it's like a light goes off inside her. It shows in her eyes. A kind of crushing sorrow. And it affects her physically."

"In what way?" asked Ray.

"Headaches. A violent shivering. Or sometimes she just closes her eyes and makes tight fists as if she's fighting something." Seraphina glanced at Ray, and then glanced away. "It probably has nothing to do with what happened Tuesday. Perhaps I shouldn't have said anything."

"I'm glad you did. Have you ever questioned Theresa about these moods?"

Seraphina nodded. "And when I do, she just smiles and quips about practicing for Halloween. Or says something equally evasive. But it's a forced smile and her explanations are given with little heart. And the days these moods hit, she spends hours in the chapel."

Moisture welled in Seraphina's eyes. She turned and walked heavily down the wide corridor, crossed the cafeteria and led Ray into a small office off the kitchen. "Sister Theresa runs the meal program from here, Mr. Fredrick." The nun retrieved a folder from the middle drawer of a filing cabinet, took a seat at a gray metal desk and began writing on a pad of paper.

"I wouldn't mind having the mother's address as well, if you have it," said Ray.

The nun handed the detective the two addresses.

"Phillip Keyhoe." Ray studied the paper, then slipped it into his shirt pocket. He stepped into the commercially equipped kitchen and waited. Seraphina locked up. They weaved their way through the miniature tables and small chairs. "Do you know this Mr. Keyhoe, Sister?"

"No, I don't. I think Yavonne is the only one who ever met him."

"Maybe I should have a word with her."

"She's working in the garden. I'll take you there." Seraphina switched off the light and closed the door. They headed for the stairs. "I always dislike being in school when the children aren't here," commented Seraphina, quickening her pace.

"Which grade do you teach?"

"First."

"Have you been at Saint Luke's long?"

"Since the summer of sixty-seven. Theresa and I arrived together."

They left by the front entrance, stepping into the full light of the afternoon sun. Hearing her name, Seraphina turned and smiled at the approaching figure of a tall, graying man in a black cassock.

Seraphina made the introductions; she informed the priest that her companion was investigating the accident that had injured Theresa.

"Any progress?" asked Father Mike Killian.

"Not much, I'm afraid," answered Ray.

Addressing Seraphina, the priest asked, "Did you get a call from the repair shop about your car?"

"Yavonne talked to someone yesterday. From what I understood, they'll need to keep it at least a week." Seraphina frowned. "I'm not sure how we'll manage."

Father Mike's blue eyes danced merrily. He took Seraphina's hand, dropped a set of keys into it, cupped her elbow with a firm hand, and turned her in the direction of the rectory. "Your loaner for the duration. No charge."

Parked next to the front steps of the old red brick house was a Chevy Nova. "It arrived a few minutes ago," said Father Mike. "They mistakenly left it at the rectory and gave the housekeeper the keys. Monsignor and I were at church hearing confessions. Otherwise, I would have sent them on to you."

"How did you talk them into that?" asked Seraphina.

"I didn't. Yavonne must have."

"She never said a thing. In fact, this very morning she was checking bus schedules for transportation to her classes."

"Well, she must have done something right. Because the car's here."

Mike's attention strayed to the convent; his eyes lost a little of their sheen and his face much of its smile. "How's Theresa?" he asked.

"Tired. Sore." Seraphina seemed to want to say more. Instead, she glanced at her watch. "Oh, dear. I was supposed to wake Theresa for her medication ten minutes ago." She looked at Ray. "Would you mind if I just pointed you in the direction of the garden? I'm sure Yavonne's still there."

"Not at all."

They took their leave of the priest. Seraphina steered Ray to a stone path that ran through a stand of tall maples.

Ray continued down the path. He found himself in a large yard divided into well-defined plots of lawn, garden and patio. He crossed the lawn, spotted the nun at the far end of the garden, and headed down a row of knee-high corn. Dressed in a denim skirt, a collarless cotton shirt and wearing nothing on her head, she knelt in front of a pepper plant, humming and turning the soil with a trowel. Nearby was an old scarecrow made of a broomstick and bundles of straw. Perched on its head was the nun's veil.

Yavonne glanced toward the approaching stranger. She wiped her forehead with her arm and waited.

"Quite a garden," said Ray, after introducing himself.

"Keeps me busy."

"Have you time for a few questions?"

"Sure." Yavonne dropped the trowel into a basket of garden tools. She grabbed a rag and, wiping her hands, led the detective to the patio. They took seats on opposite sides of a picnic table. "How can I help?" asked the nun.

"I was told you might know a Phillip Keyhoe."

"We met once, if that's what you mean."

"At the church?"

"No. At the convent. He came looking for Theresa. Unfortunately, she wasn't home, so I filled in as scapegoat. He was a very angry man, this Mr. Keyhoe."

"What exactly did he say?"

"Well, when I told him Theresa wasn't home, he came right out and called me a liar." She chuckled." The last time I was called a liar, I was a teenager motivated primarily by hormones."

"What did Keyhoe do then?"

"Stamped off like a two-year-old throwing a temper tantrum. It was quite comical in a way."

"Do you know if he ever came back?"

"I don't think so."

"You don't remember the color or make of his car, do you?"

"If he had a car, it was probably parked by the church. I never saw it." Yavonne looked directly at Ray. "Do you really think he could have had something to do with what happened to Theresa?"

"As hard up as I am for a motive, I'll take any suspect who rears his head. A final question, Sister. The day Theresa drove you to the college, did you notice a car following? A green car?"

Yavonne smiled. "The only thing I saw was the inside of my textbook. I was cramming for a test."

Five

It was late afternoon by the time Ray arrived at the station. He used a side door, and followed the staircase down to the basement. A narrow corridor led him past a storeroom for old records, the Forensic Department, and the City Morgue.

Fred Foler's office was at the far end. A plaque to the right of the door read Medical Examiner. Ray rapped lightly and ambled in, only to pull up short.

Foler glanced up from behind his desk. A second man turned and faced Ray, a tall, black-suited, stout man with several chins, black-rimmed spectacles and a thick crop of ash-gray hair.

"Fredrick," the tall man barked by way of greeting.

"Sitarski," Ray replied. He turned to Foler, nodded toward the door and asked, "Got a minute?"

Sitarski grabbed the arms of his chair and pushed himself up to his full six-foot-three. "Stay here. I was just leaving." His face twisting into a smirk, he lumbered to the door. Ray made no effort to step aside, forcing the big man to shuffle out sideways. Just as he cleared the doorway, he laid a beefy, heavily-ringed hand on Ray's shoulder and said, "Don't be such a stranger."

Ray pulled back. He shut the door hard. From the corridor came a hoarse, throaty laugh.

Foler followed the scene without saying a word.

Ray stepped to the desk and dropped a small paper bag on the blotter.

"For crissake, have a seat," Foler snapped. He pulled at his ear. "You and Sitarski remind me of two bulls circling a single cow when there's a whole herd waiting to be jumped."

"Thanks for the analysis." Ray shoved the bag closer.

"Snack?"

"Work. I found it at the scene of a hit-and-run. It spent a lot of time in someone's mouth. Mind running it through the mill?"

Foler grabbed the bag, glanced at it front and back, and tossed it over to Ray. "Do you want me to eenie-meenie-minie-mo it into one of the files? Or do you have a case number?"

Ray snatched a pen from the desk and wrote the date, the case number, the name Theresa Loomis and his initials. Foler dropped the bag into a wire basket on the floor. He filled a chipped mug with coffee from a pot on a file cabinet. "If you want some, help yourself."

"No, thanks."

"No, thanks," mimicked Foler. "It's not enough that you stand there like a man with a lamppost up his butt. You got to squeak like a eunuch as well." Fred returned to his seat and scratched at his mane of thick, curly hair. "I pick my own enemies, Ray. And the list is long enough without including yours."

"Who asked you to?"

"Attitudes do a lot of a man's talking."

Moving in an exaggerated, leisurely manner, Ray stepped to the file cabinet and poured himself some coffee, then hummed his way over to the chair vacated by Sitarski, sat, and swung his feet up to rest on a stack of papers. "How's the wife, Fred?" he asked with a jaunty swing of the head.

"Divorced and out of my hair, thank you. And how's Kate?"

"Busy cooking my meals and ironing my shirts." He eyed his watch. "By now she should be done with cleaning my workbench in the basement."

"I bet if she cleans anything, it's your clock."

"Oh, did I omit that?" Ray smiled.

"Welcome back, Raymond."

Ray finished his coffee. He lowered his feet to the floor and stood, setting the cup down next to Foler's. "I'd love to stay and do dishes but I have a suspect to hassle."

Foler accompanied Ray out of the office and down the hall. Without a word or grunt of farewell, his slight, white-smocked figure disappeared through the door of the lab.

Monroe Street formed the heart of an aging residential area northeast of the city. Eleven sixty-seven was a sprawling ranch house set well back on a three-quarter-acre lot. A car was parked in the driveway. Disappointed that it was neither green nor a Pontiac, Ray parked behind it. Immediately, his mood improved. The car had a rental company sticker on the back bumper.

Ray rang the bell and heard a brief buzz resound inside. He waited, then rang again. When there was still no answer, he stepped off the porch, cut across the lawn and headed around back. From an open window he could hear strains of semi-classical music. Ray mounted the steps of a room-sized deck with built-in bench seats. He reached the screen door and peered through it into the kitchen, in time to see a tall, heavyset man with a high forehead lick something from his fingers. Ray rapped on the door frame. The man's head snapped toward him.

Ray smiled pleasantly. "I rang at the front," he said.

"Twice. And if I had wanted to answer, I would have." The man wiped his finger on a butcher's apron tied around an ample belly.

"I can appreciate that," said Ray. "Only I'm not here to chitchat." He held his identification to the screen. "You certainly don't have to let me in, Mr. Keyhoe. Only most people find it more pleasant to answer questions at home."

Keyhoe wobbled to the door and squinted at the wallet-size card. His thin lips disappeared into a pained grimace. He lifted the latch and shoved open the screen.

Ray entered a roomy, immaculate kitchen. No expense spared here. If Phillip Keyhoe used half of this equipment, he must eat very well indeed.

Keyhoe stepped back to the counter and continued his task. Ray watched silently as the big man deftly cut crust from a slice of white bread, halved and quartered it diagonally, and spread imported paté on one of the small triangles. He added a ring of onion, a strip of green pepper, another triangle of bread and skewered the lot with a toothpick.

"Entertaining?" Ray asked.

Keyhoe gave him a hard and silent stare.

Ray studied the man's profile, wishing him shorter, bearded and older. He had to settle for the hope that Keyhoe was the suspect's employer. Ray tried again. "Sister Theresa Loomis. Are you familiar with the name?"

The meat-smeared knife hovered above its newest target. Keyhoe set the knife down. He veered to face Ray directly and, to the detective's surprise, wore a sincere smile.

"Why didn't you say you were here about that?"

Ray hesitated, trying to evaluate this sudden affability. "Forgive me, but you didn't exactly encourage conversation."

Keyhoe stepped to the kitchen table, pulled out two chairs, pointed Ray to one and offered refreshment. Ray took a seat but declined the drink. Again he waited, hoping to take his cue from Keyhoe.

"It's about time something was done about this matter. Do you realize that I filed my complaint months ago?"

"And do you still feel the same way?" asked Ray.

"Why wouldn't I? I pay taxes. My mother pays taxes.

Meals on Wheels is a government program. My mother is no less a senior now than she was then."

Although he was sure he knew the answer to his question, Ray glanced about and asked, "Does your mother live here?"

"Heavens no. That's all I need. It's enough that she hounds me over the phone with reports on her bowel movements and orders to do this, do that. Come here, go there."

"My dad was the same way," lied Ray.

"It's a real pain, isn't it? Well, you know what I tell my mother? Parents should be seen and not heard. And shouldn't speak until they're spoken to." Keyhoe's eyes grew enormous; his mouth twitched. "That's what I tell her. Yes, sir. What was good for me as a kid, is good for her as an old lady." The stout man blinked hard, as though to obliterate any possible doubt in the matter.

"There was little love lost between me and my parents," Ray lied again. He dispatched mental apologies to the two people who had first taught him to delight in life.

"Same here," said Keyhoe.

"Can't be quite the same. You're at least making an effort to see that your mother gets meals. That must stem from some filial affection."

Keyhoe gave a snicker of contempt. "Let's just say I'm looking out for both of us."

"I've already talked to the nun in charge of the meals program. She seems like a sensible woman. Claims that your mother is perfectly capable of fixing her own meals."

"The queen of England is more likely to cook a meal than my mother. You know why her finances are in the state they're in? Because for years she's been eating her meals out, and I don't mean fast food, either. Do you have any idea how quickly that adds up? Even at twenty dollars a day, which for her would be low, you're talking *over seven thousand dollars a year,* most of it out of her capital, just to *feed* the old fossil."

The picture he had drawn clearly gave Keyhoe a great deal of pain.

"So you think Sister Theresa should allow your mother to get meals?"

"Absolutely."

"Have you told her so?"

"In unmistakable terms."

"When was the last time you saw her?"

"I never saw her. It was all done on the phone."

"Something doesn't jibe here. I have a statement from one of the sisters that you came to the convent. In fact she described you quite well."

"Once. And a lot of good it did me. That Loomis nun wasn't there."

"So, you have no idea what Theresa Loomis looks like?"

"No idea."

"Perhaps you've seen her at church. Are you a member of Saint Luke's?"

"I attend Mass there. But only because my mother insists that I take her."

"So you could have seen her there."

Keyhoe shrugged. "There's a bunch of them parading in and parading out. I never paid attention. Why should I?"

Ray moved his chair back from the table. "Mr. Keyhoe, I'll be honest with you. I'm not here about the meals program. I'm here about an attempt to murder the sister who runs it."

As he walked back to his car, Ray savored Keyhoe's discomfort. Being suspected of a felony had hit Mr. Dutiful Son right where he lived. The detective made a deliberate show of copying the rental agency information from the bumper sticker on the rented car.

The mother, Pamela Keyhoe, lived a half mile from her

son. Their houses were similar in size and design; each was neat, well cared for, and set back on a large lot.

Heading up the walk, Ray wondered if there was a deck out back. He rang the bell and was surprised to hear chimes ringing a familiar, pleasant tune. When there was no answer, he smiled and rang again, already intending to walk around back.

Before he had the chance, a car horn blasted. Ray turned. A Buick Park Avenue was pulling into the driveway, piloted by a woman in her sixties.

Ray started down the steps, noticing that the body of the luxury car was covered with nicks and dings and scratches and dents. It also rested partly on the grass.

Mrs. Keyhoe stepped out and stood by the car door, arms folded across a flat chest. She was a trim, well-groomed woman with hair dyed the color of salmon and spectacles the thickness of a man's thumb.

Ray started across the lawn. He had wanted only to get a look at the woman who had borne the likes of Keyhoe. That, and check the make and color of her car. Both objectives already achieved, what he needed now was a quick dismissal.

Pamela Keyhoe pursed her lips impatiently. "Yes?" she said in a stern, loud tone.

Decision made. Interviewing her would just eat time. "Are you Mrs. Marsh?"

"I am not," she answered.

With a ponderous show of disappointment, Ray looked up and down the street. "Do you know if there's a Mrs. P. Marsh living hereabouts?"

"I do not." Mrs. Keyhoe retreated to the trunk of her car, opened it, and began unloading colorful sacks bearing the logos of expensive shops.

Six

A clown-shaped magnet fixed the note to the refrigerator door.

> Ray—Homer called. He's being released
> from the hospital. I'm off to his place to help
> him get settled. There's chili in the crock pot
> if you get hungry before I get back.
>
> Kate

Ray grabbed a beer from the refrigerator and kicked the door shut. An insistent bark turned him toward the patio. Outside, Thumper sat tall and straight on the top step, his tongue lolling and breath clouding the plate glass.

"Ah. There is someone home after all," said Ray, in a halfhearted effort at humor. He crossed the kitchen and slid open the wide glass door. Thumper bounded in, wagging his backside energetically. Ray moved to the bottom step, sat, sipped his beer. Thumper joined him, nudged his hand. When Ray made no response, he nudged it again until his master ran it over his silky chestnut coat, all the while staring off into the distance.

Abruptly, Ray took a tight hold of the dog, kneading its flesh affectionately. He blinked moisture from his eyes; in a low voice he said, "You furry fellows have it made, don't you? No cooking, no cleaning up." He paused, drank more beer and added, "No funerals."

At the sound of the garage door opening, Ray finished his beer and returned to the kitchen for another.

Kate came in through the breezeway carrying a grocery bag. "Did you eat?" she asked.

"Not yet."

"Good. I picked up some corn chips to go with the chili." She gave Ray a quick, concerned glance. "Why don't you feed Thump, and I'll set the table."

Ray hauled a can of dog food from the cupboard.

"I got Homer settled," said Kate.

"Fine. Where's the can opener?"

Kate pointed to the dishwasher. "Homer said he was expecting you to call with news about a certain project. He was very mysterious about it all."

Again, she glanced at Ray. "Do you know what he's talking about?"

Ray murmured something inaudible and spooned the food into Thumper's dish.

Kate let the matter drop and saw to the chili. Soon they sat down to eat. "Any new developments on the hit-and-run?"

"We may have a suspect." Ray told her about the Keyhoes.

Kate listened attentively until he had finished, then said, "If your Mr. Keyhole is using a rental car, then maybe he owns a green Pontiac."

"I checked. He's registered as owning a Corvette."

"Maybe he stole a car."

"There's been no report of a stolen green Pontiac."

"Do you really think he's involved?" asked Kate.

"He certainly didn't drive the car. But he could have hired someone."

"Seems hard to believe. Just because his mother was refused meal delivery. Besides, from what you just said, I can't imagine she'd eat the food if she did get it. So why is the son determined to get her on the program?"

"Not for her sake, that's for sure. I'll bet he sees the program as a way to slow the erosion of his inheritance. And from what I saw of his mother's driving and the condition of her car, Son Phillip must know that his mother won't be able to renew her driver's license again. If she doesn't cook and can't get out, guess which abused son gets to choose between being chef or chauffeur."

Kate shook her head in disbelief.

Ray said, "People commit murder for weaker motives than that. Tomorrow I'll have him run through criminal records. See if he has any priors or known associates."

Ray ripped open the bag of chips and dumped some on a napkin.

"Which of the sisters did you meet at the convent?" asked Kate.

"All of them, I guess." Ray smiled. "Quite a collection of personalities."

"Did you meet Seraphina?"

"Oh, yes. She took me on a tour of the school and looked up the information on Keyhoe and his mother."

"Did you talk again with Theresa?"

Finishing a mouthful of chili, Ray shook his head. "I wish I could have. I keep thinking she knows more than she's telling. Plus, I have to admit, she's a lot of fun."

"She's that," said Kate. "And quite a speech-maker, besides. You should have heard her Sunday."

"Sunday? Are nuns giving sermons now?"

"Come to church and find out," countered Kate.

"I don't want to know that badly. Seriously, are the nuns giving sermons?"

"No. Theresa spoke at the reception for her and Seraphina. Twenty-five years of service to the parish. I told you about it last week. I even tried to get you to come."

Kate left the table and returned with a copy of the *Saint Luke's Herald*. On the front page were photos of Theresa and Seraphina, both as very young sisters in full, floor-length habits, and as older women in their modified dress. Ray turned to the inside page and read the accompanying article.

He glanced at the ads that framed the text, taking note of a two-line ad for Jim's barbershop. Ray turned again to the front page.

"So, Theresa's from the state of Washington. I wonder what brought her east?"

Kate shrugged. "Do you want some coffee?"

"I'll make it," said Ray. He carried a can of fresh grounds to the coffee maker, and was counting scoops when he suddenly stopped. "Kate, how are these church bulletins distributed?"

"The ushers hand them out at the exits after Mass. Why?"

"Because Keyhoe said he never met Theresa and had no idea what she looks like."

"Does he go to Saint Luke's?"

"Takes his mother every Sunday. Now there's something I'd go to church to see. The devout Phillip and Mrs. Keyhoe kneeling side by side with heads bent and hands folded."

After supper, Kate stayed in the kitchen, spooning servings of Jell-O, pudding and custard into portable plastic containers with lids. Then she joined Ray in the den for an hour of TV. At ten, she climbed the stairs for bed. Ray followed a few minutes later.

When Kate finished her shower, Ray was already in bed, flipping through a recent edition of *Inside Sports*.

Kate settled on her side of the bed. She located her place in Sue Grafton's *H Is for Homicide,* and started to read. Within a few moments, she was less aware of the text than she was of the room's unusual quiet. She listened for a page to turn, but heard only the rustle of curtains and the infrequent rumble of traffic. Kate turned toward her husband and found him leaning against the headboard, staring into space.

Kate closed the book and switched off her reading light, reached over and tugged at a wisp of Ray's gray hair. "I could give you a trim in the morning."

Ray tossed his magazine to the carpet and turned off his light. "I'll stop by Jim's after work." He slid down between the sheets.

Kate did the same, and lay for some minutes lost in thought. She was half asleep when Ray asked, "How is he?"

Kate turned on her right side. "He's okay."

"Is he better?"

"No."

"Then why did they release him?"

"There's nothing more they can do."

After a long silence, Ray said, "He's not alone, is he?"

"No. He has a nurse with him." Kate scooted closer to him. Turning Ray toward her, she lay in his arms. "He asked me to look for a housekeeper."

"I thought he had one."

"She's on sick leave herself." Kate tugged at a clump of chest-hair. "I thought maybe I could go and fill in until she's well."

"You mean stay there?"

"He needs more than strangers around him, Ray."

"When would you go?"

"The day after tomorrow. I'll get some shopping done. Pick you up some meals for the microwave. Unless—"

"Get a lot of Stouffer's lasagna."

"All right."

"Is that pudding for him?"

"Hmmmm," said Kate. "And the Jell-O and custard."

"He used to be a steak-and-potato man." Ray kissed Kate's pajama-clad shoulder. "Thanks for being there for him."

"You're welcome."

Minutes passed. A half hour. Neither found sleep, but lay in the gray-dark and the heavy silence, their thoughts fixed on the days to come.

Seven

Trev Steward slammed into the squad room, shouting for his partner.

Ray was seated at one of the desks, reviewing a case with two of the younger detectives.

"Ray, let's move it! A nine-one-one call just came in from Saint Luke's."

Ray dropped the case file and grabbed his jacket. "We'll take my car. It's closer." They headed for the exit at the north end of the building. "Who called it in?" asked Ray.

"Some guy named Kruger."

"Kruger?" Ray got in behind the wheel. "Who's Kruger?"

Trev shrugged. "All I know is that the call came from Saint Luke's."

Ray floored the accelerator, cutting off a delivery van as he pulled out.

"For the thousandth time, I wish you'd get a siren for this car if we're going to use it officially," mumbled Trev, watching the van tailgate in the side mirror.

"Stick your badge out the window."

"For crissake, Ray. I've heard better ideas from two-year-olds."

"You never talked to a two-year-old in your life."

A red light forced a stop at the corner of Fifth and Church Street. The van moved into the left-turn lane, came alongside Ray's Volkswagen. The burly, bearded driver leaned over to the passenger's side and gave Ray the middle finger.

Ray paid no attention.

"You deserved that," said Trev.

They covered the remaining blocks in less than a minute. Ray turned in at the church, spotted a squad car outside the school, and sped off toward it. Two uniformed officers stood at the entrance with an anxious-looking Father Mike Killian.

The priest came to meet them. "I think it was him, Ray."

"Who?"

"The man who attacked Peter. I think it was the same man who tried to run down Theresa."

"Peter. Is that the school custodian?"

Mike nodded.

Ray turned to Trev. "Call the station. Get the crime-scene unit out here, stat. And repeat the APB for the green Pontiac."

Trev headed for the squad car.

Ray faced the officers. "Anybody touch anything?"

"Not a thing."

"Good. One of you get over to the side entrance, the other stay here. No one in or out."

Mike said, "What about the people picking up meals to deliver? They're due here any minute."

Ray gave it a moment's thought and asked, "Where did this attack take place?"

"In a lavatory on the first floor."

"All right." He addressed the officers. "Anyone coming to pick up meals goes downstairs and no place else."

Ray pointed toward the half-dozen cars in the lot. "Who do they belong to?"

"The people who prepare the meals."

"What time did they get here?"

"Around eight, I think."

Ray and the priest entered the school, the latter leading the way down the wide corridor.

Ray asked, "Where's Kruger?"

"In one of the classrooms."

"Does he need medical attention?"

"I thought so, but he wouldn't let me call anyone. I think he's afraid they'll test his blood alcohol."

"We aren't talking about a fall he took because of a few too many drinks, are we, Father?"

"I don't think so. His face looks like it was used as a punching bag. Poor guy."

"Maybe he tripped down a few too many stairs."

"Maybe." Mike stopped and faced Ray. "He's had a hard life. I'd rather we believe him first, and call him a liar only when we have to, if you don't mind."

"That's easy for a priest. A detective works under different rules."

"Perhaps we could borrow from each other."

Ray nodded agreement. "All right. Let's go see what Mr. Kruger has to say."

Peter Kruger was seated at a child's desk with his long legs supported on the seat of a second. He was holding a damp rag to the side of his face. He had a split lip and a bulge on his forehead that was already the size of an egg.

Ray approached the man, noting the familiar shape in the hip pocket. He veered off and took a seat at the teacher's desk. Mike positioned himself at Kruger's side.

Put wings on the man and you'd have a guardian angel, thought Ray. He addressed the custodian, "How are you feeling, Mr. Kruger?"

The thin old man fingered his swollen lip. "I've felt better."

"Do you need a doctor?"

"No."

"Can you describe your assailant?"

"Sure can. The little punk. If I had been younger..."

"Little punk? Are we talking about a kid?"

"He weren't no kid. Had a beard grayer than my hair." Kruger removed his cap to make his point. He held it gently, almost reverently, then slipped it back on.

"Short man with a beard." Ray felt a rush of excitement. "Anything else you can tell me about your assailant?" he asked.

"Yeah. He's got a mean left hook." Peter felt his jaw and squinted with pain.

Ray pulled out a notebook and pen and began writing.

"Mean eyes and a snub nose," continued Kruger. "And he had a face that looked like it never had a decent thought or a good night's sleep."

Pleased with the witness, Ray smiled. He asked, "Ears?"

"Flat," said Kruger.

"Length of hair?"

"Long, like yours."

Ray laughed. "Mr. Kruger, a witness as good as you is as rare as fish in a swimming pool. Think you'd be up to helping a police artist sketch us a picture of your punk?"

"Sure. Long as you let me pay the bastard back a few punches when you catch him."

Mike patted Kruger's shoulder. "A joke. Right, Pete?"

"Yeah, sure."

"Tell me about the attack," said Ray. "What were you doing at the time?"

"I went into the boys' john to take a crap. First door I pushed on was locked. First one on the left. Ain't supposed to be locked. So I got down on all fours to crawl in and fix it. Only this foot lands on my face." He nudged his nose with his little finger. "I think it's broke."

"Maybe you should see a doctor."

"They ain't going to put it in a cast. So why bother?"

"What happened next?" asked Ray.

"The door flew open and he started punching me. Like I had spoiled his..."

"Spoiled his what?"

"I don't know. But he was mad. He kept punching me. Hell, and I never even tried to hit back or hold onto him or anything. I just started hollering, hoping they'd hear me in the kitchen. The next thing I know, he's out the door."

"Had you used this lavatory earlier today?"

"Nope. Used the one on the lower level."

"Do you remember the last time you were in the one where the man was hiding?"

"The day before, maybe. Maybe not. I don't keep track."

"Where's this particular lavatory located?"

"This floor. Across from the principal's office."

Ray turned to Mike. "Who's principal here?"

"Theresa." Their eyes held, priest and detective, each mirroring the other's thoughts.

"Theresa," repeated Ray. He stood up. "Peter, was he wearing gloves, your little man?"

"Nope. Bare knuckles. I know the feel."

"I think we'd better have a look at our perpetrator's hiding place. Are you up to taking me there?"

Peter eased his long legs to the floor. He stood slowly. "Ain't far. Just a couple of doors down."

With the lanky Kruger leading, they headed down the hall. Approaching the lavatory, Ray asked Mike and Peter to remain outside and not touch anything. He went in, pushing the door open with the toe of his shoe. The room smelled of disinfectant. He passed a bank of urinals, and neared the stall Kruger had identified as the intruder's hiding place. He elbowed the door; it swung open with a squeak. Ray stepped in and let the door slam shut.

Suddenly aware of something touching his shoulder, he turned. A heavily laden drawstring sack hung from a metal hook on the door. He lifted it down and carefully opened it. Inside were two loaves of dark rye, a chunk of cheese, another of salami, and a quart bottle of table wine, still three-quarters full. Imagining the prints it would provide, Ray winked at the bottle.

Ray replaced the sack. He hooked the underside of the stall door with his foot, opened it and was backing out when something else caught his attention. Something floated in the toilet: two toothpicks, broken and pointed like arrowheads.

Ray walked the short distance from the school to the convent. Gabrielle answered the bell, looking more forbidding than ever. "Mr. Fredrick. What can I do for you?"

"I'm impressed that you remember my name."

Her eyes shifted sideways with indifference.

"I'm here on business, Sister," said Ray, deciding not to waste any more time on social niceties. "I'd like a word with Sister Theresa."

"I'm afraid she's resting."

"I won't make her stand."

"Am I supposed to find that funny?"

"Sister, I'll be blunt. I'm here on official police business. And barring a doctor's injunction, I *will* see Sister Theresa."

Gabrielle's eyes grew wide with displeasure, but she stepped back and gestured for him to enter. Ray remained where he was. "Well, are you coming in?" snapped Gabrielle.

"Not until I apologize. I had no right to be so heavy-handed. I'm sorry."

The tiniest suggestion of a smile crossed the nun's face before it disappeared into a solemn expression of pained forgiveness. "Please come in," she said.

Ray followed the nun into the parlor and sat down. A quarter of an hour later he heard footsteps in the hall. He stood and waited.

Theresa entered, her brown eyes bright with a smile. She was pushing a cart set with tea and cakes. "Gabrielle prepared this for us. You must have a special charm, Mr. Fredrick. She seldom encourages strangers to stick around by serving them goodies."

"Here, let me take that. I promised not to tire you." Ray pushed the cart to the side of an antique coffee table and waited for Theresa to seat herself. He moved a straight-back chair to position himself in front of her.

Theresa's features turned pensive. "You did get the address you were after, didn't you?"

"Oh, yes. I've even been to see the man."

"What did you think?"

"That our Mr. Keyhoe had a motive for grumbling. Not murder."

Theresa tensed. Almost as though she had been threatened. She said, "I'd rather we call it an accident, Mr. Fredrick. And even if it were deliberate, maybe Gabrielle was right about why it happened."

"Either way, it's a felony."

Theresa poured tea and handed Ray the cup.

"I'm told you're the principal at the elementary school," said Ray. "That, plus the meals program, seems like an awful lot of work for one person."

"Not with the staff I have. When school is in session, I seldom do anything more for the meals program than make sure the orders are in and the paperwork done."

Ray took a sip of tea. He eyed the long pink scar at the side of Theresa's nose. "You heal well," he said.

His remark seemed to make the nun withdraw into reverie. She picked up the plate of fancy cakes and passed it to Ray, avoiding his gaze.

Ray selected one and asked, "Hasn't anyone over here been looking out the window?"

"Out the window? I don't know. Why?"

Ray took a bite and placed the remainder of the cake on a napkin. "There's been a commotion over at the school. A commotion that drew police attention. Someone attacked your custodian, Peter Kruger."

"Are you serious?"

"That little question keeps coming up between us, doesn't it?" said Ray. "Unfortunately, I am serious."

"Is Peter all right?"

"He's fine. He did take quite a beating."

Theresa leaned against the back of the sofa.

"Aren't you having tea?" asked Ray. "And these cakes are delicious. Have one."

Theresa shook her head. She said, "You have a very bad habit of stringing others along. Please. If there's more to tell, I'd rather hear it without the subterfuge."

"I'm sorry. And you're right. I guess it comes from a career in questioning people with something to hide."

Theresa dropped her gaze. She reached for the teapot. "Perhaps I will join you."

"I wish you would," said Ray.

Theresa glanced at Ray twice while she poured. "I sense that we know more of each other than strangers have a right to know. But then Kate said you had a high degree of well-cloaked sensitivity to people."

"Cloaked?" Ray chuckled.

"Cloaked. Concealed. Masked. May I call you Ray?"

"I wish you would."

"What happened at the school, Ray?"

"Peter blundered into a man hiding in the boys' lavatory. The one near your office. From the sack of supplies the intruder left behind, I'd say he was prepared to stay a while." Ray paused. "More important, from the description Peter gave, I'm certain it was the same man who tried to run you down."

Eight

Ray tapped Trev on the shoulder and waved him out of the boy's lavatory into the hall. "How's it going?"

"Great. The stall is full of prints. How'd you do down the road?"

"I ruffled feathers. But she's still not talking."

"Maybe she has nothing to say."

"Someone is trying to kill her, Trev. Who else would know why?"

"Hell, she could have seen something incriminating without realizing it."

"Yeah, I guess. Anyway, I need a favor. Mind covering for me?"

"For how long?"

"I'm not sure. Probably most of the afternoon."

Trev checked his watch.

"It's important."

"Shit, yeah. Why not?"

"Thanks." Ray headed for the exit. He was pleased with the turn the case had taken. A star witness. Prints. *Better run, little man. You're in our sights.*

Success sharpened his appetite. He decided on lunch at the P & E and turned the car toward town.

The lot adjacent to the Pub and Eatery was already full. Ray parked at the curb and entered through a side door.

The proprietor, Millie Heintz, came hurrying toward him. "Ray Fredrick, you get yourself out of here. Any man who stays away as long as you have doesn't deserve to sweep my floor. So don't even think of food." A grin sharpened the woman's obese features.

Ray tried to look properly penitent. "That doesn't sound like the Millie we all know and adore." He pecked her cheek. "Will that buy me a table?"

"Conniver. Park yourself at the bar and I'll get something cleared."

Ray ordered a beer on tap. Before he had even taken a sip, Millie's pudgy fingers had him by the arm. He slid down from the stool.

"Why you been such a stranger?" Millie asked, steering Ray toward a corner table near the kitchen.

"Lent. I gave up the cooking of my second-favorite female."

"Lent's in February, Mr. Fredrick."

"Hell, they're always moving these holidays on me."

"And it isn't a holiday. It's a religious ritual."

"You expect an atheist to know that?"

Millie squeezed Ray in a tight hug. "If Kate ever kicks you out, you come straight to me, hear?"

"Indelibly so. How's the meat loaf?"

She leaned in close. "Fresher than the fish." Millie hurried away, tweaking the cheek of a baby-faced young man in the greasy overalls of an engine jock.

Ray left the P & E with a new edge on his sense of contentment. He drove back to Church Street and pulled into the dealership. Order had returned. Used cars occupied the Fourth-Street side of the lot; selected new vehicles circled the glass-and-brick building like strands of multicolored pearls. Ray found himself scanning the lot, out of habit, for a green Pontiac.

In the showroom he was informed that Mr. Lodwick was still away. Ted Roebuck was busy with a customer in his office. Ray lingered in full view. Shortly, Roebuck came prancing out with the air of a man bearing good news. "Mr.

Fredrick. I'm glad you stopped by. I called your office earlier but they said you were out." He paused for effect and smiled generously. "I'm happy to say that it has all been approved. I spoke to Mr. Lodwick myself. All you have to do is make a selection, and have one of the salesmen write up the order and put it on my desk. I'll see to the rest. Of course, the difference will be refunded to your uncle in whatever manner he prefers." Roebuck shook Ray's hand, excused himself, and returned to his office.

Ray snagged a middle-aged salesman from a desk at the end of a bank of small cubicles and followed the man out to the lot. They spent an hour discussing models, accessories and colors. Ray left with the choice made, the paperwork started, and Kate on his mind.

Back behind the wheel of his own VW, he engaged the car phone and dialed home. An elbow out the window, the Church Street traffic in sight, he waited only to hear his own voice tell him no one was there. At the signaling beep he said, "Kate. It's me. I decided to pay Homer a visit, so I'll be home late. Why don't we plan on eating out? I'll make sure I'm back by seven." He started to hang up, stopped, and spoke quickly into the receiver. "Love you lots."

The words were barely out when an old pickup lumbered past, making more noise than a cement truck. Grimacing at the offending vehicle, Ray recognized the rusty truck from the McDonald's parking lot.

Curious, free for the day, and far from anxious to get to where he was going, he gave chase. The truck rattled along First Street, trailing fat plumes of black smoke. Ray followed, staying far back to avoid the stink.

They crossed Junction Street and approached Main. Ray considered turning around. The light stayed green. He drove on. They were nearing Washington Avenue when the truck's brake lights flashed. It sputtered around the corner and turned directly into the circular drive of the Tanglewood Library. It stopped at the entrance. As if on cue, an elderly woman picked her way down the library steps with a wooden cane. She was wizened and bent and wore a shapeless blue dress, bobby socks and saddle shoes.

The man climbed out of the truck and helped her struggle into the cab. He patted her encouragingly.

Ray watched from the curb. The truck took a side path into the parking lot and stopped in the shade of an elm. As he pulled away, Ray passed closer to where they sat. They were eating, the two of them, sharing lunch from a McDonald's carry-out.

Damned curiosity, mused Ray, heading west toward the town of Livingston. He never could tell where it would lead. He wondered where they stayed, the old man and his wife, or sister, or whoever. *Maybe she has a night job at the library, scrubbing floors, and sneaks him in to sleep on the couch in some marble lounge.*

Ray chided himself. *Keep it up, Fredrick. That's all Homer needs, a visit from a really cheery nephew.*

Ray drove through Livingston. A few miles beyond the town, he turned onto an unmarked country road. The car bumped and clacked its way up and around hills heavy with trees and shrubs and shade. He crossed wooden bridges with their creaking boards hovering above rock-strewn brooks. Sunlight dappled the road with ground-clouds, shifting and reforming, disappearing and suddenly back again.

Several miles up the road, Ray came to a rickrack fence. He stopped at a gate, got out and opened it. A sign posted on the trunk of a black oak prohibited hunting or trespassing.

Ray drove on, following a rutted track into the woods. He drove slowly, feeling almost like an intruder in this somber, overgrown world of trees. The trail led downward for several hundred yards, leveled off, and started back up. The clearing appeared at the top of a rise, opening onto a lake as blue as the sky it mirrored. And a house. A log house that still seemed like a mansion to Ray, with skylights and enormous bay windows. It stood close to the trees at the northeast side of the lake. At the edge of the water, a boathouse and a long dock sheltered a pontoon boat and a speedboat.

Ray followed the track down to the lake and along the water's edge. He drove more slowly than the condition of the track required. He stopped and watched a pair of wing-flapping kingfishers ride the air and cut the silence with their harsh, rattling calls. But the house beckoned and his mind shut out everything but what the building held.

Uncle Homer. Ray put the car back in gear and pushed on. Approaching a narrowing inlet that meandered off into the woods to become a stream, he stopped again and remembered how his uncle had helped him launch his first boat from that spot. Ray glanced toward the woods, seeing once more his father disappear into the trees under the pretense of taking a leak, really to let his childless brother learn for himself the joy of schooling a boy in the plays of a man.

They were something, Dad and Homer. Brothers to the core. Brothers in heart.

For the umpteenth time, Ray wondered why siblings had never graced his own life. Questions unasked, unanswered. His parents gone. Homer going.

Ray veered inland and crossed the stream along a narrow, trussed bridge made of squared logs and thick slats. Minutes later he was within a stone's throw of the place Homer called his hideaway. Hush Hideaway beside Hush Lake.

Ray parked behind his uncle's white Cadillac. He eyed the car parked a door's width to the right, a beige Dodge with a bumper sticker that read, "Lord, Make Me the Instrument of Your Peace." A pair of hands clasped at the end of the verse; one black, one white.

Ray trudged forward, memories fighting each other for
attention. Young memories, old memories, middle-of-the-
way memories. Some heavy, some light. All his. All precious.
All formed in this place. He reached the front door and
knocked. Waiting, he studied anew the three lines of old-
English script that were said to have been commissioned by
his great-grandmother and carved by his great-grandfather.
The lines filled the top half of a door said to have passed from
house to house, a treasured heirloom:

Silence's Song

Hearken and Heed

That Your Years Might Sing

A black woman in a nurse's uniform answered Ray's
knock, a smiling, tired woman in her fifties. "I'm Naomi," she
said. With no further exchange, but with empathy in her eyes,
she led Ray through the foyer, down the hall and into a first-
floor corner room at the back of the house. A fireplace flanked
by built-in oak cabinets stood opposite a wide, ceiling-high
bookcase with glass doors. Centered on the floor, looking as
out of place as a bathtub in a drawing room, stood a king-size
bed. A price tag still hung from the frame.

Homer sat in a wheelchair near a large bay window with
a view of the woods and the east rim of the lake. He was
dressed in summer-weight pajamas and robe. His head lay
askew on a pillow folded over the chair's cloth back. His eyes
were closed.

Naomi quietly approached the old man, touched his shoulder and whispered, "You have a visitor, sweetheart." She
closed the door, leaving the two men together.

Ray busied himself looking about the room as he searched
for something to say. "You've rearranged this room."

"A change imposed by a harsh mistress." Homer placed a
hand on his lower right side. "Ridiculous isn't it, how some
part inside you that you never see can put on the pants and give

the orders. I'm glad you came, Ray."

"Just wanted to let you know it's done. Lodwick okayed the switch. I can pick up Kate's car anytime you want."

"What kind of a car did you choose?"

"Olds Calais. Top of the line. Winter white, to quote the sticker. How do you want this handled?"

"Kate doesn't know, does she?"

Ray shook his head.

"Tell them to bring it here. They can take the delivery cost out of the price difference."

"All right."

"Can you have it here before Kate arrives tomorrow?"

"I'll try. So Kate told you."

"She called this morning." Homer glanced out the window. "You have no idea what this means to me."

Ray settled at the head of the bed, sitting partly on a pillow.

"Pull over a chair," said Homer.

"I'm not staying that long," said Ray. "I've got a lunatic running around trying to kill a nun."

"Pull over a chair anyway. You're messing the bed. Naomi will think that you don't respect her work."

The armchair slid easily over the hardwood floor. Ray angled it to face the window as well as his uncle. He sat down, keeping himself near the edge.

"Your case sounds interesting. Who's the nun?"

"Theresa Loomis."

"Theresa?"

"You know her?"

"We sat on a committee together at Saint Luke's. Along with Father Mike and a couple of other people." Homer's face abruptly tightened and his eyes squeezed shut. He touched a button on a small device in his lap. Immediately, the door opened and the nurse appeared.

"That charley horse kicking again?" she asked.

"That charley horse," answered Homer weakly.

Naomi filled a syringe at the plastic-draped oak desk

shoved against the wall. Homer readied his arm, fingers trembling, frame knotted in pain.

Ray stood and moved to the window.

"Better?" asked the nurse, a long moment later.

Homer answered, "Much. Thank you, Naomi."

"You're welcome, Mr. Fredrick."

The door clicked shut. Ray turned. A weaker, smiling Homer was wiping perspiration from his face. "God bless whoever it was discovered morphine," he whispered.

"Is a charley horse a symptom of your condition?" asked Ray.

Homer chuckled lightly. "*Charley horse* is Naomi's lingo for the pain. Now, tell me more about what happened to Theresa."

"The first incident was a hit-and-run. Deliberate and witnessed by me. Fortunately, she wasn't badly hurt. The latest attack didn't involve her directly, but I'm sure she was the target." Ray recounted the attack at Saint Luke's elementary school.

Homer asked, "Does she know who's doing this?"

"She says she doesn't."

"And you think she does?"

"I think she suspects someone. Perhaps she feels it's unfair to say anything if she's not sure."

"What makes you think so?"

"At first, it was just her odd reaction after the attack. But when I told her about the incident at the school, she showed signs of real fear. If I had to guess, I'd say it's an old fear. I've seen it before in people who live on the run."

"You sure you're not overreacting? That's hardly a way to describe a nun's life."

"I could be." Ray shrugged.

"So what happens now?"

"We hope for a line on the suspect from the prints he left. If that doesn't work, we've got to find that green Pontiac."

Nine

The squad room was almost empty. Ray glanced at the wall clock and turned to the solitary figure of Detective Dickenson hunched over a cluttered desk. "Sam, have you seen Trev?"

Sam shook his head, and shot Ray one of those sad, puppy-eyed glances that can come only from the relatively young. He bent again to his task.

"Is something bothering you?" asked Ray. His junior detective was as easy to read as the clock on the wall.

Not looking up, Sam gave a nervous shake of the head.

Ray walked the short distance to his office. He went in and closed the door, then stopped. On his desk lay a memo. An Interdepartmental Memo. The kind the chief sent to department heads when he had something official or unpleasant to communicate. Ray snatched it and read it through. He sank into the old swivel chair.

I ought to note the time, he told himself. *They say events that change your life ought to be properly chronicled.* He banged the memo down and, in a harsh heavy hand, scribbled the hour, minute, date and place. He underlined it so hard that his pen slit the paper.

The office door opened and Trev came in as carefully as a truant into a classroom. He said nothing, took a seat, eyed the memo. He tossed a candy bar across the desk.

"I had lunch," said Ray.

"Use it as a mood raiser. Works for me."

Ray picked up the small bar of chocolate. "I might need more than one."

Trev sighed heavily. "What are you going to do?"

"What I said I would. Where's the report on the prints from the school?"

Trev pointed to the in-basket. "Don't waste your time. Our computers came up with zilch, and AFIS is backlogged. So who knows when we'll hear from them. Figures, doesn't it? Perfect prints and no match."

"What about the sketch?"

"That we can use." Trev rummaged through the top papers in the wire basket. He handed Ray a penciled image of a small-faced, bearded man with mean, deep-set, dark eyes. He followed with a second drawing, a side view. "Had this made as well, since that's the view you had when you saw him near the barbershop."

"That's him," said Ray. "Although I might have given him a little less gray."

"I'll have copies out by morning," Trev interjected. "What do you want to do about news coverage?"

"Shit. Did the press get wind of something?"

"Not so far."

"Good. Let's keep it that way. We don't want to clutter up Saint Luke's with a lot of reporters and busybodies. And we sure as hell don't want to scare the perp into waiting till our guard's down." Ray folded both sketches and slipped them into his shirt pocket.

Trev scratched at his second chin. His eyes took in the underscoring on the memo. "Just give it time, Ray."

"It's been hell working in the same building with Sitarski. What do you think it's going to be like having him as a boss?"

"People change."

"Yeah, Trev. Some do. Not Sitarski."

"Nothing else has ever come up."

"He knows better than to let it. What about Keyhoe? Anything on record?"

"One drunk driving conviction. He did community service and stayed clean."

"Doesn't surprise me. What about the green Pontiac?"

"Nothing. Sam called every repair shop in the county, plus. No green Pontiac with a dented front end."

"Tell him to stay on it. Surrounding counties, the whole state. We've got to find that car. And keep that APB alive."

Trev squirmed in his seat. "I checked your vacation time. You have three weeks coming. Why not take them? Things are slack; there's nothing I can't handle." He scratched his forehead and added in a quick, quiet voice, "I checked with the chief. It's fine with him, if that's what you want to do."

"Mother Trev. To what do I owe this minding-of-my-business?"

"I don't deserve that."

"I don't deserve to be mothered."

"Shit. Someone has to keep you from self-destructing."

Sudden loud voices in the hall silenced both men. Ray stood up. "What's going on?"

"Sitarski's making the rounds. Collecting handshakes and beaming like a hairy light bulb."

"Well, let's go sully our hands, shall we?"

Trev blocked Ray's path. "I got one last thing to say before you leave. Sign off or stick around, that's your business. What you do here and now affects the whole crew. Sitarski knows how the guys in your department stick together. Cross him, embarrass him in front of the guys, and he's just as likely to take it out on the rest of us. Sam and me and the others got time to do yet. Don't muck up our lives for the fun of kicking his ass. Sitarski's a jerk. I don't like him any more than you do. I just don't want things harder than they have to be."

For a long mute moment, Ray didn't move.

The commotion in the hall grew.

Ray stepped around Trev and opened the door. He glanced

back at the man who had been his partner for so many years. Trev of the apple cheeks, standing there slack-jawed and sad-eyed, hands in his pockets and belly over his belt. Standing there with all the years of their friendship silently pleading. Ray said, "Make the arrangements, will you? With the Chief? For whatever time I'm due. I'll start tomorrow."

"Vacation?"

"Vacation."

Trev nodded.

"Right." Ray started down the hall at an even pace. Head high, gait sure. He heard his name shouted from behind. "Fredrick? Where you going? Get over here and butter up the chief-to-be!" The voice and the guffaw that followed were unmistakably Sitarski's.

"Good cut," said Kate. "I like you with your ears in full view."

Ray crossed the kitchen, turned on the tap, filled a glass, and took a long drink. "I'm ready when you are," he said, patting the attentive, excited Thumper, who had come to sit at his side.

Kate closed her library book and fixed her gaze on Ray. "You look tired."

"It's been a long day."

"Do you want to stay here? We can order a pizza."

"Do you mind? I'm really not in the mood to eat out. Besides, I stopped at the P & E for lunch."

"Oh, you did, did you? When? Before or after you invited me out for supper and seduced me with those little words you know I love to hear?"

Ray cracked a smile. "Had to have been after," he said. "I could never have uttered such things on an empty stomach."

Kate dialed the local pizzeria. She ordered a large special and rang off. "Is Homer doing all right?" she asked.

"Actually, he seemed fine, considering. Except for a sudden—charley horse. The nurse gave him a shot that seemed to help."

"You must have met Naomi."

"Homer seems to be quite taken with his nurse."

"He's lucky to have her. She comes highly recommended."

Ray took a seat at the kitchen table. "Did you know that Homer and Theresa worked together on a committee at Saint Luke's?"

"Yes." Her gaze stayed on Ray. "Is something wrong?" she asked.

"Does it show that much?"

"I'd have to be pretty dense if I couldn't read your moods by now. It's Sitarski, isn't it? He made chief."

"I'm afraid so."

"Did you know that there's not one private investigator listed in the Tanglewood phone book?"

"It doesn't bother you, the idea that I might retire?"

"What bothers me is the memory of your run-in with that man twenty years ago. I don't want a repeat, for you or me."

"He's already choosing his weapons. I can tell. He watches me like a felon in handcuffs who knows he has the right key in his pocket. Once he gets loose, he'll do everything he can to pay me back."

Ray took in a deep breath and let it out. "Maybe I should have kept my mouth shut."

"You can close it now if that's how you're going to talk," said Kate. "What you caught Sitarski doing was worse than criminal. He should have been locked up, not made head of a department."

"It was my word against his."

"The girl should have backed you."

"She was sixteen. God knows what Sitarski promised her or threatened her with." Ray took a sip of water. "It still galls me that I handed her over to Sitarski. Just so I could get home in time to watch a ball game. I should have taken her to Juvenile myself."

"You had already worked a shift and a half," said Kate. "How were you supposed to know Sitarski would do what he did?"

"Shit, and right there in the station. If I hadn't come back for my sunglasses, we wouldn't be having this sorry discussion."

"Yes," said Kate. "And if you hadn't gone back, that girl could have spent the past twenty years in some dark alley, shrinking into herself a little more each day."

"Who's to say that didn't happen anyway?"

"If it did, at least it's not because you took the easy way and kept silent."

The doorbell rang. Ray stood. "I'll get it. Let's eat in the den and watch that movie I taped last night."

"Okay. I'll bring the drinks and meet you there."

Ray tipped the kid a couple of extra singles. He carried the carton to the den and switched on the TV. When Kate breezed in and set the tray of soft drinks on the long, low table by the sofa, Ray was already feeding a chunk of pizza crust to the dog. "Any new developments on the hit-and-run?" she asked.

"Shoot. I forgot to tell you. Our little man struck again."

"Ray! How could you forget something like that? Is Theresa all right?"

He nodded. "But only because he was flushed from his hole before she happened into the school. Gave the janitor a pretty good pounding. The guy had a sack of supplies that could've lasted the better part of a week, not to mention a private toilet and plenty of space to spread out once the building was empty. Heck, I bet there's even a sofa or something in the faculty lounge."

"How did he get in?"

"That's no mystery. The door's open every day for the Meals-on-Wheels crowd. Plus, the custodian who took the beating wasn't too careful about keeping the school locked."

"Has the man been identified?"

"Not yet. We're still waiting on a response from AFIS."

Kate sighed. "Tell me again what that means."

"You know—the fingerprint I.D. computer."

They finished the movie at 9:15, and watched twenty minutes of TV before Kate's yawn ushered them into their end-of-the-evening rituals. Ray set off with Thumper for a quick walk around the block. Kate put the den back in order and was wiping the counter in the kitchen when the patio door slid open and Ray entered. He hung the leash on a hook.

Kate asked, "Are you going in tomorrow?"

"Nope. Nor any day for a few weeks."

"Do you mean you already gave notice?"

"No. Just taking my vacation time. Clear the air and do some thinking."

"What about Theresa?"

"Trev will clue me in on developments. And I'll follow up on my own."

Kate stopped wiping the counter. "You could come with me."

"To Homer's?"

"To Hush Lake. Clean air, lots of space to sit and think."

"I don't know if I could, Kate. Every time I think of Homer and what's coming..."

"Do it for the good days he has left. Don't you want to share some of them?"

"Will there be any?"

"You had one today, didn't you?"

"Yes."

"Sleep on it," said Kate. She rinsed the dishcloth and draped it over the long-necked kitchen faucet. The ring of the phone startled her out of her musings. She answered it, listened, and handed the receiver to Ray. "It's Homer. He wants to talk to you."

Ten

Yavonne perched on the low ottoman. Seraphina and Theresa occupied the sofa. To their left, Gabrielle sat stiff and proper on her straight-backed chair, with a portrait of the Pope on the wall at her back.

"I hope I didn't call too late last night," said Ray, feeling like a schoolboy in trouble as he faced the four nuns.

"Not at all," chirped Yavonne. She gave a small tug to her veil which had slipped to the back of her head. "Actually, you had perfect timing. I was watching the Friday night movie and you rang just as a commercial came on."

A loud sigh sounded from the sofa. Gabrielle Peters glared at the younger nun. "I'm sure Mr. Fredrick is not here for an account of our activities," she said. "And I hope he doesn't think we all waste our time watching movies."

Gabrielle turned a less harsh gaze on Ray. "We are anxious to know why you insisted on speaking to all of us."

"I hope I didn't come across that strongly," said Ray.

"You *didn't*, Mr. Fredrick," said Yavonne. She pointedly glanced at Gabrielle and then rolled her eyes.

"Would you like something to drink, Mr. Fredrick?" asked Seraphina, clearly eager to keep an old conflict in the family.

"No, thanks." Ray studied Theresa. She sat slouched forward at her end of the sofa, her injured arm resting like a burden in her lap. Her eyes were downcast and she looked tired. Tired and lost. Ray found himself thinking of a painting that hung in the master bedroom at Hush Hideaway. In it, a woman in a long robe held tightly to a young girl. The artist had given both faces the same haunting sadness, and had fused their forms so that they seemed shadows of each other.

Ray took his gaze from Theresa. "Last night I received a call from my uncle. Some of you might know him. Homer Fredrick."

Theresa looked up. Addressing her, Ray said, "Homer told me he served with you on a committee here at Saint Luke's."

"Yes, I remember your uncle," replied Theresa.

"He's the reason I'm here," said Ray, returning his attention to the group. "I went to see him yesterday. We talked a little about the hit-and-run and what happened at the school. He was quite concerned. Anyway, he called last night and asked me to deliver a message. He's offering his place as a kind of hideaway till the culprit is caught."

"Hideaway?" said Gabrielle. "But we are already planning to go away. On Monday. Won't that be sufficient?"

"I doubt it very much. Let me ask you this: Have any of you talked outside your group about your trip, where you'll be going?"

Sister Seraphina touched her spectacles. "I have."

"I'm sure we all have," said Yavonne.

"Therefore you may be no more secure there than you would be at Saint Luke's."

"What about Mr. Keyhoe?" asked Yavonne. "Have you spoken with him? If he's responsible and knows you're on to him, maybe that will put an end to it all."

"I talked to him. I can't consider him a serious suspect. To be truthful, ladies, the evidence we have so far leads nowhere. We have no idea who's doing this." Ray fought the urge to watch Theresa.

"Where is your uncle's place?" asked Yavonne.

"If I don't tell you, no one will slip and mention it inadvertently. I will say this: It's perfect for a holiday. There's a nice lake. The house is comfortable and large enough to hold all of you. There's a library, TV, two boats, and plenty of woods for long walks."

"Is it far?" asked Seraphina.

"A half hour to forty-five minutes from here."

Seraphina turned to Theresa. "What do you think?" she asked.

Theresa passed a glance around the group. "Since Mr. Fredrick is convinced that I'm the intended target, then it's best that I simply leave you. That way the rest of you won't have to change your plans."

"Very sensible," Gabrielle quickly added.

"I don't agree," said Ray, avoiding the nun's stern gaze. "Let me explain. In police work, one of the major factors in solving a crime is finding the motive. Well, a theory has been offered that we shouldn't ignore. This theory suggests that your—occupation—may inspire these attacks. That would mean you're all in danger. In which case, we can protect you better if you stay together."

"You mean some nut out there just hates nuns?" questioned Yavonne, drawing in her chin. "Are you kidding?"

"Our vows, Sister," said Gabrielle, pleased at having been taken seriously. "We are a walking reminder to others of their immoral, materialistic and self-centered behavior."

"Exactly," said Ray.

Yavonne searched the faces of her fellow nuns, trying hard to keep her amusement at bay. Theresa caught the younger nun's gaze, and with a small shake of her head, discouraged further comments.

Yavonne settled for a quiet *tsk*, and said no more. Her right foot slipped out of its canvas slipper. She scratched at the sole of her foot.

Ray said, "I suggest you think seriously about my uncle's offer."

"Won't we be a bit much for your uncle?" asked Theresa.

"Not to hear him talk. Uncle Homer is excited about

having your company. Which brings me to something else. My uncle wanted you to know that he is not well. Actually, he's dying." Ray paused as if he, too, needed time to absorb the sense of his words. Addressing Seraphina, he said, "You know, I just might take you up on your offer. Coffee?"

Seraphina promptly stood, her plump face bright with pleasure. Yavonne rose as well. "I think I'll get myself a Coke. Anyone else care for anything?"

Rallying her energies, Theresa eased herself up off the sofa. "I suggest we all go to the refectory. And we might even be able to coax a few of Gabrielle's scones out of hiding."

"Really, Sister," said the tall nun, "What's Mr. Fredrick to think?" She turned to Ray. "If I didn't put some away, they'd all be devoured at once. And making scones from scratch does take time." Pride resounded in her loud voice.

Theresa smiled. She took Gabrielle's elbow and ushered her toward the door. "Come on, now, Gabbie. Show us where you stashed them."

They paraded a short distance down the hall with Ray bringing up the rear. Yavonne shoved open the refectory door and secured it with a large brick covered in black cloth. The room was wide and well lit, separated from the kitchen by a waist-high wall the width of a counter. Sunlight streamed in through a bank of four wood-framed windows.

In the center of the room, a long table was set for lunch. Yavonne shoved the place-settings into the middle. Theresa motioned Ray to a seat at the head of the table.

They worked quickly, Gabrielle digging into the depths of a counter-high freezer, with one black-shod foot completely off the ground, Seraphina filling the kettle and Yavonne and Theresa setting out cups and saucers and silverware.

Gabrielle was last to take her place, and then only after sashaying in with her prized scones and plopping them down right next to Ray. He helped himself and passed the plate.

From her seat on Ray's right, Theresa said, "I'm sorry about your uncle. Father Mike said he intended to visit him in the hospital, but I had no idea he was seriously ill."

"It's serious all right," said Ray, the words ringing in his head like funeral bells.

"Then are you certain that having strangers in his house is the best thing for him?"

"I might have wondered, too," said Ray, "but he really wants you to come. He made me promise to talk you into it." He grinned. "Face it, ladies. He knows you're an entertaining group."

"What do you think, Sisters?" Theresa asked. "Shall we go?"

Seraphina nodded straight away. Yavonne bubbled about the fun of going someplace different. Gabrielle gave the matter a measure of thought and a suitable wrinkling of the brow before making the vote unanimous.

Theresa turned back to Ray. "You can tell your uncle we've accepted his generous offer." She poured cream into her coffee. "Dare we hope that you might be staying there as well?" she asked.

Ray didn't answer.

"I think we'd all feel better if you were," said Theresa.

"Could you?" Even Gabrielle's voice sounded a little eager. "Of course, if it's not possible—teachers tend to forget that not everyone has the summer off."

They were turned in his direction, the four women. Waiting. Ray tapped the table, then found himself nodding, almost against his will.

"Thank you," whispered Theresa.

"And Kate?" asked Seraphina.

"She'll be there," said Ray. "And there's a nurse to care for Homer, so you can just relax and enjoy the place."

Gabrielle suddenly pitched her hands in the air and announced, "Oh my. We've all forgotten about Mother."

There was general exclamation among the sisters. Theresa turned to Ray. "Mother Jean is our Superior General. She takes her vacation with a different group each year. This year is our turn."

"No reason why she can't come along," said Ray. "When do you expect her?"

"She's flying in Monday evening," said Theresa.

"No problem. And now that that's settled, we need to plan. First of all, absolutely no one is to be told anything about this trip."

"Surely we can tell Father Mike," said Theresa.

"All right. Father Mike. But let me tell him." Ray pulled a paper from his pocket. "I'd like to have you look at our artist's sketch of Peter's assailant. After that, I'll run through our battle plan. These may sound like extreme measures to you, Sisters, but we have no idea who our enemy is or how far he's willing to go. The trip to my uncle's place must be made in secret."

Ray handed the sketch to Yavonne. "Have any of you ever seen this man?"

He watched it make the rounds, watched Theresa as she waited her turn. Seraphina shook her head. She handed the drawing to Theresa, who studied it without emotion, and handed it to Ray. "I have no idea who this man is."

Eleven

Ray stepped out onto the porch and stretched in the warmth of the early morning sun. He watched cars buzz past and tried to feel pleased at not needing to go to work. He kicked lightly at a large terra-cotta pot with a flowering plant. He trudged down to his car at the curb, got in and drove it up the drive and into the garage.

On signal from the hand-held remote, the garage door clanged shut behind him.

Ray circled Kate's Chevy. He crossed the breezeway into the kitchen. Kate was packing the dog's dishes into a cardboard box. Head cocked and tongue lolling, Thumper sat closeby.

Ray rubbed the dog behind an ear. "I hope we're not making a mistake taking him."

"We're not," replied Kate. She closed the box. "He'll be good for all of us. Won't you, Thump?" The dog's ears twitched.

"Did you talk to Homer about him?"

"Yes, I talked to Homer. My goodness, Ray. I thought you'd be happy having the dog along."

"I'd be happy staying here. I'd be happy if Sitarski were still confined to his paper-pushing corner in Records."

"Ray." Kate studied her husband. "It's getting a little tiresome, listening to you complain. And if you really don't think we should take the dog, we'll leave him at Pam's."

"I just don't want him to be a burden on Homer."

"How is Thumper going to be a burden on Homer?"

"Barking when he needs to sleep, for one thing."

"We'll just see that he doesn't." Kate gave the box a shove with her foot. "That's ready to go."

With the dog at his heels, Ray lugged the container out to the garage and placed it in the trunk of his car. He came back to an empty kitchen. He climbed the stairs and found his wife rummaging in the bedroom closet. "This is going to be a busy day," he said.

"What Monday isn't?" Kate hauled two suitcases to the side of the bed. "I could use some help, you know."

"What do you want me to do?"

"Decide what you want to take and put it on the bed."

Ray opened the bottom drawer of the dresser and grabbed an indiscriminate armful of socks and underwear. He shifted to the bed and dropped the lot near the pillow. "I still can't figure out how the nuns talked me into this," he mused.

"Neither can I," said Kate. "Especially since you had already given me, quote, 'a definitive and unequivocal no'."

"Did I say that?"

"You know you did. So what do they have that I don't?"

Posturing like a professor about to pronounce on a brand-new truth, Ray replied, "Innocence."

Kate glanced up from her packing. "If you mean that I have none, just remember who's to blame for that." She tried in vain to keep a stern frown on her face.

"You still have a little," said Ray in a highly condescending tone. "Only not quite as much as they have."

"Well, perhaps I'll work on regaining some at the lake. I will certainly have a supply of role models to imitate."

"Won't work. Innocence is like income tax. You don't get it back."

"Thank you, Mr. Philosopher. And if you want shirts and slacks packed, you'd better get busy. Or do you intend to strut around in your skivvies and socks?"

"If I did, the nuns wouldn't have any innocence for you to

compete with."

Kate broke down and laughed. "You know, with a little effort, we could have fun at the lake."

Ray held up a pink pair of shorts. "Maybe you're right. Being the sole male among a pack of women could have a certain...*recreational* effect."

"I'm not sure Thumper would appreciate being excluded from your little male monopoly. Not to mention Homer." Kate watched the merriment drop from Ray's face, and was sorry she had mentioned his uncle.

Back at the dresser, Ray opened the second to last drawer and lifted out a short stack of summer shirts. His gaze rested on the exposed, holstered revolver. He set the shirts on top of the dresser, removed the gun, and ran his fingers along its two-inch barrel.

Kate walked over and laid a hand on Ray's arm. "Are you going to take that?"

"Probably should."

"Do you think whoever is after Theresa will try to find out where she went?"

"I think we are up against someone very serious about getting rid of her, yes. And even with all the precautions we're going to take, there is always something we can't foresee."

"Still no news on the hit-and-run vehicle?"

"Nope. And no match on the prints found in the boy's john. And, more important, no motive. That is, not one that anybody is willing to talk about." Ray put the gun back in its holster.

Kate said, "If Theresa does know something, I don't understand why she won't tell you."

"I don't either."

"Maybe Trev's right. Maybe she saw something incriminating, and doesn't know it."

"You haven't seen her under questioning. I've interrogated lots of witnesses who claim to know nothing while every facial muscle twitches with guilt."

"*Guilt?* Aren't you being pretty hard on Theresa?"

"If she knows something and claims she doesn't? No, I don't think so." Ray smiled. "Maybe I could scare it out of her."

"I don't like the sound of that."

Ray carried the gun to the bed and sat down. "I could fire a shot. Over her head of course."

"If you dare, I'll follow it with another shot and I won't miss."

"You don't have a gun."

"Who needs a gun? I'll hit you with a round of verbal bullets that will ring in your ears for weeks."

"You have to admit, it could work."

"I can't believe you're talking like this."

Ray held up his right hand. "Okay. No shooting. If you promise to redirect your ammunition, and get Theresa to talk."

"I suppose I could try," said Kate. "So leave the gun here."

Ray placed the revolver in the suitcase. "I think I'd better take it." He returned to the drawer and fished out a box of ammunition.

At a quarter past ten when Ray and Kate carried the last of their luggage to the garage. Ray fit all but one case into the trunk of his car and slammed it shut. He laid the remaining case on the back seat, called the dog, and coaxed him in beside it.

Ray walked over to the driver's side of Kate's vehicle. He leaned in through the open window. "Want to run through it all again?" he asked.

"No, but I will anyway. Just to take that worry off your face." One by one, Kate pointed fingers and recited, "I meet Theresa at the school. We pack the meals as usual, deliver one or two, then when Trev signals us from his car with a double flash of headlights to say we aren't being followed, we drive to his apartment complex. We proceed as though we are delivering meals to two different addresses, Theresa carrying one and me the other. Once inside, Theresa gives me her container, and leaves through the rear exit. Just make sure you're there when she comes out."

"I'll be there. And don't forget, you leave the meals at Trev's. Do you have his key?"

"Yes, dear."

"Apartment twelve."

"I know that, Ray."

"Don't look around or anything when you come out. Just continue delivering the meals. And if anyone stops you and asks where Theresa is, just say she decided to stay and help an elderly woman who has fallen. Don't volunteer any information. And if you can do it without drawing attention, write down their license number and description."

"I'm sure that's not going to happen," said Kate.

"Just be ready."

Kate started the engine.

"Are you clear about where and when to meet me in Livingston?"

Kate smiled and patted Ray's hand. "I've never seen you so paternal."

"I don't like involving you in a case."

"Fiddlesticks," said Kate. "Every time you came home from work with stories of criminals and courts and interdepartmental politics, you involved me."

"Not directly like this."

"Well, relax. I'm enjoying myself. And by the way, did you remember to give Trev the phone number at the lake?"

"Yes, dear." He smiled; she laughed.

"Well, here goes." Kate backed out of the garage and down the drive.

At 11:35 Kate and Theresa arrived at the Towerwood Apartments, on the corner of First Street and State. They left the car and walked to the building, Theresa balancing a brown bag and a meal carton against the cast on her right arm.

Kate led the way to the door at the far end of a carpeted corridor, looked outside and said, "He's there." She took the bag and carton from Theresa and whispered, "See you at the lake."

Theresa headed toward the brown Volkswagen parked at the front of the lot. Ray swung open the passenger door. Theresa started to get in, then stopped cold at the sight of the dog in the back. She averted her eyes, settled in and shut the door.

Ray pulled away. "Don't tell me you don't like dogs," he said.

"I do and I don't," she answered.

"It's not going to bother you, is it, his being with us at the lake?"

Theresa shook her head, keeping her gaze straight ahead.

Ray kept his speed below the limit. Every now and then, he caught a glimpse of Trev's gray Ford in his rearview mirror. At the outskirts of the city, the headlights on the gray Ford flashed twice. Ray relaxed and accelerated. "Well, Sister," he said. "It seems we have pulled things off without a hitch. So far, at least."

"This is going to be a long day for you," the nun answered.

"I enjoy escapades like this."

"Escapade. I guess that's as good a way to look at it as any."

"Homer was thrilled when I told him you and the others were coming."

"Have you had a chance to tell Father Mike?"

"Yes. Last night. And it's a good thing I did. He's already been out to visit my uncle. He could easily have returned for another visit and unintentionally brought the culprit with him."

"I hope that doesn't mean we're depriving your uncle of a priest's visit."

"No. Father Mike will call me when he wants to come out. We'll set up a place to meet. That way I can make sure he's not being tailed."

"What a lot of trouble," said Theresa in a low, tight voice. "Perhaps I should have simply gone to our Mother House."

They drove on in silence. Spotting a McDonald's, Ray got in line at the drive-through window. "Hope you don't mind a quick lunch. I'd prefer not to leave the car until we get there. And there won't be time to have a meal at the lake before I go back for the other sisters."

"This is fine," said Theresa.

Ray ordered them fries, burgers and coffee. He pulled off to a corner of the parking lot, where a clump of trees screened them from passing traffic.

They were well into the meal when Ray asked, "Where is your Mother House?"

"In Canada. Just across the border from Buffalo, New York."

"I read in the parish paper that you're originally from the state of Washington."

Theresa turned and looked out the window. "Yes," she said.

"What brought you this far east?"

"My parents died in a terrible automobile accident. I suppose I moved to—get away from the memory."

"How old were you?"

"Seventeen."

"The article said you were twenty-seven when you entered the convent. What did you do in between?"

"Am I being pumped?"

"Pumped?" Ray chuckled softly. "No. That's just me being my curious self. I guess it's part of what makes me tick as a detective. People's stories have always intrigued me. Especially when there's an element of mystery to them. Take this older man I've been seeing around town. I first noticed him at the McDonald's near Saint Luke's. He works there. Has to be close to eighty, drives an old, rusty truck with out-of-state plates, and instead of counting sheep from a rocking chair, or playing with grandkids, he cleans parking lots and sits in his vehicle trying to balance his checkbook."

Theresa asked, "Have you solved his mystery?"

"No. Haven't even talked to him yet. But I did see him again, driving down First Street. He pulled into the Tanglewood Library and ate a Big Mac in the parking lot with a woman at least his age. Wife, sister, friend. Who knows?"

"Sounds rather sad," said Theresa.

"There are a lot of sad stories out there," said Ray.

"Do you collect them?" asked Theresa in a lighter tone.

Ray smiled. "Sounds like it."

"What about your story? Is it a sad one?" asked the nun.

"Very little of it," Ray answered.

"You're lucky."

Ray glanced at the nun. "Are you lucky as well?".

She responded with a look as pensive as it was distant. Finally she said, "Today I am."

Twelve

Ray reached the Sears side of the Livingston Mall at a few minutes past two. He cruised the lanes near the section reserved for automotive repairs, located Kate's Chevy, and parked one row back.

Kate was in hardware examining light fixtures. Ray strolled over and picked up a wall socket. Without turning, he whispered, "Any problems?"

"None."

"Nobody stopped you or anything?"

"No, dear."

"Did you buy the groceries?"

"Yes, dear. Can we get going? I have perishables in the car."

"I thought you brought a cooler."

"I did. But it wasn't big enough for everything."

"Okay. Let's get you to the lake."

Ray left the mall first. Kate lingered a little longer, then left by another exit. She pulled out to the main road and turned right. For the next ten minutes, Ray trailed her up and down the streets of Livingston, keeping several cars back. When he was satisfied there was no tail, he flashed his headlights.

Ray stayed behind Kate until she had turned onto the dirt road leading to Hush Lake, then pulled to the shoulder and waited until the blue Chevy was out of sight. He made a U-turn and headed back toward town.

Less than an hour later, Ray turned into the First Methodist Church of Tanglewood. He spotted the sisters' Chevy Nova, and drove past it. Yavonne was at the wheel. Seraphina occupied the passenger seat. She appeared anxious. Gabrielle Peters had the back seat to herself and looked as though a frown had been chiseled into her face.

Ray parked near the church. He climbed the steps, tried the door, found it locked and returned to his car.

Yavonne started the engine and drove off.

Ray followed, using the same precautions he had with Kate. Twice he pulled off the road to let traffic pass, taking note of the vehicles and their drivers. He proceeded in this fashion until they were close to Livingston, then took the lead and kept it until the nuns were safely across the trussed bridge and in sight of Hush Hideaway. He waved them on and watched the small car bump its way along the track. A bank of clouds drew his attention. Thunderheads were building near the horizon.

At twenty to five that evening, Ray stopped at the Tanglewood Cafe to buy donuts and coffee. He drove to Saint Luke's and stationed himself at the side of the church.

Ray was sipping the last of the coffee when a white van turned in from Sixth Street. Red letters on the side panels identified it as property of the Burns Bakery. Ray brushed crumbs from his shirt. He watched the van circle to the rear of the convent, and then back up until only the nose of the vehicle was visible.

Ten minutes later, the van drove off.

Ray crushed the Styrofoam cup and dropped it into the empty donut bag. He started the car and followed.

The two vehicles joined the city's dance of metal with its slow starts and quick stops. When the van reached the outskirts of Livingston, it pulled into a gas station and wheeled up to an island of pumps. Ray did the same, parking his Volkswagen on the street side of the same pump.

The door of the van opened. Father Mike climbed out.

Ray stretched, then circled the car and removed the fuel

nozzle from its perch.

"How are we doing?" asked Mike, attending to the tank on the van.

"Fine. It's been such a boring day, I almost wish there had been a tail. Any trouble getting the van?"

"None. The Burnses are used to our borrowing it for church business."

"Was it big enough for the nuns' luggage?"

Mike smiled. "I'll tell them you asked that."

Ray replaced the nozzle. Screwing on the gas cap, he said, "Thanks for the help. I just didn't want anyone seeing the nuns packing suitcases."

"There wouldn't have been room for their luggage anyway. Not in that little Nova they're driving." Mike topped off the tank. "I appreciate what you're doing for Theresa."

The two men paid for the gas and returned to their vehicles.

"I'll just follow you to the turnoff," Ray said. "You know your way from there, don't you?"

Mike nodded.

"You'll be sure to check with me before you make any other trips to the lake? Even if my uncle calls and asks you to come?"

"Absolutely." Mike grew serious. "I'd sure like to know what's going on."

"I would, too." Ray looked at his watch. "We'd better get going."

A few miles east of Livingston, the van turned onto the road leading to the lake. Ray drove past it and pulled into a roadside stand. He browsed over the trays of produce, watching the traffic, but no other cars took the turn. He bought a small basket of tomatoes, lingered a little longer, and left.

Ray reached the Tanglewood Airport with a half-hour to spare. Inside the small terminal, he found a seat in the lounge. A bowl of chili, a foot-long frankfurter and a beer occupied him for fifteen minutes or so. Ten minutes before the Mother Superior's plane was due to arrive, Ray began to fidget with his napkin. He tapped the side of the chili bowl with his spoon. A man at the next table gave him a hard stare. He dropped the spoon and left.

Gate Three was at the west end of the terminal. A crowd milled about, all quietly anxious for their own reasons. Ray turned toward the window in time to see a bolt of lightning split the darkening sky.

A plane taxied into view. Ray pulled a small envelope partway out of his shirt pocket and pushed it back. He shifted with the crowd closer to the gate.

The door opened. A stewardess emerged, then a passenger, a stocky, middle-aged man wearing an expensive suit and tugging a wheeled carry-on case. He trudged purposefully along the short, roped-off corridor.

More passengers appeared within a few seconds, rushing for the concourse like horses coming out of a starting gate. Ray moved twice to get a better view, all the while jiggling the keys in his pocket.

He spotted her just as she reached the door: a petite woman with a slight hump across the shoulders. Dressed in the familiar dark skirt, white blouse and blue veil, she walked with a cane and carried a small purse.

Ray weaved his way toward her. By the time he was free of the crush, the elderly nun had moved off to one side and was anxiously scanning the crowd.

"Mother Jean?" said Ray.

She turned her tired face his way. "Yes?"

"I'm Ray Fredrick. A friend of the sisters. They asked me to meet you." He handed her an envelope. "Sister Theresa said to give you this."

Mother Jean glanced from the envelope to a bank of chairs a few feet away. "Perhaps I'll sit for a minute," she said.

Ray accompanied the nun and took a seat next to her. He waited while she read Theresa's note.

Mother Jean breathed a small sigh and said, "Theresa writes very little. Except that you're going to take me to join them." Her tired eyes studied Ray. "Something's wrong, isn't it?"

Choosing his words cautiously, Ray answered, "There is a problem, yes."

Ray rapped at the door and opened it. Naomi and Kate looked up from the two-person task of changing sheets on the oversized bed. Kate tiptoed past Homer, asleep in his wheelchair. She stepped into the hall and closed the door. "Goodness, Ray, you're all wet."

"No kidding." Ray swiped at a trickle of water running down his cheek. Kate grabbed his arm and moved him off the hardwood floors and into the kitchen.

"Where's Mother Jean?"

"In the foyer with the rest of the flock." Ray smiled. "I didn't know nuns cackled. Reminded me of kids gathering around the candy man."

Kate kicked the kitchen door closed. "Would you behave?"

She pulled a dish towel from a drawer and handed it to Ray. "Did you get this wet walking from the car to the house?"

"I got this wet trying to remember where I parked at the airport." Ray wiped his face and rubbed his hair hard with the thin towel. He looked down at himself. A smile broke on his face. "Well, hell, here's my chance to legitimately strip."

"Keep your voice down, please."

"Which room did you put us in? I could have changed by now if I'd known where to go."

"You're not going up the stairs as wet as you are. That's all we need, someone to slip and fall on the water you've tracked inside." Kate opened the door to a long, narrow pantry and shooed Ray in. "Get your things off and I'll bring you a change of clothes." She tossed in a few more towels and shut the door.

Twenty minutes later, Kate returned to the kitchen. She rapped on the pantry door, identified herself, and stepped in. She was greeted by the spectacle of a totally out-of-sorts, barefooted Ray, perched low on a twenty-pound sack of potatoes, and draped haphazardly in towels printed with pastel teapots.

"Nice of you to make it back before tomorrow," murmured Ray.

Kate shut the door. She set the change of clothes on a low shelf. "Sorry. I was waylaid by the sisters. They wanted me to meet Mother Jean."

Ray tossed the towels to the floor and started dressing. Kate looked away and said, "I think we might have a problem."

"Homer?"

"No. Mother Jean. Too many stairs to climb. We'll have to fix her up downstairs someplace."

"Can't it wait till tomorrow?"

"I didn't mean right this minute."

Ray sat back down on the potatoes and started putting on his socks. "Where's Thumper?"

"In our room, for now. I thought we could set him free in the house later, maybe after everyone has retired."

"Good idea. A little extra security can't hurt." Ray fussed with a knot in one of his shoelaces. "I hope you put us in Homer's old room."

"I intended to. And I would have if I'd known that Mother Jean would be better off on the first floor. Anyway, we were one room short, so two of the sisters are sharing the room with the largest bed."

"As if you and I don't equal two."

"I know, but we're used to sleeping together."

"What room are we in?"

"The blue room."

"I suppose that means we share a bathroom with one of the nuns."

"Well at least we have the room with the best view. And it has a full-size bed. That's big enough."

"Not if you still mean to recapture your innocence."

Kate stepped closer and landed a kiss on Ray's cheek. "I didn't really want it back. Come on. You should say hello to Homer before he settles in for the night."

Thirteen

Kate slipped quietly out of bed.

"What time is it?" Ray murmured without opening his eyes.

"Early. Go back to sleep. I'm just going down to get breakfast for the sisters."

"Can't they get their own?"

"Ray, they're guests. I can at least pamper them on their first morning here."

An hour later Ray was jolted awake by the phone ringing in the hall. He bounded out of bed and opened the bedroom door. Across the corridor a second door opened. Ray quickly retreated into his room. The ringing stopped. He shuffled to the bathroom, found the door locked from the inside, listened for a moment, and knocked. No answer. "Great," he muttered.

Ray dragged himself to the window. The sun had yet to clear the trees crowding the eastern shoreline. He spotted Thumper sprawled flat at the side of the boathouse, tied to the limb of a willow. *We'll go for walks,* he promised. *Get you used to the place so you can run free.*

Ray settled on the edge of the sill, scratching his bare chest. The lake looked restless and choppy. Wind-driven water splashed against the boats and the dock. Toward the north shore a small craft bobbed in and out of view as if engaged in a game of hide and seek.

A rap at the door turned Ray from the window.

Kate stepped in and closed the door after her. "Get dressed and come on down. I've already started your breakfast."

"I would if I could get into the bathroom."

Kate tried the handle. "I'll go unlock it."

"You might remind Gabrielle that she's not the only one using it," called Ray as the door closed.

Ray glanced up and down the hallway. Gabrielle's door was closed, as was the door to the master bedroom across the way. The other two bedrooms were blocked from view by a section of wall that cut into the corridor.

Ray descended the wide hardwood stairs to the crackle and aroma of bacon frying. His shoes squeaked loudly at each step. He entered a large nook with a bay window and a view of the woods. Eight chairs, some mismatched, stood around a long oval table. Two places were set.

Ray slipped into the kitchen and poured himself some coffee. He sauntered over to where Kate stood, laid a hand on her arm. "Much longer?"

"A lot longer if you don't get out of my space."

Ray took two giant steps back, paused and took two more for good measure. "Who phoned?" he asked.

"Father Mike."

"Why didn't you call me?"

"Because he asked to talk to Theresa."

"What about?"

"You're very much the busybody this morning."

"It comes with the territory. Are you going to tell me or do I have to go find her and ask?"

"He wanted to know what to do about their car. The repair shop called to say it was ready. They also want the loaner back as soon as possible."

"She didn't take it to them, did she?"

"Of course not. She's waiting to discuss it with you. Which reminds me. Homer wants to see you after you've eaten."

Bacon grease spattered Kate's apron. She reached for a

roll of paper towels. "I probably shouldn't say this, and you shouldn't get your hopes up, but Homer seems to be feeling a lot better. He even wants Naomi and me to take him out for a stroll this morning."

"Oh he does, does he?" His brief smile was little more than a shadow.

"Why don't you come with us?" asked Kate.

"If I'm around."

"Why wouldn't you be?"

"You're burning the bacon." Ray disappeared into the nook and took a seat facing the window. A sudden flutter of wings brought a red-crowned sparrow to perch on the outer sill.

Kate brought him a stack of pancakes embellished with bacon. "Are you washed?" she asked in a mock-motherly fashion. Ray grabbed for the plate, and Kate let it go.

Ray sliced into the cakes. He eyed the other place setting. "Thought you were going to join me."

"That's for Mother Jean." Kate sat sideways on one of the chairs. "You two are the only ones who slept in. Even Homer was up early."

"I'm on vacation. And Mother Jean had a long flight."

"She looked awfully tired. I hope she's all right."

"She'll be fine." Ray sliced another mouthful. "I bought tomatoes yesterday but they're still in the trunk."

"Good. We can use them for lunch."

"I hope you're not going to be saddled with all the cooking."

"Does that mean you're volunteering?"

"I have to patrol the grounds."

Kate smiled. "No, I'm not going to do all the cooking, Ray. I'm taking breakfast; Yavonne and Seraphina are seeing to lunch; and the other two will tackle dinner."

"When do you want to bring the bed downstairs for

Mother Jean?"

"Obviously we have to wait till she gets up. Besides, she might not want us to move her."

"Let me know."

"I will."

"Appreciate the breakfast."

"I appreciate your being here."

Ray carried his dishes to the kitchen, rinsed them and placed them in the dishwasher. He asked, "Do you know where I can find Theresa?"

"Probably in her room."

"Which is?"

"The master bedroom."

Ray mounted the stairs. He rapped lightly on the door to Homer's old room. When Seraphina answered, he greeted her and asked to speak to Theresa.

"Theresa's not here. She went down to visit with your uncle." Seraphina fidgeted with the silver band on her ring finger. "Mr. Fredrick, may I talk to you?"

"Certainly, Sister." Ray stepped into the room and realized that there was only one chair. "We can talk in the loft." Turning to leave, he noticed that the bed had no pillows. "Don't tell me housekeeping forgot to give you pillows."

"Oh no. We have them; they're in the closet. It's just that Theresa has a phobia about pillows. And I don't really need one." A sudden twitch of the nun's mouth betrayed the last part of her statement as more charity than truth. Seraphina closed the door.

"Curious phobia," said Ray.

"It is. And she's had it for as long as I've known her."

Ray led the nun toward the opposite end of the corridor. They circled the stairwell, climbed a few steps and entered an elevated corner room with wide windows and a skylight. It was thickly carpeted and furnished with bean bag chairs, a pair of love seats, and a complete, state-of-the-art entertainment system, including a large-screen television.

Settled on the love seat, Seraphina blinked nervously. She touched her glasses and turned toward the view of the lake. "This is such a lovely spot. Your uncle is very lucky. Well, I mean…"

Her gaze found the carpet. "I'm really worried, Mr. Fredrick."

"About Theresa?"

The nun nodded. "Last night she hardly slept at all. And when I woke this morning, she was sitting on her side of the bed, fully dressed and staring at that oil painting on the wall."

"The Little Girl Lost?" questioned Ray.

"Yes. She seems haunted by that image of the sad-looking woman and child." Seraphina's plump bosom rose and fell. "I just don't know what to do to help her."

"I'm not sure I do either," said Ray. "Is there anyone she might be willing to talk to?"

Seraphina folded her hands. She looked from the floor to the window and back to the floor as if searching the room for the right thing to say. Her gaze locked on her shoe. She said, "Father Mike and Theresa are very close."

"Do you think he could get her to open up?"

"Yes. If anyone can."

"I'll talk to him. But on only one condition."

Seraphina's eyes grew wide with alarm.

"You and the others will stop calling me 'Mr. Fredrick.' You don't want anyone to confuse me with my uncle, do you?"

Ray switched on the stereo. "Another thing. Homer would be hurt if he thought that you and the other sisters weren't taking full advantage of this room. It's his favorite."

Homer responded to the knock in a voice from an earlier

and healthier time. Ray let himself in and joined his uncle and
the nun. He smiled when he realized that the two of them,
seated on opposite sides of a footstool, were engrossed in a
game of poker.

"Grab a seat and we'll deal you in on the next hand," said
Homer.

Ray eyed the pile of buttons in front of Theresa and
estimated that they outnumbered her opponent's collection
by three to one.

He parked on the edge of the bed. "What do I have to do,
rip up a few shirts?"

Theresa's tired eyes smiled. She reached to the side of her
chair with her good hand, and brought up a square tin the size
of a cigar box. She shook it, rattling its contents, and lifted the
lid with her right hand. "Take twenty," she said, passing the
button tin to Ray.

He laughed and began counting. "Where in the world did
you come up with a box of buttons?"

"They're Gabrielle's. She never goes anywhere without
her complete collection of sewing equipment. Just don't let
her know what we're doing with them. She thinks I'm
repairing your uncle's wardrobe."

Ray waited till Theresa and Homer played their hand, and
said, "I hear Father Mike called."

"Oh, yes. He called about our car. It seems it's ready to be
picked up. The service department phoned the rectory when
there was no answer at the convent. They also want the loaner
back as soon as possible. Yavonne volunteered to drive it
back, but I didn't think you'd want that."

"You were right. I'd better do it."

"I'm sorry to put you through another trip to Tanglewood,"
said Theresa.

"That's no problem. But you could do me a favor."

Theresa faced Ray and waited.

"Thumper needs to be walked around the property, close to the house. The sooner he's familiar with the area, the sooner we can let him run loose."

Theresa snatched up the cards and began shuffling them into the open hand of her injured arm. "I'll speak to Yavonne. I'm sure she'd love to do it."

Addressing his nephew, Homer asked, "You're not going this morning, are you?"

"I wouldn't think of it. Are we still on for eleven?"

"Eleven sharp."

"You sure you're up to this?"

"I haven't felt this good in weeks. I think I'm afloat on the prayers in the air."

Homer chuckled freely, making a raspy, familiar sound from happier times. Ray listened as though it were a favorite song. He felt a rush of gratitude for the chance to hear it again.

Abruptly, Homer placed a hand on his nephew's arm. "I have a favor to ask. I've been hankering for a good haircut, especially now that I feel like getting around a little. Think you could find a barber willing to make a house call?"

Ray hesitated, wanting neither to squelch his uncle's mood nor to bring strangers onto the property. He said, "Kate could cut it."

"Do you let her cut yours?"

"No."

"Case made." Homer thought for a moment. "But only if you know someone who can be trusted. I don't want to put anyone in danger." His eyes shifted to Theresa.

"I know someone," said Ray. "You'll have your haircut. And as long as we're talking safety, I've been thinking about your nurses. All these people coming and going make me nervous."

"I'm way ahead of you," said Homer. "Naomi's agreed to stay and be on call twenty-four hours. All I really need is someone to give me my injections and see to a few other things. And Theresa and the sisters have volunteered to fill in, if needed. Now, can we get back to the battle for the buttons?"

Ray watched Theresa deal surprisingly well with her left hand. Picking up his cards, he asked, "When does the cast come off?"

"Not for another month."

Ray frowned at his card. "How do you like your room?"

"It's very nice," Theresa answered, feeding the cards singly into her right hand.

"Where did Kate put you, Sister?" asked Homer.

Ray answered, "She and Seraphina have your old room." Quickly addressing the nun, Ray said, "What do you think of that painting? The one of the woman and child?"

For what seemed like a long time, Theresa studied her hand. Finally she said, "It's very striking."

"It was painted by a friend of my grandfather's," said Homer. "Used to hang in the living room till I got hoggish and hung it upstairs."

Ray fixed his gaze on Theresa. "It's been a Fredrick tradition to ask people what the painting suggests to them. My mother saw the woman and girl as the same person. She thought the woman was sad from the loss of her carefree childhood. Did anything strike you?"

Theresa shook her head and closed her hand of cards. She picked up the deck and looked Ray calmly in the eye.

"All right, gents, how many cards will you take?"

Fourteen

Using the phone in the upstairs hall, Ray dialed his barber in Tanglewood, got a busy signal, and hung up. Behind him, a door opened.

Gabrielle passed and nodded politely. She held something small and black in a balled fist. Ray glanced at his watch. It was ten to eleven. He dialed twice more, then gave up. He hurried down the stairs and out the front door. He wouldn't dare be late for this. Gabrielle and Homer would have his hide.

A sizable smile on his gaunt face, Homer allowed Naomi to cover his legs with a light yellow shawl.

"Crocheted it myself," boasted the nurse.

"Are you sure you're up to this, Homer?" asked Kate.

"I'm sure. Let's go."

Kate opened the door. Naomi pushed the wheelchair into the hall. They passed the staircase, passed the living room and dining room, crossed the foyer to the front door. On the porch, Naomi locked the wheels of the chair, removed the shawl and draped it over her shoulder. Slowly, Homer stood. Kate took his arm while Naomi lowered the chair a step at a time and hurried back to take the invalid's other arm. Cautiously, the three of them descended.

The sun had yet to crest the tallest trees and lay down long shadows from the house to the lake and across the water.

"Shall we walk along the shore?" asked Kate.

"No. I want to check the boats. I'm thinking maybe I might be up to a ride on the pontoon boat sometime soon."

Kate regarded the swells and intermittent whitecaps on the

lake uncertainly. She stole a glance at Naomi. In response, the nurse's smile did nothing but expand. Her strong black fingers tightened their grip, her steps quickened, and they moved on at a more rapid pace.

Naomi wheeled the chair to the foot of the dock and stopped in the shade of an old willow.

They watched the moored boats rock in their bed of water, and listened to their periodic *thump* against the tire-lined pier.

"I bought that pontoon boat just last year." His voice was a little sad in spite of his effort to be cheerful.

"Sure is nice here," mused Naomi. She shook her head. "Sure is." Her gaze roamed the water and wilderness that surrounded them. "How come yours is the only house, Mr. Fredrick?"

"Because most of the land along the shore is swamp. There are a few cabins deeper in. But they're used chiefly by hunters. This section is the only lakeshore property fit for building." Homer was silent for a time, then said, "That's why they named it Hush Lake. Not much noise hereabouts but what the wind and the forest and its wee folks manage to make." Homer's head tilted and he smiled. "Wee folks," he repeated. "My granddaddy used to rock me and my brother by the hour and spin us tales of the beaver and the beetle and the birds and how they worked and played on Mother Earth, and earned their food and shelter by trading respect."

Kate jumped. Homer's liver-spotted, hairy hand clutched her arm. "What's wrong?" she asked.

Naomi remained calm. "Is that Charley fellow coming, Mr. Fredrick?"

Homer shook his head. He gestured toward the boathouse, and in a tight whisper said, "Someone's in there. I saw a shadow at the window. Wheel me around to the side door. That's the last time that scalawag is going to steal from me."

"Let me go get Ray," said Kate.

"It'll take too long. Grab some stones. The three of us can

handle whoever it is."

Naomi instantly began gathering stones along the path, her backside and thighs looming large as she bent to the task. Kate watched in disbelief.

"Hurry, Kate," whispered Homer. "We don't want the rascal to get away."

Kate looked back at the house, hoping to find help. At Homer's continued prodding, she leaned over, looked longingly again at the house, and picked up a few stones.

Naomi piled her collection on the huge red handkerchief Homer had spread over the shawl. With squinting eyes and a pursed mouth, she set about gathering more.

"Now, wheel me up to that side door," Homer directed. Naomi obliged without a moment's hesitation.

"Really, Homer, I think we should get Ray," whispered Kate.

Homer simply handed her another fistful of stones. He turned to Naomi. "Ready?" he asked.

"Ready, sweetheart," she answered, brandishing her ammunition.

To Kate's dismay, Homer raised an unsteady foot and gave the door a weak kick.

A full-fledged uproar followed. Shouts and whistles and tools banging on empty cans. Ray was first to emerge, wearing the size and type of grin one would expect from a kid at his first Christmas. Gabrielle was next out, a black whistle still clutched between her teeth. She gave one final piercing blast.

The rest of the household, except Mother Jean, piled happily through the door. Homer leaned his head back and laughed. When Kate faced him in total befuddlement, he pulled a set of car keys from his pocket and handed them to her. "A gift to my surrogate daughter. Go on in."

Ray followed Kate into the boathouse, watched with pleasure her misty-eyed surprise on seeing the new car, then marched to the shore end of the boathouse and raised its garage-wide door.

Homer took his lunch with the group. After the meal, he willingly went for a siesta.

Yavonne accompanied Ray to the side of the house. She opened the door of the Chevy Nova, removed a box of tissue, a map, and a packet of gum. "I'll be glad to get the other car back. This thing has the pick-up of a turtle."

Yavonne handed Ray the keys and the repair order.

Ray glanced at the yellow sheet. "Lodwick's, eh?"

"They give us a good discount. Mike worked out a deal with the new owner. In return, the dealership gets free advertisement in the church paper."

Abruptly, Yavonne asked, "Was anything said about money? The five-hundred-dollar deductible will need to be paid."

"Theresa arranged for me to meet Father Mike at the rectory. He'll go with me to get the car, and put the charge on the parish account."

"Theresa said you'd like your dog taken for a walk," said Yavonne.

"Right. Just around the property." Ray hesitated before saying, "Theresa doesn't seem too keen on pets."

"Oh, no. We used to have a cat at the convent. It's just dogs she doesn't seem to want around."

Ray reached Tanglewood in the middle of the afternoon. He drove directly to Saint Luke's. Catching a glimpse of the caretaker at the back of the school building, he parked close by.

Peter dragged a trash barrel up to the dumpster, then faced his visitor. He took off his cap and scratched his head. "You catch that fellow yet?" he asked.

"I wish I could say yes," answered Ray. "Any chance you saw him again, hanging around the area?"

"Nope. If I had, you wouldn't need Old Lady Justice to dish out those hand-slapping penalties she calls punishments."

"You don't approve of our correctional facilities, Mr. Kruger?"

"No, I don't. Seems mighty queer when a government takes damn fine care of its criminals and lets its lame and sick and old walk the streets." With surprising ease, Peter hoisted the barrel and shook its contents free. He banged it a final time on the lip of the dumpster and let it fall to the ground. It rocked to a stop.

To change the subject, Ray asked, "Do you bunk here?"

"Nope. Got myself a cheap pad in a rooming house on Junction Street."

"How are you feeling?" asked Ray, studying Peter's scarred face.

"Crummy. Not like I was prizefighter material before. Now I can't even blow my nose in comfort. Well, what the heck? One more gripe added to the list ain't anything new." His hand reached around to his hip pocket, before he caught himself and brought it back. He screwed up his face and yelped in pain. "Ain't even allowed to enjoy a good scowl," he grumbled. Amused by his own remark, Peter allowed himself a careful smile. "See you got a haircut," he said.

Ray's eyes brightened. "I don't want to go around looking like our little punk of the pit-stop."

That brought a chuckle from Peter. Tossing prudence to the wind, he yanked his flask from his pocket, uncapped it and offered Ray a swallow.

Not wanting to spoil the moment, Ray made a show of reaching for it, then dropped his hand and declared, "Better not." He winked. "Old Lady Duty's got eyes like a mother-in-law."

"Ain't never had one, but I know what you mean." Peter took a surprisingly wee sip, capped the flask and replaced it. He grabbed the barrel, started toward the school, then turned back and called out, "Say, thanks. Kind of nice to be asked about my health."

The rectory door opened and a tall, thin man examined Ray over the rims of his half-glasses.

"Afternoon, Father," said Ray.

The priest looked pointedly at the distinctive rose-colored buttons and piping along the front of his cassock. "Monsignor," he corrected.

"Beg your pardon." As he held up his badge for inspection, Ray had a sudden vision of his interlocutor and Sister Gabrielle holding court in church. He suppressed a smile. "Would you please tell Father Mike that Detective Fredrick is here to see him?"

"Father Killian is in the church." Monsignor punctuated his response by pursing his thin lips. Clearly, police presence on church grounds did not suit his ideas of propriety.

Ray thanked him and crossed the blacktop to the side door of the church building. The sudden change from sunlight to dim interior stopped him just inside. He waited for his eyes to adjust, then advanced toward the main aisle, his steps resounding on the hard stone floor. He halted at the end of a pew. Far up front and a few feet from a large marble altar, a thin column of fire flickered from inside a red globe.

Before he could start up the aisle, Ray heard the sudden sound of quiet sobbing. Tensing, he tracked the sound to an ornate, rectangular structure that protruded from the side wall and stood more than seven feet high. Its central door and two side openings were closed with a curtain. Ray instantly retreated to a seat in a back pew.

Shortly, a bowed woman came into view, gripping a wad of tissue. She took herself to the far side of the church and knelt in front of a statue of the Blessed Virgin.

A door opened and closed. Father Mike faced the altar and knelt for a long moment on one knee. Then he headed in Ray's direction.

Ray left by the side door. Waiting at the bottom of the

round stone stairs, he watched Mike descend. The detective was struck by the childlike quality of the priest's blue eyes, and by the shine in them that suggested tears.

Ray lowered his gaze.

"Sorry you had to wait," said Mike.

"I hope I didn't disturb anything." Ray fell in with the priest as he started toward the rectory.

"Do you mind if I take a minute to change?"

"No. Go ahead." Midway, Ray said, "I met your fellow priest."

"Monsignor?" Mike shot Ray a sideways glance. "I suppose he was annoyed at having to answer the door. The housekeeper is usually there to do it, but she had to do some shopping."

Ray followed the priest into a small office at the front of the rectory. "Have a seat," said Mike. "I'll just be a minute." He unbuttoned his cassock and hung it up. Underneath he was wearing a yellow pullover and black slacks.

Ray asked, "Have any strangers been asking about the sisters?"

"Just the car-repair people." Mike slipped into a pair of sandals. "How are things at the lake?"

Seizing the moment, Ray answered, "Disturbing."

Mike took a seat at his desk.

"In what way?"

"Oh, the setting seems safe enough. But danger doesn't always come from the outside. Sister Seraphina came to me this morning. She's very worried about Theresa. And, to be truthful, so am I." Ray ran through what he had learned from Seraphina, and added a few of his own misgivings.

"The trouble is, Father Mike, unless Theresa confides in someone and helps us put the whole matter to rest, who knows what might happen?"

Fifteen

Accompanied by the priest, Ray drove the block and a half to the Lodwick Dealership. He eased the car into a space near the service department. The men met at the rear of the car. Mike said, "Having this place so close has been a godsend."

"They certainly work fast for you." Ray handed the priest the keys to the borrowed car and the work sheet for the nuns' Chevy. They stepped through a doorway into the service area. An Olds Ninety-eight stood at the far end, its driver and a service rep gesticulating next to its raised hood.

Mike headed for the customer's lounge. At the cashier's window, he identified himself, handed over the keys for the loaner, and the paperwork for the damaged Chevy.

"Was your loaner satisfactory?" inquired the cashier in a voice that could have worked equally well with a comment about the weather.

"I'm sure it was," replied Mike.

"May I ask where it's parked?"

"Just to the right of the entrance."

The cashier swiveled to her computer and typed in the number on the work order. She glanced twice at the screen, then squinted at it. "That's strange."

Ray leaned over the counter, trying to see the screen.

"Is something the matter?" asked Mike.

"I hope not. Were you contacted by our department?"

"Yes. Yesterday."

"Mmmmm." The cashier slid out of her chair.

Mike looked at Ray. "I hope you haven't come all this way for nothing."

Ray's attention stayed with the cashier until she had disappeared through a door marked Service Manager. In no more than a minute, she reappeared, looking pleased with herself.

"Computer glitch," she offered by way of explanation. Again, she entered the work-order number. The desk printer came to life with a loud hum and a clatter, and spewed out a page of text.

"You have a deductible of five hundred, Father." The cashier circled the amount due and passed Mike the customer's copy of the bill.

In return, Mike slipped her a laminated card with his name, identification number, and the logo of the dealership, and directed the amount be charged to his account.

The cashier made a note of the number and handed the card back. "You're all set," she said. "If you'll wait outside the lounge, your car will be brought around shortly."

They left the waiting room and stationed themselves on an apron of raised concrete. Suddenly, Mike heard himself addressed from the dealership side of the service area. A man headed their way, an expensively dressed, broad-faced, balding man in his late sixties.

"Father Killian. What a nice surprise." The man shook Mike's hand like an old friend, and faced Ray with a look of keen interest. Mike introduced the two men.

Simon Lodwick smiled warmly. "Fredrick," he repeated. "Why does that name ring a bell?"

"You recently authorized an exchange of purchases for my uncle, Homer Fredrick. Which he very much appreciated."

"Homer Fredrick. Yes, I remember. Just this past week, wasn't it?"

"Last Friday," said Ray.

"I'm sorry I wasn't around to handle the matter myself. It's uncanny how personal emergencies surface at the worst of times." Lodwick brushed his wide, trimmed mustache and said, "I seem to recall that your uncle was hospitalized. How's he doing?"

"At home and resting," said Ray, not wanting to say more.

Lodwick brought his attention back to Mike. He spotted the receipt in the priest's hand. "I see you've had some problems of your own. Engine trouble?"

"No. The sisters' car was in an accident last week. They had it in for body work."

"Accident? Was anyone hurt?"

"Not seriously."

"Good. Well, tell the sisters to expect a follow-up call in the next few days. Just to be sure there are no complaints. A dealership is only as good as its service department."

"Actually, they're on vacation," said Mike, with a side-long look at Ray. He chose his words carefully. "But if there's a problem with the car, I'll make sure they call you personally when they get back."

"I'll be disappointed if you don't. I want Lodwick's and Saint Luke's to have nothing but praise for each other. And if your parishioners provide sufficient business, perhaps we can discuss a more substantial discount."

The nuns' Chevy squealed to a halt inches from where they stood. A young man climbed out and hurried off. Mike settled on the passenger's side. Ray squeezed behind the wheel and adjusted the seat.

Simon Lodwick circled the car, ostentatiously inspecting the body work. He ended up at the passenger window. "I'm happy to say that even I cannot tell which part of the frame was repaired." He shook hands with the priest. "Good-bye, Father. And Mr. Fredrick, my best to your uncle."

Ray put the car in drive.

Addressing Lodwick, Mike said, "I hope you received the copy of the *Herald* I dropped off."

"I did. And your people did a marvelous job placing our ad. I only hope your parishioners find that Lodwick's displays the same professionalism." He stepped up on the concrete strip, raised a hand and said, "Drive safely. There are a lot of maniacs on the road."

Moving with his usual shuffling gait, Trev Steward entered the Cafe and made straight for a booth at the back. He squeezed in across from Ray. "I wish you'd choose a table."

"I like booths."

"I don't."

"Next time, get here first."

"Sure. Like I don't know you called from here." The waitress took Trev's order for coffee and a donut. "So, what's up?" asked Trev.

"Not much."

"Then what am I here for?"

"To enjoy my company. What's happening at the station?"

"A lot of what always happens. Plus the usual undercurrents that come with a change."

"Has Sitarski been enthroned yet?"

"Tomorrow." Trev smiled. "He stopped by the office this morning. Told me to make sure you knew you're invited for chow."

"Don't tell me he's giving himself a party."

Trev shrugged his wide shoulders. "The departments are."

"Do you think I could sneak in a stink bomb?"

"Just come in person." Trev smirked. "That ought to do it."

"I could send each department a note of condolence," said Ray. "Or maybe I'll just take out a page in the *Observer* and let the citizenship in on their misfortune."

"You always did think the world of your own opinion. Did you get me here so you can rattle off your latest litany of complaints?"

"I got you here to give you a break." Ray took a sip of coffee and set the cup down too hard. He grabbed some napkins from the dispenser, soaked up the spill and said, "Did AFIS ever get back on those prints from the school john?"

"Yeah. Just another zero to add to our collection." Trev looked away, then turned back and said, "Your friend, Keyhoe, filed a complaint about you harassing him and his mother."

"Hell, all I asked his mother was if she knew where so-and-so lived."

"Well, he reported it as cloak-and-dagger harassment. He's even hired himself a lawyer. Sitarski got wind of it this morning, and wants a hearing."

"You got to be kidding. On what grounds? Besides good old-fashioned vengeance."

"It'll fizzle out," said Trev. He scratched at both sides of his nose. "The guys want to know if you're coming back."

"Why? Have they had their fill of you already?"

"Seriously, are you?"

"I don't know. I haven't really thought about it. Isn't that what vacations are for? To get your mind off the job?"

"I guess." Trev turned to the window with its view of early afternoon traffic. "I didn't see your car out front."

"I'm driving the nuns' Chevy. It had to be picked up, and I didn't want them doing it."

"This the same car involved in the hit-and-run?"

"Yeah."

"Where'd they take it? The last time I had a car in for body work, it took a month to get it back."

"Lodwick's."

"Lodwick's? Where the hell is Lodwick's?"

"That's the Cadillac-Olds dealership over on Church Street. Lodwick is the new owner."

"They must have money, going to a dealership for repairs."

"They get a discount. Some deal worked out between

Saint Luke's and the dealership. Heck, maybe I should go back to church just for the financial benefits. Parishioners get the discount, too."

"The day you go to church will be the day I go on a diet."

"Damn, if that isn't a double-whammy motive for me to give my knees some exercise."

Sipping coffee, Ray played with the salt and pepper shakers, shoving them up against the catsup bottle.

Trev said, "What the hell is wrong with you? You're as fidgety as a rat in a cage."

"I don't know. Something's got me spooked and I'll be damned if I can figure out what." Ray called the waitress over for a refill of coffee.

"Maybe that's your problem," said Trev, pointing to Ray's cup. "Caffeine. Either that or Sitarski."

"Sitarski be damned. I'm worried about the nuns." Ray rapped the table.

"Do you think you might have been tailed?"

"Who knows?"

"Want me to follow you out of the city?"

"It would help."

"Are you leaving from here?"

"No. I have to find my uncle a barber."

"You mean to take back with you?"

Ray shrugged.

"Is that wise?" asked Trev.

"No. But I didn't have the heart to refuse him. He's got little enough to look forward to." After some thought, Ray said, "I suppose I could blindfold the barber. Give him some spiel about a star witness in protective custody."

"How will you explain the nuns?"

"Maybe convents make good hideouts."

"You think this barber is going to buy all that?"

"Come on, it's not such a bad story. But no." Ray shook his

head. "It won't work. The hit-and-run happened outside this guy's shop. He saw Theresa."

"Keep her out of sight."

"Won't make any difference. They all dress the same. He's bound to suspect."

"So just tell him the truth," said Trev. "Unless you think he's involved."

Ray laughed. "Jim? Never in a million years."

"Swear him to secrecy. Haul out a Bible and an F.B.I. manual and lay it on thick."

"Yeah, maybe that's the best way to go. I don't mean the books. I mean telling him the truth."

Trev said, "So you have to drive the barber to your uncle's, take him home, and drive back."

"Obviously."

"You're turning into a taxi service. Couldn't happen to a worse driver." Trev finished his donut. "I should get back." He stood up. "Give me a call when you're ready to roll. I'll meet you at the rear of the station."

"Make it the library. With the way things are going, I'm bound to meet Sitarski if I show my face there."

"All right, the library. And when you bring the barber back, give me a call and we'll do the same."

"Might not be till this evening."

"Good. You can buy me supper. Oh, yeah. I almost forgot. Just before I left to come here, the switchboard took a call for you. They put it through to me."

"Who was it?"

"Someone who knew your extension. When I said you were on vacation, she hung up."

"A woman?"

"A *she* usually is."

Sixteen

Ray found that Main Street had lost its detour signs and regained its usual traffic flow. Business at the bakery was in full swing, with cars parked at the curb as well as at the side of the building.

It was the same at the barbershop. Ray parked at the back and entered through the rear door. Two barbers were busy with clients, but Jim was nowhere in sight. Ray approached the nearest barber. "Is Jim around?"

"He's gone for a bite."

"Do you know where?"

The barber pointed his scissors toward the house behind the shop.

Ray made his way across the wide gravel lot. He climbed the half dozen dilapidated steps and knocked. He heard a beep that sounded like a microwave timer, then a reedy voice called, "Who is it?"

"Ray Fredrick."

Jim bustled through the living room and up to the door, holding a spatula chin-high in his hand, and looking thinner than ever without his barber's frock.

His voice quivered with concern. "Is your haircut all right?"

"My haircut is fine."

Jim shoved open the door, and invited his visitor in.

"I see you have your business back," said Ray.

"Yes. I'm so pleased. Especially for the boys. For me it's a hobby; for them it's their bread and butter." Noticing Ray's lingering glance at his four-day-old attempt at a mustache,

Jim self-consciously touched the fuzzy band of hair. "You don't like it."

"It looks fine."

"I thought it might make me look older."

"I think it does."

"Do you?" squeaked Jim happily. He pivoted and examined himself in the glass of a framed portrait of a family of Chihuahuas. "A friend of mine suggested it," he said. He continued to scrutinize his reflected countenance in the corner of the glass. As if suddenly remembering he wasn't alone, he whirled around to face Ray. His large eyes widened. Jim sniffed the air and said, "I think I'm burning my lunch."

Motioning Ray to follow, he crossed a sparsely furnished living room with drawn drapes and a lot of dust. In the hall, he broke into a run and disappeared through a door at the far end.

Ray followed at a leisurely pace. He glanced through open doorways into the rooms he passed. Two were untidily furnished bedrooms cluttered with the playthings and paraphernalia of boys in their early teens. In the larger room, the bed was unmade. A framed photo on the dresser caught Ray's eye. Sending a quick glance down the hall, he slipped in. The picture was a long shot with a snow-capped mountain in the background. One of the figures seemed to be a younger Jim. He stood with his arm around another boy of the same height and build and protruding eyes, but with both his hands masking the lower half of his face.

Ray joined Jim in the kitchen. The barber stood at the stove, frowning at a frying pan full of smoke and something that had started as a grilled cheese sandwich.

At the side of the stove, a fat dog slept on a stained, yellowed pillow. "You have a dog," said Ray.

"That's Peaches. She's kind of old."

Carrying the frying pan at arm's length, Jim dashed to the

sink and set it down.

"I seem to have bad timing," said Ray.

"I always do this," said Jim in lighthearted self-disgust. "My own fault. If I hadn't always let Owen do the cooking, I'd be better at it now."

"Who's Owen?" asked Ray.

"My brother." Jim spoke the words with a touch of melancholy.

"I didn't know you had a brother."

Jim fixed Ray with his big brown eyes. "Owen never wanted me to speak of him. Not while he was living here, anyway. I guess there's no harm now." There was a pause. He added, "Owen and I are twins."

With the speed of a nervous hare, he was out of the kitchen; and just as quickly, he returned. Jim handed Ray the photo that had caught his visitor's attention minutes earlier.

"I'm ruining your lunch," said Ray, taking the picture.

Focused again on his task, Jim gathered cheese and bread and butter from the refrigerator. He opened a cupboard and pulled out a pan twice the size of the first one. He skewered a gob of butter, dropped it into the pan and switched on the burner.

Out of the corner of one eye, Ray watched warily as the butter began to sizzle. He stood the photo on the table, and reached across for that day's copy of the *Tanglewood Observer*. Something fell to the floor. Ray reached down and retrieved the *Saint Luke's Herald*. "Do you belong to Saint Luke's parish?" asked Ray.

"Sort of," replied Jim. He plopped the sandwich into the pan just as the butter was beginning to change color, then hovered with a spatula at the ready.

Ray felt the urge to wish him luck, decided he'd better keep still, and glanced over the day's headlines.

With a swoop of the spatula that sent hot butter over the

surface of the stove, Jim rescued his sandwich from the pan and plopped it onto a waiting plate. He finished the ritual with a whoop of triumph.

Ray folded his hands to keep from clapping.

Jim opened a counter-top microwave, removed a cup, and carried it and his sandwich over to where Ray sat. His face beamed as if he'd won a gold medal at the Olympics.

"It looks good," said Ray, stretching the truth.

Jim was back on his feet. "Want me to make you one? Won't take but a minute."

"I just had lunch," replied Ray quickly.

The barber plopped back down, grabbed his sandwich and took a large bite.

Ray filled the time with small talk until his host had finished his sandwich, then said, "Jim, I have a favor to ask."

Jim came out of his house dressed in dark slacks and a beige shirt with billowing sleeves, carrying a black satchel.

"You didn't have to dress up," said Ray, as Jim climbed in on the passenger's side.

"I wanted to. This is kind of a special occasion. First time I've ever gone on a house call to cut hair."

"Well, you'll make my uncle's day. That's for sure."

"He isn't *too* sick, is he?" asked Jim uncomfortably.

"He's well enough to want his hair cut." Ray waited for the traffic to clear, then cut across both lanes and parked in front of the bakery. "I'll just be a second."

The bell chimed as he entered. Two young ladies in white uniforms were waiting on a line of customers. Carol Burns peeked out from the back room, saw Ray and hurried over.

"Happy return to normal," called Ray.

"And not a moment too soon. Another week and we would have gone under."

"Mrs. Burns, did you by any chance call me at the station earlier today?"

"Call you? No. Did you want me to?"

"Only if something important came to mind about the

accident." Ray eyed a long loaf of dark rye. He ordered three and asked Carol to box up a dozen and a half assorted pastries. While she was busy making the selections, Ray slipped a quarter into the phone near the door and dialed Trev.

It was after five when they reached Hush Hideaway. Jim had finally stopped chattering and seemed absorbed with the view of the tree-lined lake.

As they approached the house, Ray noticed two of the sisters down by the water, fussing with what looked like folding tables.

Ray ushered Jim into the house and down the hall to his uncle's room. He rapped and entered. The room was empty. He closed the door and crossed to the kitchen. Kate was forming ground beef into patties. At her side, Thumper watched with the rapture of a four-legged connoisseur.

"Where's Homer?" asked Ray. He set the bread and pastries on the counter.

Kate greeted Jim. Answering Ray, she said, "Homer's in the loft listening to music."

"In the loft? How did he get there?"

"Yavonne and Naomi carried him up. He said to bring Jim right up when you got back."

Ray started for the door. Kate said, "Come back down, hon, when you get Jim settled."

Kate was seated at the table nursing a cup of coffee when Ray returned. "I poured you one," she said

Ray reached for the mug. "Who's been in my pastries?" asked Ray, eyeing the cut string.

"I took a peek. That was nice of you." She paused, then added, "Guess what?"

"I've had a long day. I'd rather just be told."

"We're having a party."

"Everybody's having parties," murmured Ray.

"What are you talking about?"

"Sitarski's being instated tomorrow. There's going to be a party. And I'm invited." His voice had an edge of self-pity.

Kate stayed silent for a long moment. "Well, I'm talking about a party you'll *enjoy*. A cookout."

"When's this supposed to take place?"

"Tonight. In an hour."

"Count me out. When I drive Jim back, I'm having supper with Trev."

"Homer's expecting you to be there."

"What's he want me to do with Jim?"

"Invite him to stay. And if you can't talk him into it, I will. Besides, you have to pick up Mike. Homer wanted him to come. Mike will drive to Livingston and wait for you at the McDonald's there."

Ray shook his head. "What would we do for landmarks without McDonald's."

Kate glanced at the kitchen clock. "You should leave in ten minutes."

"Heck, the more the merrier. To hell with discretion."

"Ray... You ought to be glad Homer's feeling so much better."

"I am. But what about Theresa's safety?"

"Nothing's different. Jim was coming anyway. Mike will wait to be met, just as you asked."

Ray walked over to the counter and selected a cheese Danish. Seated, he said, "Whose idea was the party?"

"Homer's."

"He does seem better." Ray took a bite of the pastry. For a moment he imagined prayer as invisible waves of electricity flittering in and out of rooms, and up and down stairs, putting a shine on life. He drank some coffee. "Did Thumper get out for a walk?" he asked.

"All afternoon. First with the leash, then without."

Ray called the dog and fed him the last piece of pastry.

"I took my new car for a trial run," said Kate. When Ray frowned, she quickly added, "Just around here. I was never out of sight of the house."

"How do you like it?"

"Do you need to ask?"

"How's Mother Jean?"

"Fine. And we don't have to move her. She said stairs aren't a problem if she moves slowly."

"I saw that old couple again."

"The ones in the pickup?"

"Yeah." Ray stood. "I better call Trev and tell him not to look for me until late." He brought the kitchen phone back to the table and connected with Trev on his first try. That done, he dialed information and asked for the number for Sue Darnell. "Who's she?" whispered Kate.

Ray wrote the number down and replaced the receiver. "The gas station attendant who might have seen the green Pontiac before the hit-and-run. Someone called me at the station. I just want to make sure it wasn't her."

Kate kept quiet while Ray spoke to the woman. When he hung up, she asked, "Was it her?"

"She didn't even recognize my name. Kate, be extra careful until I get back."

The sun hung low in the sky. Ray had returned with Mike, changed into jeans and a brown pullover, and gone to the boathouse to check on fishing equipment, in case they found time to do a little fishing after the meal.

Echoes from a single shot tore through the woods.

Ray was out of the boathouse in an instant.

Birds fluttered over the crowns of trees west of the house. Elsewhere, the long shadows fell across undisturbed water and forest. Ray took off at a run for the trees. Kate slammed out the front door just as he passed. She glared at him.

"Ray, did you—"

"No, I didn't. Where's Theresa?"

"I don't know."

"Find her."

"Where are you going?"

Ray waved toward the woods. He rounded the corner of the house and cut into the trees, shielding his face with a raised arm. The woods had grown quiet again, the crunch of leaves under his feet the only break in the stillness.

Ray had hardly worked up a sweat when he saw a figure ambling along a path. Ray stopped and stared. "Jim? What are you doing out here?"

The barber blinked. "I'm just out for a walk."

"Didn't you hear the shot?"

"Was that a shot?"

"What did you think it was?"

The barber's eyes bulged as he considered the question. "Backfire?" he offered.

"Out here in the woods? Did you see anyone else around?"

"No. Is something wrong?"

Ray sighed softly. "Everything's fine. Let's get back to the house."

Kate ran to meet them as they came into the open. "I can't find Theresa," she blurted. "I looked all over the house."

"Have the others seen her?"

"Seraphina said that Theresa went up to her room for a few minutes after they set up the tables for the picnic, then said she was going for a stroll by the lake."

Ray raced for the shore. He reached the group of card tables and chairs and makeshift grill. He called the nun's name.

"Yes?" The voice came from his right.

He wheeled to see Theresa was standing in the pontoon boat, her arm in its white cast bright in the glow of the evening sun. With her good hand, she gripped tightly a ball-point pen and a notebook covered in faded black cloth.

Seventeen

"When it comes to worrying, you are your dad all over again," said Homer.

A wheel of his chair snagged on a stone. Ray drew the wheelchair back and skirted the obstruction. "That *was* a shot I heard," he said.

"And you'll hear a lot more if you stay here long. Poachers love these woods. The law doesn't give them much trouble."

They reached a wide, sandy area lit by spotlights mounted in a nearby tree. Naomi bustled over to them, retrieved the yellow shawl from the back of the wheelchair, and scolded Homer as she covered his legs.

"It's summer, for heaven's sake," Homer said.

"That cool wind off the lake don't know it," Naomi replied.

Homer shooed her away and scanned the picnickers like a miser contemplating his treasure. "So many special people." He glanced up at his nephew. "Let's go fishing tomorrow."

"Do you think that's wise?"

"I no longer have the time or the inclination to worry about that. Maybe we could go out on the pontoon boat, if you can get it running."

Mike stopped to greet Homer and thank him for the invitation. He helped Ray move the wheelchair through the sand and over to a train of tables set for ten. The air was full of the sound of the waves and the chatter of birds.

"Burgers are about ready," announced Gabrielle from the grill, where she and Thumper hovered with equal interest.

Homer clapped for attention. "Gather around, everybody.

I'd like to say grace." He bowed his head, scratched once at a bushy eyebrow. "Lord, this prayer isn't going to be about food or prosperity or weather. Instead, I want to give thanks for the last few days. For friends and for a quality of joy I had almost forgotten. Amen. Let's eat."

Naomi set a container of custard in front of her patient. He pushed it aside. "Take that mush away, woman. I'm going to have a burger."

"Mr. Fredrick, you want a burger, you get a burger." Naomi took an open-faced bun to the grill and selected the thinnest of the sizzling patties.

Mother Jean approached Homer. She hooked her cane over the back of the chair on the old man's left, and sat down with her plate of food. "You're very gracious to have us here, Mr. Fredrick," she said.

"It's a matter of luck, and all of it's mine," he answered.

Theresa settled across from Mother Jean. Soon the old gentleman had both nuns busy answering questions about their order and their Mother House in Canada.

Ray filled his plate and wandered just outside the reach of the lights. He studied the dark woods surrounding the house. Seconds later, Kate was at his side. "Would you please go back and sit down? You're going to turn this from a party into a funer—" She stopped short of finishing, and gave Ray a feeble shove toward the table. Her hand felt something hard. She said, "I suppose it's better there than in the house."

"I'd say so." Ray felt through his shirt for the grip of the thirty-eight. "You know, she's like a sitting duck with these spotlights on."

"We can't eat in the dark, Ray." Kate glanced toward the table. "What if I get Theresa to sit on the lake side, would that make you happy?"

"It would help. At least most of the shoreline is swamp."

Kate called Theresa aside and told her of Ray's worry. The

two traded places, with Theresa moving to the opposite end to sit with the lake at her back and the tall figures of Mike and Ray between her and most of the shoreline.

Jim chattered nonstop. He seemed to have an unending supply of stories collected during his years behind a barber chair, and when he got warmed up, he was genuinely entertaining.

Toward the end of the meal, Gabrielle excused herself and started for the house. She returned with two rhubarb-meringue pies. She sliced and served the pies from her place at the table, her eyebrows arching contentedly as murmurs of pleasure quickly followed.

A stillness settled on the group as they enjoyed the dessert. When conversation once again began to flow freely, Naomi leaned forward and looked down the table at Homer. He responded with a nod. Naomi eased her chair back and stood. She started for the house, disappearing into the dark.

Yavonne heard it first, the far-away sound that became music as it grew closer. The tune had an uplifting beat that matched their mood of laughter and companionship. Naomi came striding happily down the path, toting a portable stereo with its volume turned up high. Thumper sprinted off to meet the nurse, and barked and pranced about her happily.

"Tonight, we are going to dance," announced Homer.

Naomi kicked off her sandals and set the stereo on the ground, then clapped and rocked from side to side. "Come on, people! Let's show Mr. Fredrick that we're really havin' fun at his party!" Her infectious smile beckoned to the others.

Feet and fingers and forks began to keep time with the music. Only Yavonne responded by removing her shoes and coming forward. When the others didn't follow, Naomi shook her head as though to scold. She danced her way up to Kate, curtsied, coaxed her into removing her shoes, drew her up with a tug and a laugh, and urged her onto their sandy dance floor. She moved on to Theresa and Gabrielle, Seraphina and Mike and Jim. No one refused her, not even Ray.

They danced on the sand, singly at first, then in a circle and holding hands, round and round, forward and back, finding in the pull of the music a common partner.

Mother Jean moved her chair next to Homer. The two of them laughed and watched and listened, often clapping hands.

Mother Jean leaned close to her host. "It's such a delight, the age-old alliance of movement and sound."

Homer smiled and said, "My earliest memory as a child was my mother dancing with me in her arms." In a more melancholy tone he added, "Just now I'd give anything to be out there with them."

Mother Jean nodded; for a long moment, her hand covered his.

Ray and Mike carried Homer up the wide porch steps and set him in his wheelchair. The priest returned to the picnic area to help with the cleanup. Ray pushed Homer's chair into the house and down the hall, the two of them cloaked in a shared silence.

Stepping forward to open the door to Homer's room, Ray saw pain on his uncle's face. "Do you want Naomi to give you a shot?" he asked.

"Not yet. It was just a twinge. And there is something I want to do while I have all my senses."

They entered the room. Ray switched on the light. "Shall I help you into bed?"

Homer shook his head and smiled through a pallor that worried Ray. He said to his nephew, "It was a good party, wasn't it?"

"It was a great party," agreed Ray.

"The last time I saw you dance was at your wedding."

Homer bowed his head, as though the memory of it lay at his feet.

At Homer's direction, Ray wheeled him close to his desk and switched on the small lamp. "I should go see about driving Jim back to Tanglewood," Ray said.

"Is Father Mike staying the night?"

"No. I'll be taking him back to his car in Livingston." Ray glanced toward the door.

Homer's hand latched onto his nephew's. "I love you, boy."

Ray breathed in deeply, then leaned down and wrapped himself around his uncle. He stayed like that for some time, bent low, feeling his uncle's arms around him in a weak grip, the old man's hair tickling his ear. Ray drew back, his face flush with emotion. "I hope we have another of your parties soon," he said.

"We will."

Ray left the room and closed the door. He swiped at a lone tear. Hearing movement in the foyer, he slipped into the hall bathroom. He reappeared a few minutes later, jiggling coins in his pants pocket and holding his head a bit too high.

Kate and Seraphina and Gabrielle were in the kitchen putting away leftovers and condiments and doing the dishes. Ray stood in the doorway and announced, "I'll be leaving shortly to take Mike and Jim back."

"We'll need eggs and milk for breakfast," said Kate, her smile apologetic. "Do you think you could...?"

"Okay. I might be back pretty late, though. I told Trev I'd join him for a drink."

Ray found Jim on the porch, chattering with Naomi about his brother. The barber's satchel was at his feet. Ray mentioned that they would be leaving soon. He descended the porch steps and started toward the lake.

Yavonne was spreading sand on the fire. "You haven't

seen Mike, have you?" Ray asked.

Yavonne pointed toward the dock.

In the far reach of the light's glow, Ray could make out two motionless figures, inches from the water's edge. One was Theresa; the other, Mike.

Ray chatted with Yavonne. When she left to go in, he ambled over to the boathouse, stepped inside, and in the faint light coming through a side window, fussed with one of the fishing poles. Carrying the pole, he moved to the window facing the water.

Mike and Theresa had advanced to the deck of the pontoon boat. Theresa sat on a bench seat at the stern; Mike sat next to her. Ray kept his eyes on the nun. He saw her shake her head in that continuous fashion of a person not wishing to believe something. She turned toward Mike, providing Ray a profile; he wished in vain for sufficient light to read her face.

Ray locked the boathouse. He started for the house, feeling a stir of expectation. *Get her to talk, Mike,* he urged silently. *It's her best hope now.*

Jim and Ray were seated together on the top porch step when the tall figure of the priest came around the corner of the boathouse. Ray waited for Theresa to appear. When she didn't, he started down the steps, only to have Jim do the same, bringing his satchel with him.

Ray stayed within the reach of the porch light and waited. When he saw the priest's face Ray's hopes rose higher than they had since the case had begun; Mike's eyes held that same misty sheen he had seen at the church after the priest had come from the confessional.

Ray asked, "Where's Theresa?"

"She'll be in soon." Mike glanced at Jim. He looked at his watch. "I should be getting back. I was supposed to be on call an hour ago. Monsignor is going to be...*vexed.* When we get to Livingston, Jim could ride with me back to Tanglewood."

"Thanks, but I'm going that far anyway." Ray led the group to where his car was parked. Theresa appeared at the side of the boathouse. Ray started the engine and waited until the nun had mounted the porch steps before pulling away. "Mike, can I call you tonight?"

"How about in the morning? Say ten? I shouldn't tie up the rectory phone tonight, in case there's an emergency."

"That's fine." Ray resigned himself to waiting a few more hours to find out if Mike had broken Theresa's silence.

Eighteen

Ray drove with the windows open and the cool night breeze full on his face. He thought of Trev and their hour together and the jokes they shared. The car rattled along the country road, drowning out the chirp of crickets and the play of the wind in the trees. The headlights caught a rabbit scampering into a thick tangle of scrub. On the lake side of the second bridge, he stopped the car and listened to the gurgle of water churning over bedrock. His eyes found the dashboard clock. Twenty to one. He wanted to stay longer, enjoy the quiet, but Kate would be waiting up. He listened to the stream for a last moment and drove on.

Reaching the rise that looked down on the lake and the house, Ray's heart skipped a beat. A light burned in every window on the first floor.

Ray accelerated down the slope. He sped along the shore and came within a foot of plunging into the small cove that connected with the out-flowing creek. He regained the road and crossed the final bridge.

Kate was standing at the bottom of the steps in her pajamas and bathrobe, her small frame silhouetted in the pale light of the porch. She moved to meet him at the car. She was crying. No sound, just tears running freely down her face. She took him in her arms, held him tight and whispered, "Homer's gone."

They stood that way for some time. At last Kate relaxed her grip. "He just went to sleep and that was it. Naomi found him a few minutes ago. We haven't called anyone yet, nor told the sisters."

"I'll call. You can tell the sisters. But not just yet." Ray stepped back.

Kate touched a tear on his cheek. "I'm sorry."

He nodded. Bent with pain, he climbed the porch steps. He pushed through the screen door, crossed the foyer and headed down the hall.

Naomi sat at the side of the bed. She was clad only in a multicolored cotton nightgown, and was holding Homer's hand. She was singing softly an old song full of sorrow and longing for a better home.

Ray stood beside the nurse. He steadied his gaze on the lifeless form; on the hand that still gripped the yellow shawl; on the iron-gray hair, the hawk nose and the freckled face. He thought of the heart and soul and humor and warmth of the man and wondered where it rested now. Were there grave-yards in the sky, celestial dump sites mirroring those prolif-erating on earth? Or did the master of the universe reuse the precious material, and send souls further out to another home? He fixed on the latter and prayed for a good trip.

The singing stopped.

Ray said, "He was very fond of you."

Naomi responded with a smile. She gave the old man's hand a final soft pat, laid it across his breast and left the room.

Ray knelt. He closed his eyes and let his mind play with the memories that he was thankful still to have. He thought of Homer and his dad and their parents and grandparents. And in a choked voice, he whispered, "Out partying again, eh, Uncle Homer?"

In accordance with the directives and arrangements made by Homer Peter Fredrick, there was no funeral. His remains were cremated. The following day a short memorial cer-emony was held near the lake. Father Mike Killian officiated and, at the request of the deceased, wore neither collar nor cassock nor solemn black suit.

Kate sat with the nuns and Naomi on folding chairs in the shade of the willow. Ray stood at the back of the group leaning against the tree's trunk. His arms were folded, and his gaze held to a distant shore.

When the ceremony was concluded, the women returned to the house for a light lunch.

Ray walked down to the water's edge. Mike joined him. "Will you stay on here?" asked the priest.

"Only till my uncle's affairs are in order."

"What about the sisters?"

"Mother Jean suggested that they all go to their Mother House. They're leaving the day after tomorrow." Ray glanced at Mike. "We never did talk. About Theresa, I mean."

"I know. We can now, if you want." A stomach-growl brought a smile to the priest's face. He patted his mound of belly and shrugged.

Ray said, "I'll go get us some sandwiches. Do you want beer?"

"Beer's fine."

Ray returned with plates of sandwiches and chips and two cans of cold beer on a cookie sheet. They sat on the vacated chairs, using two as tables.

Ray sipped his beer and waited.

Mike said, "You were right. Theresa is holding back something. Something that happened years ago. What it was, she wouldn't tell me. Perhaps she couldn't tell me. I could see it hurt her—almost physically—to approach the subject."

The priest munched a potato chip and continued. "Theresa's not convinced that what's happening now has anything to do with whatever happened back then. I'm not sure she'd tell us about it even if she were certain. It would be like reopening a door to devils and demons and terrors that it took her decades to close. She said, 'It's a memory with the power to tear me apart. Death would be more welcome.'"

Mike turned toward Ray. "Theresa and I have been close friends for almost as long as we've known each other. I've always felt that something lay heavy on her heart. She's never said what. I never asked."

"So, maybe it's best that the sisters do go to Canada, to their Mother House," said Ray. "Maybe Theresa should stay there."

"Saint Luke's will be a sadder place if she does."

"There's nothing more I can do. Not with what I have to work with."

"I understand." Mike followed the flight of a lone sparrow. "There's one other thing we might try," he said. "Just maybe, and I emphasize *maybe*, Theresa would agree to write down what she cannot bear to say out loud. Just an outline. No details, but maybe enough to give you a lead."

Ray said, "I'll need dates. Places. And above all, names."

"Dates, places, names," repeated Mike.

"Tell her that the information will be for my eyes only. And I promise to be discrete in checking it out."

"I'll tell her."

"I wonder if it has anything to do with her parents' auto accident," mused Ray.

"I don't think so. She told me about that years ago. So obviously this other thing was even more devastating."

"Tell me about the accident," said Ray.

"Theresa was eighteen when it happened. They went on a trip. The parents. Theresa stayed home to get ready for college. They never came back. Their car was crushed when a cement truck went out of control. They didn't die right away. Theresa stayed at their bedside for nearly two weeks. She said that, at the end, they were going mad with the pain. Her mother could still use one arm. Theresa said she couldn't go near her because she would grab hold and beg her to shoot them or smother them or do something." Mike stopped speaking.

Ray said, "I used to wonder what I would do if my uncle got that bad."

"You were lucky that it didn't come to that."

"*Luck.*" Ray drew a line in the sand with his foot. "It seems obscene that a four-letter-word should call the shots when it comes to peoples' pain. This one's lucky because he died in his sleep. Another's unlucky because his death came after days or weeks or months of misery. And it's all in the hands of luck and the happenstance of genes and the positions held by medicine and science and religion at the time of their death."

The priest chuckled softly. Surprised, Ray faced him. Mike said, "Remember our meeting at the school? We talked about how, as priest and detective, we borrow from each other in our work?"

"I remember," said Ray.

"Well, I think you have borrowed more than your share from my end."

Ray smiled with affection at his friend. They finished their meal. Ray stood. "I guess I should make an appearance up at the house."

Halfway up the path, Mike asked, "When will you scatter your uncle's ashes?"

"Tomorrow. If I can get the pontoon boat working. Kate and Naomi and the sisters want to come along. What about yourself? That boat can carry all of us, easily."

"I'd like to, but I can't. I have people scheduled for instruction."

Wednesday dawned hot and humid. The lake was like a sheet of glass, stirring only at the touch of a dragonfly or the bustle of a beetle.

After breakfast, Ray made his way to the dock. He installed the pontoon boat's colorful canopy and carried an extra can of gas to the boat's deck.

Theresa was the first of the others to join him. She stepped onto the wide, carpeted deck, looking surprisingly rested and holding a dandelion in her good hand. She asked if she could do anything to help.

Ray resisted the answer that came to mind. Instead he said, "There's nothing left to do. As soon as the others come down, we can go."

Theresa sat on the bench seat to her left. Ray examined the ropes that kept them moored. Theresa asked, "Did your uncle have children?"

"No. And his wife died years ago. In fact, I'm his last living relative, and he was mine." Ray tugged on the rope. "What about you?" he asked. "Do you have a lot of nephews and nieces and related folks scattered around?"

Theresa smiled. "You are a very hard worker."

Ray released the rope and faced the nun. "I've been known to take hold and not let go." He smiled. "What about it? Do you?"

"No. Unfortunately, both my parents were without siblings. And I was an only child."

The hum of a plane drew their attention skyward. "I've always loved that sound," said Theresa. Her gaze dropped to the yellow flower, moved out to the encircling forest and the still waters. "It's very beautiful, this place."

Voices rang in the distance. Theresa glanced landward. Gabrielle and Naomi were coming toward them, the latter carrying a small, covered urn. Yavonne and Seraphina were descending the steps of the house.

Ray started the engine. "What's it like around your Mother House?" he asked.

"Hilly. Some trees, but nothing like this. And although we

don't have a lake, there is a small pond by the cemetery."

Gabrielle climbed aboard, with Naomi following. Ray kept his eyes from the urn cradled in her hands. He unhooked all but one of the ropes. When Seraphina and Yavonne were aboard, he asked, "Is Kate still coming?"

Yavonne replied that she was. The group waited, thankful for the shade of the canopy. No one spoke. Naomi hummed softly to herself.

Finally Kate appeared. She climbed on board.

Ray released the last rope and shoved off from the dock with his foot. The boat slid sideways. He geared into reverse, cleared the dock, changed gears and headed for open water. The air filled with the harsh drone of the motor. Well away from shore, Ray killed the engine. He looked at Naomi and found her eyes on him. She raised the urn in his direction, questioning him with her gaze. He shook his head. The nurse stepped to the bow. Ray asked, "Would you mind singing that song again?"

The nurse removed the lid and began to sing. She shook the ashes from the urn. The gray cinders drifted downward to cloud the still surface of the water.

They heard the shot and saw the cast on Theresa's arm shatter in the same instant. The nun fell backward like a statue, hitting the water head first. A second shot ripped metal from the engine casing. Gas and oil poured into the water.

Kate cried out and fell to her knees. Naomi dropped the urn into the water and gripped the side to keep from following it. Gabrielle leaned overboard, grabbing for Theresa.

Ray jumped in feet first. He reached the nun just as she sank from sight. He brought her head out of the water. He gripped her blood-soaked blouse and reached for the looped rope at the side of the craft.

Nineteen

Ray waited outside the closed door of room three-eleven. A nurse passed, gave him a brief glance and moved on. The door opened. Kate appeared, sitting in a wheelchair and hugging an overnight bag. Above her right eye was taped a square bandage. Ray relieved Kate of the bag. The nurse aimed the wheelchair toward the elevators and chatted about the wonderful summer weather Tanglewood was having.

Ray followed behind Kate and the nurse. He looked twice at his watch as they rode the elevator down to the main floor, where he rushed ahead to fetch the car.

Kate thanked the nurse and eased into the car on the passenger's side. Ray pulled away from the hospital. "Are you sure you're up to this?" he asked.

"I'm sure."

"Did you ask the doctor?"

"Yes, dear. He said I could do whatever I normally do." Kate glanced at her husband and asked, "How are you doing?"

He didn't answer. Kate picked a loose thread from the sleeve of Ray's suit.

Ray joined a line of cars pulling into Saint Luke's. He parked as close to the church as he could. He came quickly around to Kate's side and helped her out.

Monsignor Becker said the Mass, assisted by a drawn, older-looking Father Mike. After the gospel, Mother Jean rose from her seat in the front pew and climbed the sanctuary steps. Her cane made soft tapping sounds on the floor.

Mother Jean bowed respectfully toward the altar and stepped to the massive, hand-carved podium. Except for the top of her veiled head, she all but disappeared.

A faint murmur of amusement rose from the congregation. Mother Jean drew back from the confines of the speaker's box, and came to stand at the sanctuary rail.

Monsignor Becker handed his lapel microphone to the nearest altar boy, whispered in his ear and shoved him in Mother Jean's direction. Mother Jean accepted the mike, and gave the boy an encouraging pat on the shoulder. She introduced herself to the congregation, thanked them for being a family to the sisters, both in their day-by-day lives, and in their grief.

"I haven't all that much to share. Theresa has already said what needed saying in the way she lived among you. She knew the pain of loss that you and I now feel. She was in her teens when her parents died.

"She knew, as well, the secret to survival. She shared her approach with me in one of our many talks. I want to share it with you now."

Mother Jean took a moment to collect her thoughts, then continued. "Theresa said that in our lifetimes, God touches us in many ways. But none are as personal and caring as the way He touches us through each other. That is what pains us most when someone dies—being deprived of the special 'God-Touch' that person brought to us in life. Finally she said, and I quote, 'Aren't we lucky that, to be touched anew, we have only to struggle forward, and open ourselves again to others.'"

Mother Jean left the sanctuary and walked past the casket to her place in the first pew.

The ritual for the repose of Theresa's soul was concluded a little after eleven. With no funeral procession to follow, the congregation was invited by Monsignor to partake of a lunch prepared by the ladies of the Altar Society and served in the church basement.

Ray stayed close to Kate as they descended the stairs. The

large hall was set with long tables and plastic chairs.

"Do you want me to get you something to eat?" Ray asked.

"I'll get it," Kate answered.

They got in line near a table set with salads and cold cuts and steaming dishes of different entrees. The hall was slowly filling with the buzz of people happily distracted with food and chatter. Ray spotted Jim Wheeler and another familiar face from the barber shop. The two men were several places ahead of them in line.

Kate filled her plate. Ray did the same and led the way to an empty table at the rear of the hall.

"I'll miss the sisters when they leave tomorrow," said Kate.

"Too bad they didn't leave the day before yesterday." Ray dragged out a chair and sat. He grabbed a pickle from his plate and bit off a chunk.

A hand clasped his shoulder. He turned to look into the sad blue eyes of Father Mike. Beside the priest stood Simon Lodwick. "I'm sorry it ended this way," said Ray, noticing an inflammation where the priest had nicked himself shaving.

"We all did what we could to prevent it," answered Mike.

"I suppose you're right."

Mike removed his hand from Ray's shoulder. "You remember Mr. Lodwick."

"Yes, certainly." Ray shook the man's hand, and introduced him to Kate.

Lodwick said, "Father Mike told me about your uncle. I'm sorry."

"Thank you."

Mike asked Kate how she was feeling, then excused himself, saying that he wanted Monsignor to meet Mr. Lodwick before he left.

Ray picked up his fork. "Are you sure you don't want to go home and rest?" he asked Kate.

"Would you stop fussing? The doctor would have discharged me yesterday if there hadn't been a mix-up with my x-rays."

"That doesn't take away the fact that you were comatose for twenty-four hours."

"Just unconscious," corrected Kate. She smiled. She opened her purse and pulled out a small plastic bag. Inside was a piece of metal the size of a nail clipping. "The doctor thought I'd like to have this as a conversation piece."

"You're lucky it didn't hit your eye," said Ray.

He speared a meatball with his fork. "I wish I could figure out how the killer found her at the lake."

"Is it possible that your barber told someone?" asked Kate.

"I went to talk to him yesterday. He almost wept when I implied that he might have."

"Well it's over with. And you did everything you could."

"Obviously, it wasn't enough."

Kate touched his arm.

Ray glanced up and said, "I should never have let Theresa join us on that boat."

"She asked to come," said Kate.

"I know. And I never even gave it a thought. It was as if her reasons for being there had disappeared."

"Ray, you were in mourning. It's not a time when the mind functions normally."

Ray halved the meatball. "If only that second shot hadn't hit the motor. She might have lived if we had reached shore sooner."

"You did what you could. Even by swimming to the other boat at the dock, you put your life in danger. What if he had decided to take you off the case then and there? You were an easy target."

"Everyone was."

"May I join you?" Mother Jean pulled out a chair, hung her cane on the back and sat down.

"Have you eaten?" asked Kate.

"Not yet."

Kate stood. "Let me."

"I'll go," said Ray.

"I want to," said Kate. "I feel better moving around."

Mother Jean nodded. "All right. Thank you. Just nothing too greasy."

Kate hurried away.

Mother Jean leaned forward in her seat. "Thank you for what you tried to do for Theresa," she said.

"I wish I could have done more."

"You still can."

Ray faced the petite, elderly nun. "How do you mean?"

"Find the person who took her from us."

"There's nothing I'd like to do more. Only Theresa took the information I needed to the grave."

"Perhaps not."

Mother Jean handed Ray a square of lined paper. "Seraphina found this in their room at the lake."

Quickly, Ray unfolded the thin sheet. On it were three short lines written by hand:

Date: August 9, 1951

Place: Northpointe, Washington

Name:

After the last word were several dark jabs of a pen's point.

Mother Jean smiled at the rush of excitement in Ray's face. She said, "There is also a file at the Mother House that could help."

"What kind of file?" asked Ray.

"When the sisters enter, they fill out forms with personal data: next of kin, persons to contact in case of an illness, and so forth. There should also be progress reports submitted by those who trained her in the postulate and novitiate."

"You are beginning to make my day," said Ray.

"Good." The nun's broad smile showed her pleasure.

"What year did Theresa enter the convent?" asked Ray.

"I think it was around 1957. I know it was shortly after she graduated from college. In fact, that's where I first met Theresa. At our college in Connecticut. I taught there for a few years."

Ray tapped the date on the paper. "Six years after what happened in Northpointe."

Kate slipped a plate of food in front of Mother Jean. She took one look at Ray. "Well, you suddenly look full of life." She regained her seat, looked across at Mother Jean and said, "I believe I should be a little jealous. This is the second time sisters have done for Ray what I couldn't."

An engaging blush rose over the nun's lined features. Kate reached across the table and squeezed her bony, veined hand. "Whatever it was you said, thank you for saying it."

Using both their cars, Ray and Kate drove the sisters to the airport on Saturday, July twenty-fifth. Courtesy of Sloane's Funeral Home, Theresa's remains had arrived earlier, and would travel on the same flight.

Yavonne accompanied the skycap with their luggage to the check-in counter. The rest of the sisters and the Fredricks took a seat nearby and waited.

Back with the group, Yavonne passed out the tickets. They started toward the gate, moving slowly out of respect for the eldest among them.

A plane was just taxiing in from the runway. Kate, Yavonne, Gabrielle and Seraphina strolled to the window to watch.

Mother Jean gratefully took a seat. Ray did likewise.

Mother Jean asked, "When do you think you'll come?"

"It will depend on how soon I can get my uncle's affairs in order. But I'll aim for this coming Wednesday or Thursday."

"You won't need a motel, if you don't mind the simple accommodations of our guest house."

"Book us in." Ray watched the plane glide up to the gate. He glanced at his watch. "Looks like your plane's on time."

The elderly nun wrote a phone number on a piece of paper and handed it to Ray. "That's my direct line. Call me with the particulars of your flight. I'll have someone meet you."

Trev hung up the phone, grabbed a nine-by-twelve envelope and a copy of the *Tanglewood Observer,* and left the office he occupied as interim chief of detectives.

Some minutes later, he entered the Tanglewood Cafe and headed toward an occupied table at the rear. Trev greeted Kate warmly and sat.

"Do you want something to drink?" asked Ray.

"Of course." Trev gave the waitress his order. He adjusted his chair for additional room, then passed Ray his copy of the *Observer,* folded to show a four-by-five sketch of the man suspected of killing Theresa Loomis. In the lower half of the page was another photo, the one that had appeared in the *Saint Luke's Herald* to commemorate the nun's twenty-five years of service to the parish.

A sidebar gave a number to call if anyone had information pertaining to the case.

Ray handed it back. "Did you have it—"

"Yeah," interrupted Trev. "I had it run in all the local papers in the state."

Ray grabbed for the envelope Trev was guarding under his arm.

"Ask politely."

Ray turned to Kate. "You ask him. You've always had more influence than me."

"I'm glad to hear that. Makes up for having to play second fiddle to the sisters." Kate smiled broadly at Trev and received the envelope without needing to say a word. She handed it to Ray.

He pulled out a copy of the autopsy performed on Theresa Loomis by the Livingston medical examiner. "That's no help. We already knew the bullet passed straight through. It's probably at the bottom of the lake."

"You checked the floor of the boat, right?" asked Trev.

"Yeah. The Livingston police checked it over." Ray turned to the page detailing the site where the suspect had waited for his opportunity. He swore softly. "I see they found more toothpicks. Have Foler contact the Livingston Forensics Department and see if there's a match on the saliva."

"Already been done. The man who killed Theresa was the same guy who hid in the john at the school. All we have to do now is find him."

"Did you put a guard on Kruger?"

"Yep. Had to fight with Sitarski to do it though."

Ray looked up from the report. "I wish we had a make on the gun."

"Must have been a high-powered rifle with a good scope."

"Even with good gear, the shooter had to be a real marksman to make that shot," added Ray. "Might not be a bad idea to have someone check out the firing ranges around. I don't think our man was tall enough to have been in the military. By the way, did you hear anything more on Keyhoe and his lawyer?"

"Not a word." Trev pointed at the report. "Check out the last page, bottom paragraph."

Ray flipped to the back page. His eyes widened as he read.

"What is it?" asked Kate.

"You won't believe it."

Kate reached for the report. Ray let go. He said to Trev, "At least the case is heading in a definite direction."

"Cesarean section?" blurted Kate. She looked from Ray to Trev, her mouth agape. She said, "Maybe it's a scar from some other kind of surgery."

"If there was any doubt, they would have said so." Ray tapped the table. "And where there's a child, there's a father."

Twenty

Thumper lay with his head on his paws and his nose hanging over the edge of the porch. He lifted an eyelid at the sound of the cars. Doors slammed; the dog didn't move. Even when Kate and Ray approached the steps and called, Thumper did little more than send them a look that could have shamed a saint.

"I think we are being punished," said Kate.

Ray crouched and patted the dog's head. He settled next to the dog. Kate took a seat on the opposite side. They stroked the big red dog, and watched diminutive breakers tease the shore of the lake. Out on the dock, a wood duck preened itself, then cocked its tail, and flapped its way into the water. Ray said, "I wonder why birds never look old?"

Kate sent Ray a sidelong, quiet smile and said, "Maybe they would, if they lived as long as we do."

Ray shifted his position. "The lawyer's coming by tomorrow."

"On Sunday?"

"He said he didn't mind. And I want to get things moving so we can take off."

"When are the sisters expecting us?"

"The middle of next week."

Kate opened her purse. She handed Ray an envelope with his name on it. "Homer gave me this the night he died. He asked me to give it to you after he was gone and things had settled down." She stood up. "I'll go see to supper. Something simple."

Ray settled his gaze on the familiar, squiggly script. He

pulled a penknife from his pocket and slit open the envelope. He removed a single sheet of paper.

My dear Nephew,

I read someplace that to tell another how you really feel, you need the easy pace of a letter. Sweet words for a man with much in his heart that begs to be said.

If you have been to the lawyers, you'll know by now that I died a very wealthy man. I died also a man with much self-reproach. Funny how one day you wake, find yourself dying and view the profits of a lifetime as just so much smoke. A fleeting veil of paper and numbers that hide from view what is of real value.

During these last few weeks I've tried to find a way to feel good about allowing my money to sit unused. An idea came to mind when Kate told me of your situation at work. It took shape after a conversation I had with Sister Theresa. She told me I had a compassionate nephew who was both a detective and a collector of sad stories.

Would you allow this old man to use you to make amends for his sterile life? In my name, would you use my money and make something good happen?

I don't mean for you to walk around and give it away. But to use it to free yourself first, and then apply your talents in assisting others in their struggles.

The thought of you out there, working at my behest and as my detective, thrills me beyond words. What do you say? Is it a deal?

With the promise of watching over you and Kate from above, and with more love than I ever imagined was in me to give, I remain now, and after I'm gone,

Your Uncle Homer

Ray descended the steps and walked down to the lake. The

dog followed, keeping his distance. Ray stood at the edge of the shore, his eyes filling with tears. He folded the letter, slipped it back into the envelope and into his shirt pocket. Gazing out over the water, he gave a slow nod, almost a bow, and whispered, "You're on."

Thumper came alongside and nudged his hand. Ray squatted and hugged the dog. He snuffed slightly, took a swipe at his nose with the back of his hand.

Up at the house, the screen door slammed. Ray straightened. Kate came toward him, carrying a tray of sandwiches and cans of beer. "Let's go sit on the pontoon boat," she said, allowing Ray to take the tray. Her eyes met his. She offered a misty-eyed smile, then led the way, staying close to the sandy shore.

They climbed onto the dock and into the boat. They sat on the bench seat facing west, setting the tray between them. The sun shone through the break in the trees that marked the path of the creek. Ray blinked at its brilliance. He handed Kate the letter and took a sandwich from the tray.

Kate read it. She closed her eyes. Ray took her hand and kissed it. She folded the letter carefully, handed it back, and blew her nose, but said nothing. The boat rocked softly, every now and then thumping against the side of the dock. They ate and watched birds fly swooping arcs, and ducks paddle playfully about.

After the sandwiches were gone, Ray said, "Did you ever feel guilty about being lucky?"

Kate laughed. "Too often." She touched the bandage above her eye.

Ray moved the tray from between them. He scooted close to Kate and put his arm around her. She lay her head on his shoulder. After some minutes, he said, "You were right."

"Which time are we talking about?"

Ray tightened his hold and smiled. "When you said that

there would be good days left. I'm glad I came."

The lawyer arrived at ten the next morning, read the will naming Ray as sole heir to Homer's estate, answered what few questions the Fredricks had, and was gone before eleven. At 11:15 Kate announced that she was thinking of making the 12:30 Mass at Saint Luke's. "How about coming with me?"

"I'll come with you to town. Not to church."

"Think of it as a way to say thanks for your blessings," prompted Kate.

"I did that last night, while you were asleep." Ray rubbed his knees energetically. "I might even have overdone it."

Kate smiled. "Well, let's go. I don't want to be late." She took keys from her purse, dropped them in Ray's hand. "I'll let you drive my new car."

They left the dog loose in the yard and drove off. Kate asked, "Did Homer pick it out himself?"

"I helped."

"When did all this take place?"

"About a week before Homer sprang his surprise."

"I wish you wouldn't go so fast on these bumpy roads."

Ray chuckled and slowed down.

They arrived at the church at 12:10. The eleven o'clock Mass was just letting out. They agreed on a time for his return, and Kate watched Ray merge with the departing vehicles.

Ray spent an hour driving the streets of Tanglewood before he spotted what he was looking for: the old, rusty truck with the out-of-state plates. It sat in the lot adjacent to an all-night drug store. Ray pulled in beside it and got out to inspect the other vehicle. Except for some maps on the seat, the cab was empty. He surveyed the strip mall with its collection of small businesses.

Ray started with the drug store. He marched the length of the store, checking all the aisles. He retraced his steps and checked again. The elderly pair were nowhere to be seen.

A clock caught his eye. Within ten minutes, he had to leave to meet Kate. Walking at a quick clip, Ray covered the rest of the mall. The only other store open was a yogurt and ice-cream shop. He studied the crowd milling near the counter. No one looked older than thirty.

Ray walked to the road and took a quick visual inventory of the buildings in the area. None offered a clue. Hands in his pockets, he pivoted toward the truck. His mind began to click off the possibilities: they had gone for a walk; they were at a restaurant on a side street.

His attention shifted repeatedly from his watch to the truck.

Ray moved to the rear of the vehicle and rapped on the curtained window of the camper top. He tried the handle of the gate and was surprised to find it unlocked. He lowered it, crouched low, and peeked in.

"Oh, shit." Ray scrambled into the bed of the truck. They were both there. Holding hands and lying side by side on a floor of blankets and pillows. Near the woman stood two worn suitcases and a small cook pot with an attachment for a cigarette lighter. There were two Styrofoam cups, both empty except for a single tea bag, a box of McDonald's cookies, opened but untouched, and two aspirin bottles. Ray hefted them quickly. Both empty.

Ray crawled forward and felt the woman's arm for a pulse. She was alive. The man too. Frantically, he felt the man's pockets, found keys, and crawled backwards, bumping his head on the edge of the camper top. He slammed the gate, raced to the cab and took off with a rattle of fenders and a squeal of tires.

Ray parked the truck at the emergency entrance to Tanglewood General. He flashed his badge at the guard. "I'm transporting two elderly people overdosed on aspirin."

Within seconds, Ray was helping an orderly pull the woman out of the camper. She was shod in bobby socks and loafers with soles as thin as paper. She wore a silver-flecked, black silk dress with a matching bolero. They laid her on a gurney and a nurse wheeled her quickly away.

The man was sockless, his shoes fastened with twist-ties pulled through the top eyelets. His well-creased slacks and yellowed shirt smelled of moth balls. A red bow tie all but hid his neck. Ray and the orderly eased him onto the stretcher and into the waiting hands of the hospital staff.

Ray went straight to the desk, showed the receptionist his badge, and handed her a credit card.

Reading her name tag, he said, "Joyce, could I count on you to see that the old couple get whatever they need? I'll be back to fill you in on the particulars just as soon as I can." Ray pocketed his badge, left the credit card and took off for the exit.

Except for a few scattered cars, the church parking lot was empty. Ray slipped in through a side door. Women milled around the altar, removing candlesticks, arranging vases.

He left, scanned the grounds. He noticed the nuns' Chevy parked at the rear of the convent.

Ray climbed into the truck and drove it clinking and rattling across the lot to the rectory.

Mike answered the door and gave Ray a warm smile and the warning, "Kate's been worried sick."

"Where is she?"

"In my office. Calling all over town."

Ray entered the small room. Kate's back was to the door. She was bent over the desk with the receiver to her ear.

"Hon—"

Kate spun toward him, dropping the receiver back in its cradle. "Are you all right?"

"I'm fine."

"You were supposed to be here an hour ago."

"I know. I'm sorry."

"What happened?"

"Can I tell you as we drive? I should get back to the hospital."

"Hospital? Why?"

"Come on." Out on the porch, Ray said to Mike, "You know, if you're not busy, you might want to come with us."

Mike nodded, asked nothing, and said, "Give me half a minute."

Kate squinted at the old truck idling at the porch steps. She descended the stairs and looked around for her car.

Ray stepped to the passenger door of the truck and opened it. Before Kate could speak, he said, "Your car's fine. This belongs to that old couple I've been telling you about. I found them in the back. Overdosed on aspirin."

Kate heaved herself up into the high cab. Ray climbed behind the wheel. Soon Mike hurried out the door, in his Roman collar and a black suit of clothes. He climbed in next to Kate and slammed the door shut.

Ray kept his speed to the legal limits and his eyes on the gas gauge. The indicator was close to the *E*.

A mile from their destination, Ray said, "Check the glove box, will you, Kate? See if there's anything in there to identify this couple."

With little more than a touch, the door dropped open. A handful of pay stubs fell to the floor. Inside the compartment were a can opener, a half-full bottle of cough syrup and an old wallet.

Twenty-one

It was after three when the Fredricks and Father Mike Killian left the hospital for the Pub & Eatery. Millie brought menus and setups, and would have included some home-style teasing, but she recognized the seriousness of their mood. She settled for a few friendly words and a suggestion that they try the special.

Their orders placed, Mike faced Ray and asked, "Do you know this couple at the hospital?"

Ray shook his head. "I've noticed them around town. Didn't even know their names until we found his wallet."

"But he's been talking about them for a week," said Kate.

Ray asked, "How were they when you left?"

"Regaining a lot of their color," the priest replied. "They're not fully conscious yet. The old man does keep mumbling something about his broom. The doctor's encouraged."

The threesome were served lasagna, crisp rolls and salad. Mike poked at his food. He said, "Mother Jean showed me the note Theresa left. She said you intend to go to Northpointe."

"As soon as we can. But first we're going to the Mother House. We may be able to leave next week." Ray drank some coffee. "Did you ever hear Theresa talk about Northpointe?" he asked.

"Never."

"Did she ever talk about her years growing up in Washington?"

"She mentioned it. It wasn't a subject she ever elaborated on."

"What did she like to talk about?"

"People. Especially the ones she met delivering meals. Children. She was very fond of children."

"Did she ever talk about what she did between her parents' death and the year she entered the convent?"

Mike set his fork down. "I understood that she entered soon afterwards."

"I'm afraid not," said Ray. "There's a gap of several years we can't seem to account for." He considered telling Mike about the C-section scar. He studied the troubled eyes and the tired face, and decided bringing the man more pain served no purpose.

The priest returned his steady gaze. "Whatever it is that you find, Ray, please keep me informed. It means a lot."

The Fredricks dropped Mike at the rectory and were back at the hospital by five.

Joyce was off duty. Her replacement phoned for information on Karl Dunn and his wife, and told the Fredricks that both patients were conscious. She gave them the room number and directions to the ward.

The old couple were in adjacent cubicles with the curtain between the beds pulled back to the wall. They were eating Jell-O out of plastic cups.

Ray handed the old man his wallet and received a glower in return. He introduced himself and Kate and asked, "How are you feeling?"

"Not as good as we could, if you had let us be." Karl stared past his visitors.

Kate said, "Your truck is parked in our drive, so don't worry about it."

The old woman whispered a word of thanks. Her cheeks were sunken and her eyes struggled to stay open.

Karl continued to stare past the Fredricks.

Ray pulled up two chairs.

"Just more bills we can't pay," snapped the old man. "That's what your meddling's brought us." His large, scarred chin shot forward.

"Karl!" his wife admonished. "Just because things have gone bad for us, doesn't mean we have to be impolite." She tried to smile at Ray. She said, "I'm Molly Dunn. And I apologize for Karl."

"The plates on your truck tell me that you are from Minnesota," said Ray. "What brings you this way?"

"Warm weather. We wanted to get down to Florida before winter. Only we ran out of money for gas. Karl's been working and saving his pay so we can finish our trip. Only we were robbed." Molly's face twitched with the painful memory. She said, "They hurt Karl. They took every penny we had but the few dollars I had in my shoe."

"Jackasses."

"Father. You know how I feel about such language." Tears welled in the woman's eyes. She reached for the box of tissues on a nearby table.

"Do you have family in Minnesota?" asked Ray.

There was a long pause before Molly answered, "We have a son but he's—"

"That's not their business, Molly." Karl turned a sad, almost apologetic smile on his wife.

"Where are you staying here in town?" Ray asked.

"At the Waldorf."

The Fredricks exchanged glances. The silence lengthened. Karl began to fidget in his bed. When a nurse passed, he shouted, "Okay if I get up to go?"

She stepped to the bed and watched attentively as Karl set his feet to the floor and pulled the hospital gown tightly around himself. She stayed at his side as he stumbled to the bathroom; his bony behind was barely the size of a child's.

Kate leaned toward Molly. She laid her hand lightly on the

old woman's arm and said, "We're going to go. I just want you to know that your hospital bill will be taken care of. And that when you're discharged, you'll have a place to stay. I promise." She leaned closer and hugged the old woman's shoulders.

They left the hospital and headed for the parking lot. Kate said, "I think the world is seeing a new generation of the brave and the strong. And they are not the young."

The Fredricks returned to Hush Lake for a quiet evening. Mid-morning on Monday, they were back in Tanglewood. They drove to Saint Luke's, entering the property from Seventh Street. Passing by the convent, Ray noticed that the nun's Chevy was no longer at the side of the building.

They parked alongside several other cars in front of the school, and went in. They were met by the aroma of fresh coffee. Ray took a long whiff. Kate explained that drinks and donuts were always provided for the kitchen staff and those who deliver the meals.

The two walked the main-floor hall, looking and listening for signs of the caretaker. They reached the stairs at the far end of the building. Starting down, Ray said, "I don't like this. Trev told me he had a guard on Kruger. If anything happens to him, we'll be minus our sole witness."

They reached the bottom of the stairs. On the right was a door marked Maintenance. Ray opened it slowly and flipped on the light. Enormous boilers and water tanks filled two thirds of the room. He called the caretaker's name. No one answered. He checked a side door. It opened on a closet cluttered with buckets and mops and a machine for polishing the floors, as well as a sink the size of a bathtub.

"Maybe he's working on the grounds," said Kate. Suddenly she smiled. "I bet I know where he is. In the cafeteria having coffee."

Kate was right. The officer and Kruger sat facing each other over a plate of donuts and mugs of coffee. Ray and Kate approached. Looking up, the officer straightened. He waited like a man not sure of what to expect.

"Anybody going to invite us to sit down?" asked Ray.

Kruger slapped the seat of the chair next to him, then took off in the direction of the kitchen. Kate and Ray sat across from the guard. "All quiet?" asked Ray.

"Pretty much so."

"No doubt you've been told who to keep an eye out for."

The officer showed his copy of the drawing of Kruger's attacker.

"Fine. And do you mind finishing your coffee at a different table? There are a few things I have to discuss with Peter."

The guard left. Kruger returned with two coffees and additional donuts. He set them down, sat and said, "Thanks."

"You're welcome. But for what?"

"My guardian angel over there. And he's a hell of a listener."

"Just don't be passing him that bottle of yours. At least not while I'm around." Ray smiled.

"By the way, this is my wife, Kate."

Kruger doffed his cap. "Ma'am."

Ray passed a cup to Kate, and took a sip from his. "I need a favor," he said. "Some friends need a decent place to stay that won't cost too much. Any ideas?"

"Sure. Right where I live. Been a Vacancy sign in the window as long as I've been there. But it ain't the Ritz."

"Is it reasonably safe?"

Kruger guffawed as though Ray had told him a particularly lewd joke. He said, "With Lucy around, it's safer than a locked cell."

"Who's Lucy?"

"The landlady. Got the first flat just as you come in."

"And you're sure there's a vacancy."

"That's what the sign says."

Junction Street crossed town from east to west. Kruger's apartment building was at the east end. Little about the old building was inviting.

The Fredricks climbed the short stoop to the entrance. The vacancy sign leaned against the inside window on the right. Cobwebs covered one corner of it. Ray opened the door and they stepped in. Instantly, a hall door opened. A large woman filled the doorway. She had stick-like legs and breasts as big as melons. A cigarette dangled from her lower lip, its smoke curling up past hard, gray eyes.

"Good morning," said Ray.

"Whatever. What do you want?"

"We noticed your Vacancy sign in the window."

The woman eyed the Fredricks as if they were items for sale. She removed the cigarette and allowed her mouth to twist in amusement. She said, "I got a plant there too. So what?"

"We're looking for a room."

"Sure you are. And I'm looking for a silver spoon to stir my tea."

"Mr. Kruger referred us," said Kate. She reached out a hand. "I'm Kate Fredrick and this is my husband, Ray."

The woman took Kate's hand. "Lucy Hammer," she said.

"This room is for friends of ours," said Kate. "And from what Mr. Kruger says, we thought this place would be ideal for their situation."

"Oh, they're poor, eh?" Lucy spun around and was gone. Kate and Ray waited outside the open door. The landlady tramped back with a key in hand. "Down the hall. Last door on the right. Only one not rented. Two hundred a month. Cash up front. First month I don't get paid, your friends are gone."

She handed Kate the key. "Check it out, if you want."

They walked down a clean, uncarpeted hall with walls the color of putty. They opened an unmarked door and entered. The place smelled of smoke and disinfectant. There were a bedroom, a bathroom and a twelve-by-twenty space that served as living room, kitchen and eating area. The only furniture was a card table and three chairs.

Kate walked to the window and looked out. Below was a narrow yard with clotheslines and trash cans. Further back was an alley.

"Do you think they'll like it?" asked Kate.

"I'm more worried about getting old Karl over here for a look. You can be sure he won't stand for a handout. Besides, Homer didn't want money given away. He wanted people helped."

"Karl has a job, doesn't he?"

"If he didn't quit, or get fired."

Kate stepped over to a stretch of cupboards and a counter. She started opening the doors. The cupboards were empty but clean. Kate looked in the oven. It too was clean. She said, "That truck of theirs still runs. Maybe we could get both of them jobs helping out with Meals on Wheels."

"I thought those were volunteer positions."

"Some are salaried. And even if the program can't pay them, we could give them so much a week through Father Mike. As for this place, we'll pay the first month and tell the Dunns it's a loan."

"Yeah, that might work."

"I just thought of something else we could do," said Kate. "My old car. I'd like them to have it." She smiled. "We'll trade it to them for the truck."

Ray joined Kate in the kitchen. He kissed her on the tip of the nose. "I think we just made Homer's first week in eternity a little happier."

Twenty-two

The Fredricks flew nonstop to New York on the Thursday
following Theresa's funeral. They transferred to a Canadian
airline and landed at an airport outside Small Falls, Ontario
at seven in the evening.

Yavonne was there to meet them, along with Sister Myriam,
a squat, broad woman with pink cheeks and a permanent
smile.

They retrieved their luggage and headed for the exit.
Yavonne went for the car while the others waited.

Sister Myriam made small talk on the subject of soil
preservation, and about steam heat as opposed to gas. She
chattered happily away and didn't stop until Yavonne appeared at the curb behind the wheel of a large station wagon.

With equal energy, Ray and Myriam stowed the luggage
in the rear of the wagon. Myriam took the passenger seat, and
the Fredricks climbed in back.

Yavonne merged easily into the sparse traffic. Her companion draped an arm over the back of her seat, faced the
Fredricks, and asked, "Is this your first time in Small Falls?"

Kate nodded and would have said more, but Myriam went
immediately into a brief history of the area that included the
date of its incorporation as a city, the names of its founding
fathers, and the reasonable cost of such everyday expenses as
heat, water and electricity. "But they rob us blind when it
comes to building material," she added, quoting the price of
two-by-fours, nails and poured cement.

The first twenty minutes of the drive took them past farms
green with vines and stalks of corn. Ten miles farther on, the

road divided orchards of apples and cherries.

Myriam recited the statistics on the amount of produce exported from the area.

Yavonne caught Ray's eye in the rearview mirror and smiled sympathetically. She said, "Myriam, why don't you offer the Fredricks some mints and maybe some quiet time to get their bearings."

"Oh, my. Have I been—?"

"Just a little," cut in Yavonne.

Myriam's mouth twitched with self-reproach. She passed Kate and Ray a sack of candy, and faced front with a determined set to her shoulders.

Kate handed back the sack. "How big is Small Falls?" she asked, receiving, as she spoke, a kick from Ray. She kicked him back.

"Twenty thousand people," said Myriam. "It's a lovely city. Our sisters moved here from Toronto at the turn of the century."

The road meandered around small hills with pockets of grazing cattle. Coming over a steep rise, Yavonne pulled to the shoulder and stopped. "Small Falls," she announced, nodding toward the still distant town. Pointing to her left, she drew attention to a group of buildings that looked like a college. "And that's our Mother House."

"The property was given to us by the family of one of our sisters," offered Myriam.

They drove on. Just shy of the city, Yavonne took an unpaved road through fallow fields and over train tracks. "This is the back way," explained Myriam. "We used to farm these fields before—" She stopped herself mid-sentence and clamped her mouth shut.

They neared a small cemetery. Dozens of gravestones circled a gazebo-like structure with a granite altar. At the outer rim was a freshly dug grave. Close by was a pond in a stand of trees.

The boundary of the complex was marked by a waist-high stone wall and old trees growing at even intervals. Yavonne drove past the buildings, identifying them in turn as the infirmary; the main building housing offices, refectory and chapel; living quarters; and the visitors' quarters, a two-story red brick structure with a full porch, ornate windows and a mansard roof.

Yavonne parked in front.

Mother Jean and Sister Seraphina immediately appeared on the porch. Myriam shooed the Fredricks up the steps, then saw to the luggage with Yavonne's help.

The old nun took hold of Kate's hand. She touched the small bandage over Kate's eye. "You're looking better," she said. She took Ray's hand as well. "I'm so pleased you've come."

"You have the whole place to yourself," said Mother Jean. "Which normally isn't the case, especially in the summer. But then, more and more of the sisters are outliving relatives and friends."

They entered a short foyer with a staircase on the right. Mother Jean explained how, years back, when she was a young nun, the house had been renovated and made into apartments. She led them down a carpeted corridor and stopped at the last of three doors. "We put you in here. It's the largest of the units." Mother Jean opened a door marked with an *A*. The apartment consisted of a bedroom, a bathroom and a large room containing a kitchenette, dining area and an island grouping of couch and chairs. The ceilings were high and rounded, and the rooms were furnished in the style of the thirties. Seraphina walked the guests into the kitchenette and informed them that there was a pie in the refrigerator, as well as food for snacks and small meals.

"We'll leave you to settle in," said Mother Jean. "Gabrielle is fixing your supper. Shall we fetch you in a half hour?"

"That would be fine," said Kate.

"Oh, yes." Mother Jean reached into her pocket. She handed Ray keys for the apartment, and a piece of paper with *Memo* printed across the top. She said, "About an hour ago, a Mr. Steward called. He asked that you call him back as soon as possible."

Kate walked with the nuns out to the road. She looked around. "It's very nice here," she said.

"It's been home to many people," said Mother Jean. She pointed to the central building. "When I came here in the late thirties, that was the only other building, besides this one."

After the sisters left her, Kate stood for a long moment in the shade of an elm. When she returned to the apartment, Ray was just replacing the receiver. "What did Trev want?"

"They found him."

"Found who?"

"The man who attacked Peter and probably killed Theresa."

Kate took a seat on the couch. "Already?"

"He was floating in a swamp not far from the turnoff to Hush Hideaway. They think he's been dead since the day of the shooting."

Ray joined Kate on the couch. "They also found the gun. A high-powered Winchester with an expensive scope."

"How did he die?" asked Kate.

"Trev's waiting for the autopsy, but it looks like he drowned." Ray rubbed his face with his hands.

"Are they sure it's him?" asked Kate.

"Peter identified him. Trev was sure even before the identification was made. The drawing was a perfect likeness. It's him all right. Trev is going to send me a photo as soon as I call him back with a fax number."

"So it's over." Kate leaned back. "I was looking forward

to going to Washington."

"Who says we aren't?"

"You still want to go?"

"It sure beats going back to Tanglewood. Right now, anyway. Besides, there are still too many unanswered questions. Who was he? Why was he after Theresa when she didn't even know him?"

"Maybe she did," said Kate.

"No. I know she didn't. When she saw the drawing, she was as curious as the rest of us about who he was."

"Did they find the car?"

"No car. Which could mean he took a bus or a taxi, or he hiked. Or someone else drove."

"That would give him an accomplice," said Kate.

"Exactly."

Kate ran a finger along the arm of the couch. "Maybe it's Keyhoe."

"If he were involved in all this, I doubt that he'd be making so much fuss. Killers don't usually call attention to themselves."

"What fuss?" asked Kate.

"He filed a complaint. Said that I was harassing him. Even hired a lawyer."

"You never told me that."

"Because it's stupid. He has no grounds. Anyway, the Livingston Police are checking to see if anyone spotted the dead man in the area on the day of the shooting. They're also flooding the town with his picture; and the local news is carrying the story on the tube."

"Could he be from out of state?" asked Kate.

"Not if he owned that green Pontiac. It had Michigan plates."

"Do they know his name?"

"Nope. He had nothing on him. Forensics is checking his

clothes to see if they give us anything." Ray stood and stretched. "It sure would be nice to have a name. And a motive." He walked into the bedroom and bounced on the bed. "Not bad," he announced. "I wonder what Gabbie is fixing us to eat!"

Ray and Kate slept late the following morning. Kate sat up with a start. She nudged Ray, looked at her watch. "Can you believe it's after eight?"

Ray laced his fingers behind his head. "I haven't slept this well in weeks. Must have been last night's prolonged session of community exercise."

Kate punched him in the chest. "With that kind of a description, you could lose your participation privileges."

"Prolonged session of tender touching?" offered Ray.

"That's better." Kate scooted to his side and settled in his arms. "I'm glad we're getting away for awhile."

"I'll tell Thumper. And by the way, did you buy extra dog food?"

"Yes, dear."

"Well, it's important. You know he stops eating if we change brands."

"I know, dear." Kate pulled at a clump of chest hair. "I wonder how the Dunns are getting along?"

"They'll be fine. Peter has already lined Karl up for poker. And I'm sure those two will be busy for weeks swapping gripes."

"We better get up." Kate slipped out naked, threw on her robe, and hurried into the bathroom.

Ray propped himself against the headboard and yawned.

"How long do you think we'll be here?" called Kate.

"For as long as Gabbie does the cooking."

Kate stuck her head back into the room. "Seriously."

"Two days. Maybe three."

They were dressed and out the door by nine. The sky was cloudless and the day already heating up. The Fredricks headed for the building where they had dined the evening before. They met Myriam coming from a small, flat-roofed structure at the back. She walked with them up to the door, chatting about the cost of repairing boilers, and was off in a different direction as soon as the Fredricks went inside.

"When are you going to tell Mother Jean about the killer?" whispered Kate.

"I don't know." Ray hurried along, pulled by the aroma coming from down the hall.

As soon as they entered the empty refectory, Gabrielle strode in bearing plates of homemade hash browns, sausage links the size of a man's thumb, and eggs scrambled with onions, peppers, cheese and mushrooms.

She proudly placed the food on the table set for two and graced with freshly cut flowers. "How did you know we were on our way?" asked Kate.

Ray was already seated and working on his first mouthful.

"Mother called me. Her office faces your place. She also asked that I bring you by after you've eaten."

Twenty-three

The Fredricks followed Gabrielle up a wide, polished staircase. At the landing was an enormous stained-glass window depicting the Ascension of Jesus Christ amidst onlookers dressed in costumes of the twenty centuries that had since passed.

Gabrielle showed them into a large outer office on the second floor, and left them in the hands of the sister secretary, a woman not much older than Yavonne. She, in turn, led them into an adjoining room.

Mother Jean came around the desk and greeted the Fredricks warmly. "Did you sleep well?"

"Very well," said Ray. "Thanks largely to the marvelous quiet, and to my wife."

Kate blushed and cut in, "You know, Mother, you're spoiling us with these fancy meals and lovely surroundings."

"Then I'm pleased." The petite nun turned toward a side window with a view of the cemetery. "Later, perhaps you'd like to visit Theresa's grave," she said. "We buried her Monday." Her gaze stayed on the view. "I was thinking last night, there must be more than a hundred sisters out there whom I knew well."

Shaking her head, she turned back to face her guests. "Forgive an old lady her reveries." She removed a manila folder from a desk drawer and handed it to Ray. "Theresa's file, the one I told you about."

Ray thanked her. He flipped through the pages, noticing that some were typed, others hand-written. "Do you know if Theresa ever went by a surname other than Loomis?"

"I'm not sure I understand what you mean."

Ray laid the folder on his lap. "Mother, are you aware that Theresa had had a cesarean section?"

"Cesarean? How—" Mother Jean looked at Kate.

Ray said, "From the autopsy report. I see you didn't know."

"No." The nun's fingers found her ring. She turned it slowly. "No," she repeated. "I didn't know." There was a pause. Suddenly she said, "Surely not while she was a sister?"

"It's an old scar," said Ray.

"But still, we should have been told." Mother Jean rested her head against the back of her chair. "Is that why you asked if Theresa had ever gone by another name?"

Ray nodded. He held up the folder. "Is there anything in here about her having been married?"

"Nothing. And I doubt that you will find it very helpful. I read it through yesterday. Nothing seemed unusual, except for a few disciplinary problems during her postulate."

"Like what?" asked Ray.

"You must understand that when she entered the congregation back in the fifties, everything was uniform and regulated. The sisters dressed the same, followed the same rules, kept the same schedule. We also had dormitories divided into cubicles for the postulants. During the night, curtains separated the beds, but during the day, the curtains remained open. It seems that Theresa always made her bed without its pillow, which she kept under the bed in a plastic bag. And even after she was told to do as everyone else, she didn't.

"Regardless, she made it to the next stage of her formation, the novitiate. Sister Charles was novice mistress at that time. And when Theresa continued to make her bed in the same manner, Charles simply took the pillow away. She was never one to fuss about insignificant things."

"Sister Charles. You and the sisters talked about her at Hush Hideaway. Isn't she the oldest sister still living?" said Kate.

"That's right. She's been mother and grandmother to many of us in our lives as sisters. A real super-nun, even now at the age of a hundred and one. Would you like to meet her? I could take you there now."

"I'd like that," said Kate.

Mother Jean rose and retrieved her cane from the back of her chair. "The infirmary building is just a short walk."

They moved to the outer office. Mother Jean spoke to her secretary. "Ann, if anything urgent arises, I'll be over at the infirmary. And tell Sister Florance that I'll see her this afternoon. Check my schedule and give her a time." She thanked the young nun. They left the office and walked to an antiquated elevator with a cagelike door. It descended slowly, with disquieting creaks and groans.

The infirmary, a two-story building of recent construction, stood at the west end of the complex, a few hundred yards from the cemetery. Wide ramps flanked the stairs at the entrance.

Mother Jean rested a moment, taking a seat in one of three wheelchairs just inside the door. With the Fredricks standing close by, she said, "This was constructed five years ago and it's already too small."

"How many sisters are here?" asked Kate.

"Well, let's see. There are ten in the Alzheimer wing, three under controlled psychiatric care, another thirty-five in the section for the sisters too infirm to care for themselves, and another twenty hospitalized for one thing or another. Unless my math is going the way of my eyesight, that makes sixty-eight."

Mother rose. "Shall we go see Sister Charles?" They passed through a set of double doors. A nurse glanced in their direction from an island counter of files and monitors. She smiled and waved a greeting.

Mother Jean approached a door on the left. A small slot held a card with the name *Sister Charles de Jesus*.

Mother whispered, "Sister Charles has been here several years. She has terminal cancer. I should warn you, she's not always coherent."

Kate and Ray followed Mother Jean into a small white room with a bed, night stand and chair.

Sister Charles was covered with several summer-weight blankets. She wore a white kerchief on her head. Her cheeks were sunken and her eyes deep-set and closed.

Mother Jean walked over to the bed and placed her hand on the thin, veined arm that lay atop the covers. Sister Charles opened her eyes, saw Mother Jean and offered a weak smile. "Tell me we're both in heaven," she whispered.

"That's not such a bad thought," answered Mother Jean. "But, no, we're both still waiting."

"Maybe tomorrow." The old nun's eyes closed and she took several deep, rattling breaths.

Mother Jean ran her hand lightly along the veined arm. "Charles, I brought you some visitors."

Sister Charles opened her eyes wide and she smiled. Her gaze settled on the Fredricks. Mother Jean made the introductions, explaining that Ray and Kate were helping to unravel what happened to Theresa.

"Ah, Theresa." Charles raised her head. Mother Jean arranged the pillows to give her more height. Charles said, "Theresa and I were just talking. She said they're getting things ready for me."

"Did you tell her how chilly you get here and that you're hoping for a warm place?"

"Now, Mother, if I had said that, they might get the wrong idea as to where I want to go."

Sister Charles' eyes twinkled. She looked over at Kate. "Come here, my dear," she said. Kate walked over to the side of the bed. "You have a nice smile," said Sister Charles. "It's one of the few things I can enjoy these days. A smile like yours."

Suddenly Sister Charles de Jesus closed her eyes; her hand knotted the spread. Her mouth opened to release a weak moan. Mother Jean held tightly to her hand.

Kate retreated to Ray's side.

Mother Jean opened a bottle of pills and placed two in the elder nun's palm. She poured some water. Charles swallowed the pills separately. Her head fell back against the pillow. She seemed suddenly asleep.

Ray leaned toward Mother Jean and whispered, "We could visit another time."

Mother shook her head and whispered back, "She's much better today than I've seen her in a while."

The tension eased in the face of the bedridden woman. She opened her eyes, looked up at Mother Jean and said, "It's like false labor, this waiting. When the pain starts, I say to myself, now, finally, it's time. Then, I find it isn't." She bit her lower lip. Suddenly her eyes were on Kate and Ray standing at the foot of her bed. "Have we no chairs for our visitors, Mother?"

Ray followed Mother Jean into the hall and came back carrying two chairs. "Place them here, young man," said Charles, touching the side of the bed nearest her. "There, that's fine. Now, what can I do for you two youngsters besides embarrass you with my illness and age?"

Kate was about to protest when Sister Charles reached out, took her hand and said, "Forgive me. I'm being too free with my words, a sometimes regrettable side effect of my condition. What can I do for you children?"

Ray answered, "We need to know more about Theresa. More about her past, and what made her tick."

"Tick," echoed Charles. "Time." She paused and looked beyond them as if to take inventory of her memory. Her eyes found Ray and she motioned for him to draw nearer. Whispering as if she were sharing a confidence, she said, "I've trained many sisters. But Theresa was my favorite." Charles nodded to herself. In a louder voice, she said, "I'm not surprised you're curious about what made her tick. She was always a puzzle to me as well."

"How do you mean?" asked Ray.

"She could be so serious, and yet so full of humor. She had a glow of innocence, yet a dark side that was worrisome. And as much as she was a very private person, at times she could be delightfully open. I remember once her telling me about how, at the age of ten, a teacher drilled her class on how God was to be loved first and most of all. She went to bed that night and cried herself to sleep simply because she knew it was not God she loved most, but her mother and father." Charles suddenly stopped and turned a little to one side, as though to curl up with her memories.

"And the dark side," coaxed Ray, "how did it make its appearance?"

Sister Charles turned slowly back to her visitors.

"How did the dark side make its appearance?" he repeated.

Charles laid one hand on the other. "It's not a thing that's easily described."

"Try. It could help." Ray waited.

Charles turned her gaze to the ceiling. "It didn't happen often, but every once in a while Theresa would go off on her own. Sometimes I would find her alone in chapel, other times in an empty classroom. She would be standing or kneeling or sitting, her face as white as death, eyes shut, and hands fisted as though to fight."

Sister Charles began to blink rapidly; then her eyes closed.

"Touch her hand," whispered Mother.

Kate took hold of the wrinkled hand. Sister Charles opened her eyes, looked at Kate, then at Ray and at Mother Jean. "How nice," she said, "you've come to visit."

Mother Jean took the Fredricks to the refectory for a snack. They served themselves coffee and banana bread from a sideboard laden with pastries, butter, and jars of jam.

"Oh, dear," said Mother Jean, glancing past the Fredricks. Coming in their direction, moving with the aid of a walker, was a very old, plump, humped-back nun. She shuffled herself and her walker over to where Mother Jean sat, and smiled angelically.

"Sister Pierre," said Mother Jean, in a forced acknowledgment of the nun's presence. She introduced her to the Fredricks, and told them Sister Pierre was curator of their museum.

Pierre beamed at the fresh visitors. With the jubilance of a cat who's caught a mouse, and in a voice that veritably squeaked, she said, "You will come and visit, won't you?" She gripped her superior's arm with short crooked fingers. "Mother, you will bring them down, won't you?"

"Perhaps they haven't the time," said Mother Jean.

Pierre fixed her sad, pleading eyes on Kate.

Kate said, "I'd love to see your museum. We both would, wouldn't we, Ray?"

Ray nodded, still giving a good part of his attention to the goodies that remained on the sideboard.

Mother Jean said, "I'll bring them down as soon as we've finished here, Sister."

"I'll wait," announced Pierre. She shoved her walker aside, pulled out a chair and sat, her chin barely higher than the edge of the table. "You'll love our museum," she cooed.

"I didn't know you had a museum," said Kate.

Ray excused himself and headed for the sideboard.

Pierre talked as she waited patiently. "Our first sisters came from Ireland and brought with them much of their furniture and the necessities to get started. My great-great-aunt was one of them."

Pierre went on to recount how the sisters traveled by covered wagon all the way from Massachusetts to Toronto, moving soon afterwards to Small Falls, to take up residence and ownership of property left them by a sister's relative.

Mother Jean glanced at her watch. She said, "Well, perhaps I'll leave you with Sister Pierre for now, and meet you back here for lunch at one. That is, if you're sure you want to see the museum."

Pierre's mouth tightened with a small frown. "Of course they are," she said. When Kate concurred, Mother Jean rose, deposited her cup and dish in a plastic tub near the door to the kitchen, and left.

Pierre smiled continuously while Ray quickly finished his second piece of banana bread. As soon as he drained his cup, she squirmed out of her seat, took firm hold of her walker, instructed the visitors to follow, and set off. They took the rattling old elevator down to the basement. Pierre, shuffling along as happily as a toddler on a trip to the zoo, led the Fredricks through a door elaborately marked Museum of the Sisters of Saint Joseph.

"Oh, my," exclaimed Kate at the sight of an enormous space divided into completely furnished and decorated rooms. Even Ray whistled at the displays of wooden buckets, button shoes, short, narrow beds and cast-iron kettles.

Pierre basked in their appreciation. Her old eyes glowed. She took them through each room, telling of the origin of the furniture, explaining the living conditions of the time, and demonstrating the appliances of a pre-electrical age. Then she opened a wooden trunk and lifted out an old, high-collared velvet dress. Beneath it were more dresses of the same period. "These are the clothes some of our early candidates wore when they entered. If I had the room, I would put up a whole section of what was in fashion from the early eighteen hundreds until now."

Ray stiffened. "Are you saying that you kept the things worn by the ladies who entered?"

"Until about twenty years ago. We stopped for lack of room."

"So if a woman entered in 1957, you'd have her things?"

"We should have."

"Might that include a purse?"

"If she brought one."

Ray smiled. "Sister Pierre, I have a big favor to ask. Can you locate the things that belonged to Theresa Loomis?"

"I'm sure I can. As long as they weren't in the section we lost in that fire a few years back."

Sister Pierre worked herself and her walker over to a bank of wooden file cabinets at the back of the Museum. She pushed her walker to the side and pulled out the middle drawer of the middle cabinet. With her head in the drawer and her mouth taut with purpose, she searched, then proudly announced, "Section K, shelf seventeen."

Sister Pierre closed the drawer and pulled back her walker. The threesome entered a back room through a door not far from the cabinets. It was lined from end to end with shelves holding small plastic bundles, all tagged and tied and neatly stacked. Approaching the section labeled K, Sister Pierre pointed to the top shelf and said, "It should be up there."

"Is there a ladder?" asked Ray.

Pierre told him where to find it. Ray hurried off. He returned with the wheeled, freestanding ladder and a look of tense anticipation. The ladder hooked snugly onto the skirting on the top shelf. Pierre showed Ray how to lock the wheels. She and Kate stepped back to watch.

One by one, Ray tugged the bundles toward him and read the names, stirring up decades of dust, and to compound the disturbance, sneezed repeatedly. He had read the names of some twenty sisters and blown his nose five or six times before he found the name he wanted. He pulled the bundle toward him, stared at it.

"Did you find it?" called Kate from below.

"I sure did."

"Bring it down," said Pierre. Then in a sterner tone she added, "Mother won't mind. She's been wanting to give these things to the Goodwill for years."

Ray descended slowly, the bundle in one arm. He set the package on the floor and crouched beside it. Kate brushed dust from his shirt. Ray yanked on the twine; it snapped like straw. The plastic cracked and broke away in pieces. Ray calculated the time it had sat on the shelf. Nineteen fifty-seven till now. Over thirty-five years.

His hands sweating, Ray lifted a white silk blouse from the top of the pile. And there, under a pair of low pumps and on top of a green skirt, he found a purse.

It was a white purse, imitation leather.

Ray disengaged the tarnished silver clasp. He removed a yellowed lace hankie, a round rusty compact, a small comb, a tube of lipstick and a wallet.

Ray reached into his pants pocket and removed a handkerchief. He wiped his hands and the back of his neck.

"Come on, Ray," said Kate.

Ray replaced his handkerchief and opened the wallet.

It was empty except for a card under a square of stiff plastic, opaque with age. Ray slid out the card. It was a driver's license.

"What does it say?" asked Kate.

"Theresa Loomis. 27 Main Street. Seline, Connecticut. The same address is on the form in her file." Ray sat back on his heels. "Shoot."

"There's nothing else in the purse?" asked Kate.

Ray laid the wallet and card on the floor. He picked up the purse and held it open to the light. Empty. Then he noticed a turned-up corner at the bottom. He reached in, tugged on the edge, and felt the bottom flap lift. He peered in. His face broke into a full smile.

"What is it, Ray?" asked Kate, gripping his shoulders and leaning forward.

"An envelope. An old envelope."

Ray carefully removed it from its hiding place. It was addressed to Miss Theresa Loomis, 733 Center Street, Northpointe, Washington. "We have us an address," said Ray.

"Two addresses," corrected Kate, pointing to the return address in the upper left corner.

"2946 Bolder Road, Northpointe," read Ray.

"Well, open it," said Kate.

He did. Inside was a letter dated January 1, 1947. It consisted of three short, intimate paragraphs. And it was signed *Casey.*

Twenty-four

Their flight from Toronto landed in Vancouver late Sunday evening, the first of August. They stayed overnight at a hotel near the airport. The following morning, after a quick breakfast, they rented a two-door Dodge Dynasty and picked up the 401 going east. Within the hour, they were on Route 9 heading south.

It was noon when they crossed the border into Washington state. In the far distance on their left, mountains cut into the sky like the forbidden realm of giants.

"I'm glad we came," said Kate.

"So am I."

"How far is it, Northpointe?"

"We'll be there before one."

Twenty minutes later a sign directed them off Route 9 and onto an asphalt road that angled lazily around quiet foothills punctuated with farms.

Minutes later, Northpointe came into view. It was a sun-drenched, sleepy collection of crisscrossing, tree-lined streets and well-kept buildings. A sign posted the population: 4,127.

The county road became Main Street and the Fredricks had arrived in Theresa Loomis' home town.

"Shall we have lunch first or look for a motel?" asked Ray.

"Let's get settled, then we can relax over lunch."

They drove down Main Street until it became an open country highway again. Not a building they passed offered accommodations.

Ray made a U-turn in front of the roadside stand at a poultry farm. He pulled up to one of the two pumps at a service station, parked the car and got out.

A man rose from his seat on a wooden barrel. He ambled over to them, smiling as though the Fredricks were old friends. "Afternoon," he said, shoving up the sleeves of his gray sweatshirt. He unhooked the nozzle from the gas pump.

"Fill it, please," said Ray.

The meter churned away. Ray asked, "Is there a motel in town?"

"One in town. And two further south on Route Nine." The attendant discreetly glanced from Ray to Kate. "I'd stick to the one in town. The other two cater to hunters and the like."

"Mind giving me directions?"

"Just keep going back toward town. Count off four blocks past Center Street—that's the street with the traffic light—and make a right. It's on Market Street. It's called the Buggy Works. Got a lounge and restaurant. Pretty good food. And if you're into down-home, heavy eating, try Granny's on South Street."

"Thanks." Ray paid for the gas.

They drove into town, adjusting to the slower rhythm of the traffic.

The Buggy Works sat between a one-show theater and a shoe store. It was two stories high and constructed of brick. Wide steps led to a large sheltered porch housing a pair of old buggy seats with squared-off wooden wheels as armrests.

Ray trailed Kate up to the porch. They pushed through a screen door that slammed shut after them. A small boy turned and stared, his eyes widening through thick glasses with black rims. He dashed off down a narrow hall, shouting for his mother.

Ray and Kate waited near an L-shaped counter. A woman emerged through a swinging door from what seemed to be the kitchen, drying her rough, red hands on a cobbler's apron. She removed the apron, handed it to the boy and, stepping behind the counter, smiled kindly.

Kate asked if there was a room available.

Looking amused at the question, the woman responded that there was.

"Good," said Kate. "I was worried about finding a place at this time of year."

"Years back, you would have had reason," said the woman. "Now, with motels mushrooming in the bigger towns and cities, we're grateful for a trickle of business."

She opened a book and turned it toward Kate. "Just a name and address will do."

Kate began writing.

"Second floor or first?" asked the woman.

"Second," said Ray.

She opened a drawer, fished among a mess of keys and handed Kate one marked 208. "Forty-five a night," she murmured, as if afraid they might object to the rate.

The travelers mounted the stairs with their cases. They gave the room a quick inspection, approved the corner view and the cleanliness, and headed back to the first floor.

Tacked to the frame of the archway leading into the lounge was a handwritten card that read No Firearms. Kate playfully felt the small of Ray's back. "A little lower," he whispered in her ear.

She responded with a hard pinch and took the lead.

The floor boards creaked as they crossed to the bar. A man appeared through a door at the far end. His face was framed in hair as white as snow. A short-stemmed pipe full of unlit tobacco poked from the corner of a wide mouth, and a towel hugged his shoulder like a sash.

"What can I do you for?" he asked through his teeth.

"How about a beer and a hamburger," said Ray.

"I'll have the same," Kate added.

The bartender removed his pipe, turned toward the door

and shouted the order. He filled two glasses from a tap and set them on napkins in front of the Fredricks.

A sudden rat-a-tat of tiny steps sounded. The small boy from out front appeared at the side of the bartender, tugged at his pant leg, and asked, "Grandpa, can I have a pop?"

The man reached down and hoisted the boy head high. "You got a quarter?"

The little head shook no.

"You got two hands?"

The little head nodded, this time with a grin.

"Well, Chris, give me five minutes of sweeping and you got your pop." He set the boy down, and watched with pride as the little fellow scurried toward a short hall leading to the rest rooms. Instantly, he was back, carrying a broom twice his height. "Okay, Gramps," he called, watching his grandfather ostensibly check his watch and drop his hand as a signal.

Still smiling, the bartender moseyed over to the Fredricks, leaned on the counter and asked, "You folks have grandkids?"

"I wish we did," said Kate.

Ray finished his beer and set it on the counter. A call from the kitchen took the bartender away. He returned with two plates, each piled with a fat burger, pickles and french fries. He set the plates down, along with a stand of potted condiments that included corn relish. He placed his pipe on a saucer and reached a hand to Ray. "The name's Josh. Susan tells me you just checked in. That's my daughter; you met her out front. You from Seattle?"

"From Michigan," said Ray.

Josh smiled and said, "I hear it's almost as nice out there as it is here."

Ray checked the lobby for a public phone. Not finding one, he ran upstairs to their room. Kate waited on the front porch, watching a young family in overalls climb out of a truck.

Ray pushed through the door. Kate caught it before it slammed. They walked to their car at the curb. "What did you want a phone book for?" asked Kate.

"To get an address for the sheriff."

"Why didn't you just ask Josh?"

"I would have if I'd wanted the whole town buzzing about strangers who need to see the sheriff." He started the car. Hill Street was two blocks over from Market. The sheriff's office was a square structure near the town hall. It was identified by a sign with large curlicued letters carved into a bed of oak and hanging above the door.

They found the sheriff in, occupying the single chair at the front desk. He was a solid-looking young man in his thirties. The name *Marsh* was embroidered on the flap of his western shirt. Ray approached with his credentials in hand. The sheriff gave them an uninterested glance, and asked, "What brings you folks this far west?"

"We're checking into a murder. The victim was a former resident of Northpointe."

A shrug confirmed the sheriff's indifference. "From when? Last week? Last year? How far back we talking?"

"Nineteen fifty-one, or maybe as late as fifty-seven. We're not sure."

The sheriff's face lit with a smile. "Kind of before my time," he said, straightening a little. "What exactly did you have in mind?"

"We'd like to ask a few questions around town."

"I don't see any harm in that." He rose and looked at his watch. "Just keep me in mind if you come across anything I ought to know."

They drove off with the sheriff standing in the doorway.

"He didn't even ask the victim's name," said Kate.

"Thank God for small favors."

"What do you mean?"

"He could have stuck us with his own procedures, or insisted on going along. As it is, the most we have to do is stop by before we leave. And if we're lucky a second time, he won't be in.

"Now, let's check out those addresses we found at the Mother House." Turning onto Main Street, he asked, "What was the sender's address on the envelope?"

Kate carefully removed the item from her purse. "Two-nine-four-six Bolder Road."

"And Theresa's address?"

"Center Street. Seven-three-three."

"We'll try that one first." He made a right at the light.

"Wrong way," said Kate, catching the numbers on a run of small stores.

Ray pulled close to the curb, waited for a break in traffic and turned around. Seven-three-three was two blocks in from the light. It was one of a strip of bungalows occupying both sides of the street and housing small service establishments: a barber shop, a beauty parlor, a small-appliance repair shop, and an antique store.

Seven-three-three was an office for Mountain Creek Realtors. It was attractively painted off-white with green-gray trim.

Ray parked on a small asphalt pad that angled up to the side of the building from a cracked, concrete drive. The property had a narrow back yard, a shed and a leaning one-car garage occupied by a black Ford LTD.

They climbed the steps of a small front porch. In the ceiling were enormous hooks that might once have held a swing. A sign said to walk in.

The room was large with open venetian blinds at all the windows. The walls were a pale daisy yellow that went well with the olive-green carpet.

An elderly man in a suit and tie offered them a seat and

introduced himself as Keith Jensen.

Ray said, "This is a little bit of a shocker."

"Shocker?" The man blinked innocently from behind his wire-rimmed glasses.

"We had some dear friends who used to live in this house. The Loomises. Never dreamed they moved away."

Kate folded her hands and tried to show the appropriate amount of disappointment.

"Darn," continued Ray.

"I wish I could help," said the man, "only I'm not from around this area. I moved here to retire, sort of."

"I noticed most of the street has gone commercial," said Ray.

"That sometimes happens to nice old streets like this," said the agent.

"Do you know how long this office has been open?"

"At least five years. Maybe ten. I'm not sure, but I could find out."

Ray encouraged him to do so. "Could you also find out who the house was purchased from, and that person's forwarding address, if possible?" Ray put on his most beseeching face.

Jensen began scribbling on a pad with the agency's letterhead. Ray said, "Will you need a retainer?"

The agent laughed. "I should pay you for giving me something to do."

The Fredricks next stop was at a post office. They both went in, Kate out of curiosity and Ray with the hope of finding a map of the area. He did. It was in a glass case beside a display of colorful stamps. He traced a finger up and down the streets and lanes until he found Bolder Road.

Ray located the road without a problem. They followed it, heading east, driving toward the snow-capped mountains a brilliant white in the light of the afternoon sun. They had gone about a mile when Ray said, "We must have passed it."

"You think so?"

"We'll go a little farther and then head back." They rounded a hill set with boulders the size of a compact car. Ray noticed some old buildings off to the side on the right. Locating what had once been a driveway, he pulled in as far as the undergrowth would allow.

There were two separate structures and what had once been a large fenced yard. The roofs were gone. Weeds climbed up sun-bleached door frames and the grass was as high as the rotting window sills.

Noticing a sign buried in a tangle of brush, and with Kate close behind, Ray worked his way across a stretch of trash and scrub. He freed a stick and began clearing leafy shroud from the face of the sign. It was cracked and rotten to the point of crumbling. Some of the letters had faded into shadows on the wood.

"The Sportsmen Kennel," announced Ray after a long study of the letters that could still be read. The next three words were more easily deciphered and ran down the sign like three steps. *Boarding. Breeding. Training.* At the bottom of the sign was the word *Specialize*, then a bare space and the letter *G*.

"Golden retriever, Great Dane, greyhound," suggested Kate.

Ray shrugged. "Whatever. I wish there were a numbered address so we'd know where we are." Suddenly he said, "I bet this is the place."

"A dog kennel?" replied Kate.

"Sure. Why not? It could tie in somehow with Theresa's attitude toward dogs."

Twenty-five

Back in their room at the Buggy Works, the Fredricks watched some TV, dozed, and about five-thirty, left the motel to have supper at Granny's.

The restaurant was busy. A woman in jeans and a loose-fitting man's shirt seated them at a table near the kitchen. Country and western played from a quartet of speakers, one directly over the Fredricks' head. They both ordered T-bone steak, baked potato, summer squash, coffee and apple betty with vanilla sauce. Conceding to the uselessness of trying to converse, they settled down to enjoy the meal and the surroundings.

By seven-thirty, they were back at the Buggy Works. Ray suggested a nightcap. They went into the lounge. Half of the dozen tables and most of the bar seats were occupied.

Josh spotted them and had a word with a couple of customers to free a pair of adjacent stools. He finished filling an order for a large table of plaid-shirted, white-haired cronies, and worked his way to the Fredricks, replenishing drinks where needed.

"Had a good day?" Josh asked, bringing the Fredricks a brandy and a Scotch and soda.

"A real good one," answered Kate. "Nice town you have here."

"We like it." Josh brought the visitors a bowl of peanuts.

Ray asked, "Ever hear of the Sportsmen Kennel?"

"Sure. Used to be over on Bolder Road. But it's been closed for years. You looking to buy a hunting dog? There's a place out on Route Nine that has a good reputation for gun dogs."

"Do you know who owned the place, or ran it?"

"Ah, gee." Josh did a one-eye squint and said, "Not right off hand. But I know who could tell you."

"Who's that?"

"Guy named Wilkey Hamilton. Lives here at the hotel. Room two-fifty-two." Josh glanced around the lounge. "He used to come down every night till he broke his hip. Now he's down when the pain allows. I tried to get him to move down to the first floor. So far he's fought it. Says he likes the view from up there. Sees a lot of the goings-on in town from his window."

"Do you think he'd be up to visitors?" asked Ray.

"Sure. He loves having people around. That's why he moved here. He used to live on a farm outside of town. When his wife died, he moved in here for the company. He gets a yearly rate. We got three like him. Thank God. Otherwise we'd be running empty too often to stay open."

"What does he drink?" asked Ray.

"Beer."

"How about a couple of pitchers and some glasses?"

Josh filled two pitchers and set them on a tray with three glasses.

Kate removed one of the glasses from the tray. "I think I'll go to our room and read," she said.

Balancing the tray on an edge of wainscoting, Ray rapped at the door to 252.

"Friend or foe?" a voice called from inside.

"A stranger with a bribe," Ray replied.

The tapping sound of a cane followed. The door opened. Wilkey smiled at the tray. He trained his smile on Ray and asked, "You won't make a cripple dance for a drink, will you?"

"For a bottle of whiskey, maybe. But for beer, conversation will do me fine."

Wilkey scratched at himself between the buttons of a frayed shirt pulled taut over a roll of belly. He backed into the room, and gave the door a tug inward.

Ray entered. Wilkey shut the door, using the hooked end of his cane. The room was identical to the one Ray and Kate occupied, except for an armchair covered with a sheet, and a footrest blackened with heel marks.

Wilkey pointed the cane at a TV tray next to the draped chair. "Do you mind getting your own seat?" he asked.

Ray set the tray down and brought over a straight chair with arms. He filled the glasses, handed one to Wilkey, and toasted Josh and the Buggy Works.

"Old Josh send you up with the bribe?" asked Wilkey after a long, slow swallow. His lower lip stretched up to remove a smudge of foam.

"Josh said you might be able to answer my questions."

"What do you want to know?"

"Are you familiar with the Sportsmen?"

"The old dog kennel on Bolder Road? Sure. Got me some of my best dogs from there in my hunting days."

"Do you remember who owned it back in the fifties?"

"Fifties. Seems to me that just about then the place was bought by some woman. She ran it into the ground. Shame, too. Place did good business, sold dogs all over the county."

"Do you remember her name?"

"Nope."

"But you're sure a woman owned the place in the fifties?"

Wilkey leaned back and settled his gaze on the ceiling. He asked, "You talking early fifties, late fifties? What?"

"Say, nineteen fifty-one," replied Ray.

"Fifty-one." Wilkey scratched at his curly gray hair. "That was some year around here."

"Why was that?"

"You don't want to know. Bad business. Best buried and left that way."

Ray held his beer with both hands. "August ninth, nineteen fifty-one?"

Wilkey's eyes narrowed. "Are you some reporter looking to rattle old ghosts?"

Ray shook his head. "Let me tell you exactly why I'm here." Beginning with the hit-and-run, Ray passed a half-hour recounting the events that had led him to Northpointe. He kept the victim's name to the last, then in a quiet voice mentioned Theresa Loomis.

The look on the old man's face was what he had hoped to see. Ray offered the man more beer.

Wilkey pushed the pitcher away. "If you got the man who shot her, why are you here?"

"I need to be sure. I need a motive. I need to know what happened on August ninth."

"Leave it alone. What happened back in fifty-one has taken too much of the soul out of this town already."

"What if we don't have the right man?" asked Ray.

"You want to bring the devil's memory back because of a *what if?*"

"Perhaps it need not go any further than this room."

Wilkey rested an elbow on the arm of his chair and his head in his hand. *"Perhaps* is a flimsy, fickle word."

"I've come a long way."

"To feed on people's sorrows."

"To find the truth. To make sure a killer isn't partying and planning his next 'Northpointe'."

"Shit."

"Please? Having one source is a lot better than going around town with my questions. Even better than asking for old newspapers with a curious librarian breathing over my shoulder. And I've already been to the sheriff. That's probably circulating around town right now."

Wilkey set his glass on the tray. "No. I don't want to be the one to get this thing going again. But I'll do this. I'll give you a name. The name of a couple who would be hurt the most with your digging into the past. You go see them. Ask them. Nobody knows more about it than they do."

Kate was in bed reading when Ray returned. She watched her husband cross to the open window and draw aside the drapes.

"Don't tell me you didn't find out anything about the kennel. You were there an hour."

"I was busy being lectured about stirring up trouble."

"For asking about a kennel?"

"For asking about what happened on August ninth in fifty-one." Ray let the drapes drop into place and faced Kate. "Maybe we should just enjoy the scenery and leave."

"Maybe you should have yourself a good night's sleep."

Ray moved to the bed and sat facing the wall. "Theresa wanted this left alone. Trev thinks he has the man who shot her."

"What happened to putting all the pieces in place, and making sure we have the whole picture?"

"Perhaps the man who said that was just looking for a way to keep his mind off his own pain."

"We do that all our lives, Ray." Kate closed her book and set it on the covers. "What did Mr. Hamilton tell you?"

"Nothing much. But he gave me the name of a couple who he said 'had the most to suffer' if the story resurfaced."

"Then let them decide whether we should be told or not. Besides, all you really need to do is check the library."

"I know."

"Who are they?"

"Alice and Douglas Campbell."

"I mean, who are they to Theresa?"

"He wouldn't say."

"Where do they live?"

"They have a farm on Route Nine. About an hour's drive from here. I have the address."

"We'll go there tomorrow," said Kate.

Tuesday turned cool with a stiff breeze coming in off the Strait of Georgia. The Fredricks drove with the windows partially up.

They found the Campbell farm with no trouble. It sat a short distance back from the road, a white house surrounded by fields that had long since reverted to high grass and weeds and the offspring of former crops.

The house was old but in good repair. The barn wasn't so pampered and leaned a little.

Ray pulled into the drive and turned off the engine. A face appeared at a side window. Seconds later a man came toward them from the rear of the house. He was thin, of average height and wearing glasses.

"You're the Fredricks?" he asked.

Ray and Kate exchanged glances.

"Wilkey called me last night. It's a good thing he did." The man turned back toward the house and said, "Come on in."

They entered a tidy kitchen. Douglas Campbell pulled out chairs, signaled for them to sit. "I'm not going to offer you drinks and all that. I want you gone before my wife gets back."

"Thank you for asking us in," said Ray.

"You're lucky that Wilkey called. If you had come unannounced and if my wife was here, you would have been off my property in less time than it takes to cuss you out."

"Did Wilkey tell you Theresa Loomis was murdered?"

Douglas nodded. "It makes you want to send God packing. Not that we haven't already." A heavy sadness came into Campbell's face.

Ray asked Kate for the envelope and handed it to their host. "I want you to know that we are legit, and that we are not here for a story. That envelope was Theresa's. It was with the things she wore the day she entered the convent. The letter inside is signed *Casey*."

"I recognize the writing." Campbell returned the envelope.

Ray handed him an issue of the *Saint Luke's Herald* with the double photos of a young Theresa in full habit and Theresa aged and wearing more modern attire.

Campbell studied the pictures with growing emotion. His eyes clouded. "She looks happy," he said.

"I think she was," Ray answered.

"She looks almost the way she did before—" Douglas tugged on his chair, drawing closer to the table. "She was special, Theresa, only far too innocent. The world devours innocence and spits it out." Douglas took another long look at the *Herald*. "Alice used to say that Theresa grew up with too little of the negative. My wife's folks fought almost as often as they attended church. Theresa's folks breezed through a day as if it was just another Christmas.

"Alice grew up next door to Theresa. They made her place into a beauty parlor; Theresa's old house is a real estate office."

"We were there," said Ray.

"Wilkey didn't tell me how Theresa was murdered."

"She was shot. And a few days earlier, she had survived a hit-and-run attempt."

"She got her wish," murmured Douglas.

"I beg your pardon?"

"The last time my wife and I saw Theresa, she said she wished she were dead."

"Why?" asked Kate.

Campbell stood and left the room. He returned with an envelope. He took from it a single photo and laid it on the table, face up and turned toward the Fredricks. It was a picture of Theresa with a man, a child and a dog.

Ray and Kate studied the young, vital, happy faces. The dog was an Irish setter that could have been Thumper's twin.

Kate spoke first. "Then she was married."

"For almost four years. To Casey Hubbard. They went

together all through high school and married a year after Theresa lost her parents. Casey pulled Theresa through that tragedy. But he wasn't there to do it the next time."

Douglas pointed to the toddler in the photo. He smiled. "That's Phillipa. She was a charmer. Theresa adored her. So did my wife."

Douglas trained his gaze on the view of the barn from the window. Tears filled his eyes. "I suppose I might as well tell you what happened. You'll only dig it up in some old newspaper if I don't."

Campbell stood and crossed to the window. With his back to the Fredricks, he said, "Before I start, I want to make something clear. If my wife comes back, you're to leave. I'll tell her you're canvassing for a politician, or something."

Douglas ran a finger along the sash. He said, "Theresa and Casey ran a motel on Bolder Road. Wilkey said that you were over at the Sportsmen Kennel. Hubbard's Motel was a little further out, on the same side of the road. Nothing but ruins, now. It's in a grove of trees and scrub that have had forty years to work at burying the place. It's hard to spot, if you don't know it's there. Casey's parents owned it and left it to him when they died. It was a ma-and pa-place, easily run by two, with some hired help during the hunting season."

Douglas sighed and lowered his head. He took hold of the sill with both hands. "August ninth, Casey went to town for supplies. Theresa and Phillipa were there alone.

"We found out later the dog had started barking. Theresa headed for the office at the front of the house with Phillipa in hand. The barking stopped as she neared the office.

"The dog was behind the counter in a pool of blood, its head almost severed from the body. A man in a ski mask grabbed Phillipa and wiped his bloody knife on her blouse. He ordered Theresa back down the hall and into the bedroom. He taped the child's mouth, and Theresa's. Made Theresa tie

Phillipa to the dresser. Then he tied her to the bed. He switched on the radio, even took the time to find his station.

"Casey came back. He'd forgotten a gas can he wanted to fill in town. Normally he'd have got the can from the shed and left. There wasn't a car out front to indicate anyone had come.

"Only the music stopped him. He knew Theresa didn't listen to the radio during the day." Douglas turned from the view and sat on the wide sill.

A cat meowed from somewhere in the house. The sound of a passing car drifted in. Douglas finally spoke. "Casey walked in as the man was cutting off Theresa's clothes.

"Casey and the man struggled. Casey was stabbed over half a dozen times. When he finally fell to the floor, he had a hold on the man's mask. It came off.

"The man smothered Phillipa. Didn't even hesitate. He used the same pillow on Theresa, apologizing the way you would when you bump the arm of a stranger. Telling her that he had no choice."

Campbell came back to the table and sat down. "My wife was the one who found them. The dog first. Then the others. The man hadn't done his job well. Theresa was still alive. Barely. They took her to the hospital. She was incoherent for weeks. When she came to herself again, she wouldn't say another word for a long time. Alice spent hours at her side, wearing herself out with worry and trying to say something that would make a difference.

"They tried shock treatment. It helped. Bit by bit, she told the police what had happened. It was months before they got enough of a description to make a drawing of the man and circulate it. He was never found.

"When Theresa came out of the hospital, she sold the motel. Soon afterwards, she called us to say good-bye. Said she had to get far away and try to forget. She mentioned going to college. She didn't think she would be able to stay in touch.

We never heard from her again.

"Alice always thought Theresa blamed her for the fact that she survived. Between that and the shock of finding them..." He took a deep breath. "My wife had a series of breakdowns after Theresa left. We had a farm not far from the Hubbard Motel. We moved. Alice got better. She joined a club and goes out on digs. They research the old West, find old fur-trading posts, lumber camps, mines. Search for old bottles and coins. It keeps her distracted by things that don't matter.

"I'd rather she didn't know Theresa was dead."

"She'll not learn it from us," replied Kate, her voice choking with emotion.

"I suppose I could make some coffee," said Douglas.

"Thanks, but maybe we should be going."

"Yes, perhaps that's best."

Ray asked, "The drawing of Theresa's assailant, do you have a copy?"

"No."

"I have a photograph of the man we think killed Theresa. May I show it to you before we leave?"

Campbell did not answer. Ray laid the faxed photo on the table. "Do you see any likeness between this man and the man who killed the Hubbards?"

"A beard."

"Eyes? Nose? Anything else?"

"It's hard to say. This man is a lot older. And if I remember correctly, the other man's face was not so small."

"Do you remember if he was described as short?"

"Definitely tall. That I remember. Taller than Casey, and he was just under six foot."

Twenty-six

"Little Girl Lost. Just like the painting," muttered Ray.

"What dear?"

"Nothing." Ray maneuvered to pass a truck with a full load of crated, cackling chickens.

Kate opened her purse and took out the photo of the Hubbard family and their dog. "I'm glad Mr. Campbell let us keep this. Maybe Mother Jean would like to have a copy."

"Give them a copy of that and you'll have to tell them what happened."

"I took it for granted we would," said Kate.

"I'm not so sure I want to. Theresa didn't. Even when her life was in danger, and she suspected the reason, she never told. Maybe we should just honor that silence."

Kate slipped the photo back in her purse. She asked, "Do you think the man who destroyed her family is the same man who shot Theresa?"

"Definitely not."

"They both have beards."

"Yes, but the Northpointe perpetrator is six-foot tall," said Ray. He tapped the steering wheel. "Do you remember when I went to visit Theresa in the hospital? She seemed genuinely concerned until I told her the driver of the car was a short man. Then suddenly she was ready to laugh it off."

"She laughed off being run down?"

"All right, she was playfully relieved, then."

"What about Keyhoe?" said Kate. "He's tall, isn't he?"

"Taller than the man who did the shooting," answered Ray.

"Forty years ago he could have worn a beard. Did Theresa

ever meet him?"

"She said she hadn't." Ray glanced at Kate. "Maybe I'll call Trev and have him check on Keyhoe's whereabouts in fifty-one."

They passed the turnoff for Northpointe.

Kate asked, "Where are we going?"

"Bolder Road should be a mile further up. I'd like to have a look at the ruins of the Hubbard place." He located the road and made a left. They drove slowly, eyes alert. When they were abreast of the kennel, Ray turned. He kept the car on the shoulder and inched along, watching for what had once been a road.

"Stop," ordered Kate. She pointed to an old downed pole, black with decay. Ray pulled the car off the road. On foot, they followed the pole into the weeds and found an old sign, its message totally obliterated by fungus and rot and weather.

A few yards from the pole was the remnant of a road. Dirt and sand and grass all but filled the ruts. The Fredricks followed it to a stand of trees. They pushed on.

It was a strange sight, like some battle-scarred, rotting ghost. The main house still had the rectangular shape of a building. The four cabins on either side of it were peaked heaps of earth and wood and pipes and looked like ancient burial biers waiting to be set afire.

Kicking an old beer can, Ray trudged on.

"You're not going in there, are you?" said Kate.

Without stopping, he said, "Probably not."

"Well, I know I'm not." She went to stand near a tree. Ray wandered closer. He stopped a few feet from the end cabin. He crouched.

"Did you find something?" Kate called.

"Probably where they buried the dog. There's a heap of stones covering something that could have been a dog collar."

"Come on, Ray. Let's go."

He straightened, gave the ruins a final, pained glance and rejoined Kate.

Using the phone in their room, Ray dialed Trev's home number at five o'clock, Washington time. There was no answer. He tried again a half-hour later with the same result.

Ray and Kate went down to the lounge for supper. They returned to their room around seven. Kate went into the bathroom with her book and her glasses. She started filling the tub.

Ray tried Trev again. He let the phone ring twenty times and hung up. He switched on the TV, and watched a rerun of "Barnaby Jones." Toward the end of the hour, Kate emerged from the bathroom in her pajamas. She put her book and glasses on the night stand, folded down the bedspread and climbed between the sheets.

Ray switched the TV off and reached for the phone.

"You're not going to call him now, are you?" asked Kate. "It's nearly midnight in Michigan."

"What difference does it make? He's been out all evening anyway." Ray dialed.

"About time you called," said the familiar voice, seconds later. "And give me the number there right now."

Ray did so, then breathed into the receiver, "You missed me."

"About as much as I missed my last toothache."

Ray wiggled Kate's toes. "Trev said he misses us."

"Send him a kiss for me," she teased, smacking her lips hard.

Through the receiver came the words, "Cut out the horse play. Do you know what time it is over here?"

"I'm not the one who's been out all evening," said Ray.

"Yeah, well..."

Ray asked, "What's Sitarski been up to?"

"Working on his image. He acts so pompous, he must think he's the Pope. He's also trying to be granddaddy to the younger crowd that didn't know him back when. Even tutoring them at target practice. But then he always was a crack shot."

"Crack pot," corrected Ray.

"That too. So why did you call?"

"Did you get the autopsy on the little man?"

"Yeah. He drowned all right. Only the findings are inconclusive. Could have been an accident or murder. Blood alcohol of point one-eight supports the one and light bruises on the back of his neck and shoulders support the other."

"From what I'm finding out around here, I'd put my money on murder. Autopsy say anything else?"

"Yeah. His last meal was a doozy. Barbecued chicken, mounds of shrimp, raspberry meringue pie and enough red wine to float a tubful of Ivory soap."

"How much time between the meal and the time of death?"

"Two hours, give or take. Since the time of death was between ten and eleven in the evening of the day Theresa was shot, and since there isn't a restaurant around Livingston that serves such a feast, I'd say he partied at his place."

"Or someone else's." Ray sat on the bed. "How did the Livingston Police find the body?"

"Some guy called in. Said he was from out of town and had stopped on the side of the road to take a leak. Wouldn't give a name. Now, what's going on in your part of the country?"

Ray told Trev about Theresa's young days, her husband, her child and dog and their quiet life at a small motel. He described the murders.

"No shit?" said Trev.

"Makes me even more determined to get to the bottom of this whole business," Ray added.

"Forensics came up with something else that might help."

"Like what?"

"The creep's clothes were full of dog hairs. And not just hairs from one dog. Forensics counted at least ten different breeds. And when I say the hairs were everywhere, I mean on his undershirt and shorts and socks. Christ, he must have slept in a kennel."

A long silent pause followed. "You still there?"

"I'm still here."

"What's with the heavy breathing? Kate just walk out of the shower?"

"No. Something even better. You just suggested a link between the murders here and the murder there."

"Like what?"

"A dog kennel. There was one right next to the motel where the murders took place. Trev, first thing tomorrow morning, check out all the kennels in the area. Show them the little man's picture."

"Interim Chief of Detectives," grumbled Trev over the long-distance line. "A lot that means when the boss doesn't know what a vacation is all about."

Ray said, "And if none of that gets us anywhere, check with the local kennel club. See if we can get a blurb in their newsletter or something. And a classified ad in the *Observer* might jog somebody's memory. I'll get to work at this end and find out who worked at the kennel here at the time of the murders. We need to give the swamp man a name."

Ray replaced the receiver and stretched and grinned.

Kate pulled her glasses down on her nose and said, "I bet you never look this ecstatic after you talk to me on the phone."

Ray took a giant step to the head of the bed and hugged his wife.

"Would you calm down and fill me in?"

"The killer's clothes were full of dog hairs," said Ray.

"So are yours when you finish playing with Thumper."

"Yes. But mine are all one kind."

Kate's face broadened in a smile almost as wide as Ray's. She removed her glasses and put them in their case. "I think I'm catching detective fever."

Ray could hear Kate's light snoring. He turned and watched her in the weak light of the rising moon. She turned on her side; he settled back, slipped a hand under his pillow and fingered the softness of it. He thought of Theresa and how one man's warped nature had turned a pillow into a symbol of pain. He thought of the young mother tied to the bed, mouth taped, unable even to scream as she saw her child kick and struggle. Then stop. Stop forever. A sack of feathers the means of a small child's murder, a daughter's death. A little girl lost.

Ray thought of Theresa's muted wail. He saw with her eyes the pillow closing over her face. Her fight for air. The darkness.

Ray dabbed at his eyes with the sheet; he relived the scene at the lake the day of her death. Theresa with her dandelion and her smile. Theresa soaked and bleeding. His frantic swim to the shore for help. The trip back in the speedboat, only to see her take her last breath.

He recalled Theresa's words to Mike: "It is a memory with the power to tear me apart." And he remembered Theresa in the parlor at the convent, and her long silence on hearing him say, "You heal well." Perhaps, in a way, Theresa too had been a little girl lost.

Ray settled back into his pillow. At least the two of them—Theresa and Phillipa—had found each other now.

Twenty-seven

Josh brought breakfast to their table on a tray. Chris trailed behind, his small hands clutching a bowl of sugar with a spoon sticking out the top.

"Susan says to holler if you want more," said Josh.

"Will do." Ray cut a wedge out of his stack of pancakes.

"This will do me," said Kate, taking the sugar bowl from Chris, and giving him a smile for his trouble.

Josh and his grandson departed.

Kate said, "I have a question."

"That gives you ten less than me."

Ignoring Ray's comment, Kate continued. "Molly and Karl Dunn. Wouldn't you think they would be getting Social Security checks? Why are they sleeping in a car, living in a library, and working at a fast food place?"

Ray stopped chewing long enough to say, "You have a point."

"I think I'll give Mike a call after breakfast."

"What for?"

"See how the Dunns are doing. Maybe drop a hint about the Social Security checks."

"He'll want to know what we've found out," said Ray.

"Are you going to keep this from him as well?"

"I haven't even told him about the C-section."

"Ray, just because they work for the church doesn't mean that nuns and priests need to be treated like children."

"Fine. You tell them that Theresa had a husband and a child and a past."

"We all have a past. And Theresa's was certainly not one

to bring shame to her memory. Anyway, if Mike asks, I'll just tell him we're still investigating."

Kate finished her French toast and sausage. Ray ordered a second helping of everything. He sipped his coffee as he waited. He said, "Hon, if you still want to make that call, why don't you go do it now. We've got a lot to do today and I want to get started as soon as we can."

"Obviously. Why else would you order a second breakfast." She stood. "All right. But I'll be back down for more coffee." She took her purse and key and left the lounge.

When she returned, Ray was just finishing. Josh came over with the coffee pot and filled their cups.

"Did you get hold of Mike?" asked Ray.

"Yes."

"How are the Dunns doing?"

"Mike said that Molly is all smiles and a real help with the meal prep. Karl's a different story. The few days he went to the cafeteria, he sat in a corner and grumbled."

"He could go help Peter."

"He did. Until Monsignor caught the two of them in the boiler room playing poker and sharing a bottle."

"Karl could always go back and work at McDonald's."

"He won't have to. It seems that Monsignor invited Simon Lodwick over for supper last night. Karl came into the conversation. Mr. Lodwick offered to hire him as a kind of house sitter while he's at work."

"Lodwick? I don't picture him as a man who would need a house sitter."

"He told Mike that he lives alone and is nervous about leaving the house unattended. Of course that could be his way of helping out without making a show of it."

"I hope he locks his liquor cabinet."

"Is that nice?"

Ray shrugged.

"And by the way, Mike said Mr. Lodwick has been trying to get in touch with you. He wants you to call him when we get back."

"What for?"

"He told Mike the dealership owed your uncle some money on the car deal. He wanted Mike to help sell you on the idea of applying the money to a new car for yourself. Said he would give you a deal you wouldn't get anywhere else."

"Maybe I will. Homer's old car and another ten thousand cash ought to get me the pick of the lot."

"I hope you're not going to get a Cadillac."

Ray laughed. "I should count my blessings. How many men catch a wife who hates fancy cars, furs, and jewelry. Of course, you do make up for it in the shoe and dress department."

"I do not. And I thought you were in a hurry."

"That was before I took on that mountain of pancakes. What a fellow won't do to put a smile on a cook's face."

"Bull."

"Kate!"

"More coffee?" Josh asked as he approached. As he poured, Ray asked, "Josh, you've been to the kennel on Bolder Road, haven't you?"

"Sure. Years back."

"Back as far as the fifties?"

Josh laughed. "I'm not one for dates. Never was."

"Can I show you a photo?"

"Sure. Faces I remember."

"Got time to join us?"

"Why not?" Josh dragged a chair over from another table and straddled it.

Ray said, "The man is a John Doe. It's a morgue photo. I hope you don't mind."

"I saw plenty of death in Korea." Josh took the picture. He

stroked his beard and studied the black-and-white image of a narrow face with bushy eyebrows and a beard that all but covered the cheeks. The eyes were closed and strings of moss hung in the hair.

"That's a recent picture," said Ray. "You'd have to imagine him minus forty years."

"I can't even imagine myself minus that much," said Josh. Shaking his head, he handed back the picture. "Sorry."

Josh chatted another few minutes and left.

"Strike one," said Kate.

"We'll try Wilkey," said Ray.

"Go ahead. I think I'll relax with the newspaper while you're doing that."

"I'd rather you came. I think I wore out my welcome."

Kate signed the meal tab. "Let's go."

Wilkey's frown changed to a weak smile when he saw Kate. His hand rose as if to doff a hat but scratched at his head instead.

"Can we talk?" asked Ray.

"More talk? You're empty-handed. Don't I rate another bribe?"

"I thought I'd bring my wife instead."

"Campbell called me. He's already told you more than I could or would have."

"I have a photo I'd like to show you," said Ray.

Wilkey glanced back to Kate and exhaled. "All right. Come on in."

"Only got one other chair," said Wilkey, shuffling bare-footed back to his sheet-covered armchair.

Ray positioned the single chair for Kate. He handed Wilkey the photo of the mystery man. "That's the man who killed Theresa. It's possible he was connected with the murders of her husband and child here in Northpointe."

Pulling at an ear, Wilkey studied the photo. He reached for his cane and pointed it at an old framed photograph on the wall. "That was me in my twenties. Me and my wife. Look at me now. Think you'd know that young guy there and this here old far—, er, fellow are the same, if you were asked?" He handed the picture back.

"He might have worked at the kennel by the Hubbard Motel," coaxed Ray.

"He could have worked on my farm and I still wouldn't necessarily know him now."

Ray replaced the dead man's photo in his pocket. "Can you think of anyone in town that might have had business with the kennel in the fifties?"

"I suppose if I say no, you're going to show that picture to everyone you meet."

"Wouldn't you, if you were me?"

"What if I give you the name of a man who's sure to have an answer?"

"That's all I'm looking for."

Wilkey smiled at Kate. In a sprightly voice, he asked, "Do you folks have a car?"

Kate nodded.

"Big enough for an extra passenger?"

"What did you have in mind?" Ray asked.

"These bones need to soak up some sun. Last time I went for a drive was four years ago, when I came here. The man you need to talk to lives out of town."

"This man, is he a sure thing?"

"As sure as a sunset. He was the sheriff who investigated the Hubbard murders."

"Deal," announced Ray. "And we'll throw in lunch on the way."

Wilkey's mouth twitched as if he were already tasting the meal. He wiped an arm across his nose. He looked down at himself and scowled. "Can you give me time to shower and change? If I'm going to make a public appearance, I ought to fix up some."

"Sure. Say an hour? Will that give you enough time?"

Wilkey was already struggling out of his chair. "One hour. You bet."

Ray checked his watch. "Expect a knock on your door at ten."

The Fredricks showed themselves out. As Ray closed the door, the distinctive honk of an elderly man blowing his nose came from the other side.

Kate hugged Ray's arm. "I'm glad you said yes."

"I was bribed."

"Tit for tat." Kate laughed.

"Well, let's get going. I don't think he'll forgive us if we're late."

"Where are we off to?" asked Kate, starting down the stairs.

"I have some more work for our real estate agent."

Keith Jensen was standing at the front window when the Fredricks' car pulled in. He hurried back to his desk, tightened his tie and busied himself with papers.

Ray pushed open the screen door for Kate to enter. He followed her in.

Keith placed his pencil neatly in the fold of a notebook and stood. "Mr. and Mrs. Fredrick. I'm glad you came by. I think you're going to be happy with what I found out about the sale of this property." He gave the Fredricks time to be seated and handed Ray a typed page. "Hope that helps you locate your friends."

Ray made a show of excitement and read the paper. "This is great. Thank you very much."

Ray gave the paper to Kate. "I have another favor to ask.

But only if you agree to set a fee."

"All right. It will make my boss feel better about paying me to sit here all day. Some days I'm the only one who comes through that door." Jensen drew a notepad toward him. "What can I do for you?"

"What's the fee for a property search?"

"What kind of property? And where is it?"

"A business on the outskirts of town. It's nothing but ruins now, but it used to be the Sportsmen Kennel."

"Fifty dollars sound fair?"

"Fifty dollars is fine."

"Do you have an address?"

"It's on Bolder Road, just west of Route Nine. East of it was a motel with the street number two-nine-four-six. The kennel was probably two-nine-four-four or two-nine-four-two. What I need to know is the history of the property from the nineteen-twenties on."

Jensen finished scribbling. "How soon do you need this?"

"How soon can you get it?"

"Couple of hours, if I can get hold of a friend at the courthouse. If not, I'll have it by tomorrow."

"Tell you what," said Ray. "Give me a call at the Buggy Works when you have it. We'll get the message."

Twenty-eight

The Fredricks were back at the Buggy Works fifteen minutes early. Not wanting to rush Wilkey, they settled side by side on the porch in one of the carriage seats.

"Imagine us rattling down the muddy roads of a frontier town in our fancy buggy," said Kate.

"Right." Ray yawned.

"The horses stop. You dutifully climb down, hurry to my side and assist me to descend."

"Wrong. I order you to stay in your seat and I go into the saloon for a cold beer."

"Pilgrims on horseback and families in covered wagons pass us on their way to and fro."

"Prostitutes and preachers and charlatans sell us their cure-alls," added Ray.

"I hope you wouldn't need all of their services," said Kate.

"Never did care for preaching."

Kate punched his arm. She rattled on, "The good old times of well water, wood stoves and steam engines."

"Those bad old times of dirt roads and no refrigerators or TV," chanted Ray.

"I wonder what people will think of our world, a hundred years from now?" Kate said.

Ray shifted to a better position on the springless seat. "Do you know any place in Tanglewood that sells raspberry meringue pie?"

"If you mean Sister Gabbie's specialty, it's rhubarb meringue."

"I don't. This was part of the swamp man's final meal. Do they sell raspberry meringue in the grocery stores?"

"I've never seen it there."

"Maybe a girlfriend made it for him," said Ray.

"Or maybe he got it at a bakery," Kate offered.

"Good point. I think I'll have Trev check the bakeries in town."

"We'd better go up," said Kate. "It's almost ten. Did you ask Josh if he'd help?"

"No, but I will." Ray hopped down and ceremoniously offered his hand. Kate took it with equal pomp.

His door was open. Just inside and facing the corridor sat the clean-shaven, smiling Wilkey. He wore a wrinkled white shirt and a pair of green twill pants with deep, dusty creases across the legs. His cracked black belt had a buckle the size of a man's fist with the engraved letters *WH*.

"Ready when you are," said Ray.

Wilkey smoothed back his wet hair and slapped on a baseball cap with the Seattle Mariners logo.

Josh was waiting at the landing. With a stoic look on his face, Wilkey allowed the bartender and the stranger to half carry him down the stairs. Kate followed with the cane.

As soon as Wilkey was back on his own feet, he shuffled toward the exit. He took the porch steps on his own, lowering each foot carefully.

The rented Dodge was parked in front of the motel. Ray opened the door. Wilkey turned and lowered his backside onto the passenger seat. One by one, he lifted his legs in. Ray handed the old man his cane and closed the door. Kate climbed into the back seat through the door on the driver's side.

Ray started the engine. "Well, the day is yours. Which way do we go?"

"Back to Main Street. Make a right and then just keep going." Wilkey folded his hands on his lap. His gaze held the view as tightly as a young man would cling to the sight of a lover. He rubbed his cheek and smiled. Memories brightened his eyes as they passed familiar haunts. He pointed to a drug store and said, "Had my first taste of a soda right there."

They approached an elderly couple waiting to cross the street. Wilkey raised his hand and waved.

They passed the gas station where the Fredricks had received directions to the Buggy Works, then passed a lumber yard. About a mile further on, Wilkey told Ray to make a right. The road was narrow and unpaved. An old farm came into view. It had a beautiful facing of field stones and a large side chimney with matching masonry. "Mind stopping here a minute?" asked Wilkey. Ray pulled to the shoulder. Wilkey pointed, "I lived there for sixty-two years. Brought my kids up, helped feed my country, and buried my wife."

"Who lives there now?" asked Kate.

"Strangers. Nice enough people. Except when they walk the halls and rooms, it won't be in the company of all the memories the place has made." Wilkey tore his gaze from the house and the fields and the past. He gripped his cane tightly and said, "Let's go."

"Straight ahead?" asked Ray.

"Back the way we came," Wilkey answered.

He directed them down winding country roads and through towns even smaller than Northpointe. He pointed to landmarks in the life of the state and landmarks in his own life and in the lives of family and friends. He chatted endlessly of old trips, and close calls on the farm. He talked of his children, two boys making their fortunes in Alaska. Sons too busy to be in touch more than once or twice a year, or for any longer than it takes to say hello and good-bye.

Ray kept the speed to the minimum. They had been on the road for more than half an hour when he asked, "What's the sheriff's name?"

"Bailey. Les Bailey."

"How long has he been retired?"

"Ten years, maybe."

"How long was he sheriff?"

"Too long, some folks say. But he did his job. Wasn't on the job all that long when the Hubbards were murdered. Worse thing that ever happened in our town. Hubbards were good people. Loomises too. The town was really on edge after it happened."

"Was anyone ever arrested?" asked Ray.

"Don't think so."

They passed through several more towns, all larger than the last. "How far are we going?"

"Another ten miles or so."

"How is it you know where he lives?"

"He's my wife's baby brother."

Ray caught Kate's in the rearview mirror. "How come you didn't mention that earlier?"

"I was afraid you might think this was just a ruse to get me out and around for the day. But it isn't. He really was the sheriff back then."

"Heck, his being your brother-in-law will probably be to our advantage," said Ray. "Now, what about lunch? We'd better work it in before we go calling."

"Can I suggest a place?" asked Wilkey.

"I wish you would."

"It's a little further than we have to go."

"Does it have pretty waitresses?"

Kate rolled her eyes. Wilkey said, "Pretty as a picture."

Kate asked, "Clothed or unclothed?"

Wilkey laughed. "Clothed down to their ankles. It's an old lighthouse. It stands at the tip of a finger of solid rock. It's been remodeled to double its size, and has five floors of round rooms and two elevators. I was part of the work crew, way back before I met my wife. My dad was a mason. I apprenticed with him until I turned farmer."

"I'm hooked already," said Kate.

"And it's going to be on me," said Wilkey.

"Oh, no," replied Ray.

"Either it's on me, or you find the place on your own."

Ray laughed. "I guess that decides that. Your treat. I pay for the drinks and dessert and tip."

"Deal." Wilkey rubbed his hands together and sat straighter in his seat.

The restaurant was called the Wayfarer. It stood at the end of a narrow, crooked peninsula that extended into the Strait of Georgia like a single finger pointing from a fist of stone.

They parked in a lot at the base of the finger. Before they were even out of the car, a young man in an oversized golf cart arrived to pick them up. Ray and Kate took the narrow seat in the rear. Wilkey sat with the driver, pride reshaping his face as they bumped along the concrete walkway to the lighthouse proper. Up close, the tower of windows and stone seemed mammoth . The sea was calm and the outcropping of rocks at the base of the wall glistened in the late morning sun.

"I helped build this place," said Wilkey to the driver.

"That right, sir?"

"Yeah. My dad was the master mason. Wilkey Hamilton, Senior. There used to be an old photo of him and his crew hanging in the lounge."

"It's still there," said the driver.

"No shit? They still rent out the top floor for overnight stays?"

"They sure do. Only they stopped taking reservations. That floor's booked until nineteen ninety-six."

The driver dropped them off at the door and scooted off in his cart for other clients.

Wilkey moved to the side of the door and motioned to the Fredricks. He pointed to a *W* etched in a seam of cement between two stones in the rounded wall. "My signature," he said.

Ray held the door for Kate and the old man. They were met by a hostess costumed for the eighteen hundreds: blouse with balloon sleeves, embroidered vest, and skirt with more pleats than Kate could count in a minute. She escorted them into the elevator and to a room midway up the tower. The room was ringed with booths that sat four. In the center a tiled table with marble shelves held carafes of coffee, berry pies and custard-filled cakes.

It was after two when the electric cart returned Wilkey and the Fredricks to their car. Ray backed out of the parking space.

Kate put a hand to the old man's shoulder. "Thank you for bringing us here."

"You're welcome," said Wilkey, holding his head high.

Ray drove a cobbled street back to the main road. Kate kept her eyes on the lighthouse for as long as it remained in view.

They had been driving for another ten minutes when Wilkey directed them down an unmarked road on their right. "Better go slow," he said. They neared a fork in the road. Wilkey pointed left.

"Where does this lead?" asked Ray.

"To a few farms. Les has a place out in the sticks. He's not much for company."

"Should we have called?" asked Kate.

"He doesn't have a phone."

"Is he on his own?"

"Yeah. Always has been."

They passed a dairy farm. The road wound its way higher into the green hills. "Up there to your right," said Wilkey, indicating a small stone house with a shake roof. It was hedged in on three sides by trees. Large chimneys climbed both ends of the structure. The windows were small and covered from the inside.

The Fredricks and Wilkey approached the house. The door was a weather-worn plank with a brass handle and forged arrow-shaped braces. Ray knocked. They waited. He knocked again.

"Out back!" The shout was rough.

They moved slowly, letting Wilkey take the lead. They crossed a soft bed of pine needles, rounded the far corner. A dog growled from his place next to a woodpile. The same rumbling voice silenced it with a word. Then the owner of the voice appeared, eyed Wilkey, and said, "Well, look at you. You always said you'd never let a cane cross your palm."

"I'll leave it to you in my will, Les."

"Who'd you bring with you?" Les stepped away from the tree and a partially skinned rabbit pinned to the trunk by a nail, cleaning and sheathing a hunting knife as he spoke. He was a man of medium height and small build. He had hard craggy features and eyes that could silence a magpie with a single look.

"These here are the Fredricks. They're from Michigan."

Les gave the visitors the benefit of a nod. "You bring them here to introduce them to your favorite brother-in-law?"

"I brought them here 'cause they want to talk to you. Mr. Fredrick's a detective."

Les grew more attentive. He wiped his hands on his faded jeans. "Got I.D.?" he asked.

Ray held out his identification card and badge. Bailey squinted at them and asked, "Why so far from home?"

"I'm on a case that could be connected with one you worked, back in the fifties."

"Oh, yeah? How connected?"

"Two crimes. Possibly the same murderer. In your case, it was the Hubbard family."

Les stiffened. He looked at Wilkey, back at Ray. "Casey Hubbard?" he asked.

Ray nodded.

"And who's the victim you represent?" Bailey asked.

"Theresa Loomis Hubbard."

The hard eyes disappeared briefly behind closed lids.

When they appeared again, they seemed softer.

"Wilkey, you and the lady go sit in the shade. We'll be back in a few minutes." Bailey led Ray into the one-room house. He pointed to a cluttered table and a single chair, and seated himself on a wooden stool. His mouth worked as though he were chewing gum. "How did she get it?" he asked.

"A single shot. Out in the middle of a lake. She was with my wife and a few others on a pontoon boat. The shooter got the engine with a second shot. Otherwise she might have made it."

"Theresa Hubbard. She must have been about sixty, by now."

"Sixty-two," said Ray.

"She was in her twenties back when I knew her. Nice lady. I used to hunt with Casey. Damn." Bailey pulled his stool closer. "What made you connect the two cases? The shooter could have been aiming at you and missed."

"First, there had already been one attempt on her life. So there's no doubt that she was the target. Second, I can't find any reason why anyone would want her dead, except to get rid of the only witness to what happened here in fifty-one."

Bailey was silent for a moment. "At least she put in forty years of living before he did it. Did she have a family?"

"Of a kind." Ray passed Les the side-by-side portraits of Theresa the nun.

"No shit," said Les. "Who'd have figured it. I had half hoped that she'd stay around here and let me take care of her."

"I need help," said Ray.

"Anything I can do, you've got it."

"I have a snapshot of the man we believe killed her. His body was found in a swamp."

Bailey frowned. "If that's so, why are you here?"

"Until yesterday, I knew nothing about the Hubbard murders and had no motive for the shooting. Before Theresa died, she wrote two things on a piece of paper. A date—

August ninth, nineteen fifty-one—and the name of the town of Northpointe, Washington."

"But if you have the murderer—"

"We think there may be someone else involved. And I think that person is the man responsible for the Hubbard murders."

"You got the photo with you?"

"In my pocket."

"Good." Bailey slid off his stool. He crossed to a cot with a sleeping bag and a pillow. He reached under the cot and came back with a handful of smudged, coffee-stained papers. He pulled a sheet from the stack and set it on the table next to the snapshot. It was the composite sketch of the Hubbard murderer. They studied the two faces.

"No way these are the same man," said Ray.

"Hell, the noses alone make that clear," said Bailey.

Ray said, "So the man we have is not the man you were after."

"Damned shame. It's galled me all these years that he got away. That's how come I kept the file. Well, kept a copy of it, anyway."

"Did you find out anything at all about him?" asked Ray.

"Not a damn thing. All I had was this composite. And I didn't have it till months after the fact. Showed it all around town. Whoever he was, he wasn't from around here. I even had the composite carried in papers all over the state. Didn't get me one call."

"How was he dressed the day of the murders?" asked Ray.

"T-shirt. Jeans. Theresa said he stunk of whiskey. Said he was real muscular. And tall."

Ray tapped the photo he'd brought to the table. "This guy's barely five foot."

"Mutt and Jeff of a sort," said Les.

Ray tapped the photo again. "This guy had dog hairs even on his underwear."

Bailey shrugged. "I probably do too."

"Yeah, but his were from maybe ten different breeds." Ray saw the light go on in Bailey's eyes. He said, "The Sportsmen Kennel."

"Right next to the motel," added Bailey.

Ray asked, "Any chance you interviewed the folks there?"

"First place I went. Figured if anyone saw the murderer, it would have been them."

"Who did you talk to?"

"The owner. Some woman." Les found his notes of the interview. "Fay Forester. Spinster veterinarian. Ran the place with a couple of boys from the high school. Part time work. I talked to both of them. Only one was around the day of the murders. He didn't see a thing. Said the witch of a boss would have tongue-lashed him for putting out less than four hours of nonstop slave labor. He was all day in the kennels, cleaning them. The other one was home. His folks backed him up.

"Something else about that kennel. This Fay Forester was mauled to death later that year. From the evidence we collected, it was just a matter of her being with the wrong dog at the wrong time. She was a real mean lady. Never did find the dog. The cage door was wide open. With as much open country as we have around here, I never really expected to."

"I talked to Douglas Campbell," said Ray.

"Surprised he let you."

"His wife was out of the house."

"How's she doing?"

"Struggling."

Bailey picked up the *Saint Luke's Herald*. "A nun, eh. What a waste."

"I think you're wrong there."

"You knew her?"

"For a very short time. But it was long enough to be impressed." Ray glanced around the room. "Don't you get lonely out here?"

"Seldom. When I do, I make a trip to town and hang out till I'm cured. Which usually takes half a day and a fifth of Scotch. I like it here, away from everything. Had my fill for far too long as sheriff."

"I'm close to retiring myself," said Ray.

"Hard business, law enforcement."

"Anything else you can tell me about the Hubbard murders?"

"Fire some questions and we'll see."

"What time of day did all this happen?"

"Early evening."

"What did Theresa say about the killer's behavior? I mean, was he in a rage? Out of control?"

"Rage? No. Acted more like he was mad at Casey for making him do what he did. No, he was in no rage. He was a man covering his tracks. Killed the little girl with no more emotion than me skinning my rabbit. He even sweet-talked Theresa, told her he was sparing her pain by using the pillow. Like he was doing her a favor. And that she ought to understand that her husband forced him to kill them.

"If I had to describe the freak, I'd say he's calculating and cool and a user of others."

Suddenly Bailey slapped the table. "Son of a bitch. I almost forgot." Again, he shuffled through the papers. He pulled out a sheet of fingerprints and handed the page with its swirling smudges to Ray. "These were taken from the bedroom. None of them belonged to the Hubbards."

"I had no idea you had prints," said Ray.

"Yeah. That's what's kept me looking. The hands that made these are out there somewhere waiting to be slapped into cuffs. These prints will do it if we can find him." Bailey gathered the papers and slipped them into a folder. "Here. Take it. Make a copy and send it back when you get a chance. Better still, send it back stamped Case Closed."

Twenty-nine

Susan was in the lobby with Chris when the screen door opened and Wilkey and the Fredricks entered. She hoisted the boy on her hip and stepped forward to meet the threesome. Addressing Ray, she said, "You had a call about an hour ago."

"From Mr. Jensen?" Ray asked.

"He only left a first name. Trev. He said to have you give him a call as soon as possible."

Ray thanked her and headed for the stairs.

Kate accompanied Wilkey into the lounge and over to a booth. Josh brought them two tall glasses of beer and a bowl of pretzels. "Did you have a good day?" he asked, directing his question to the old man.

Wilkey pinched his lower lip. His eyes shone as he answered with a simple and emphatic *yeah*.

"Let me know when you want to go upstairs. I'll give you a hand."

"Thought I'd stick around down here and have supper first," said Wilkey. "See the boys."

Ray appeared in the doorway and beckoned to Kate. She excused herself and joined him.

"What did Trev want?" she asked.

A grin spread across Ray's face. "Remember how I suggested he canvas the kennels in the area?"

"I remember how you ordered him to do so. Yes."

"It paid off. He located the swamp man's den. The owner of one of the kennels he called had heard about a man missing in Ohio. A kennel-supplies salesman who works the Midwest had told him about it."

"But you said the green Pontiac had Michigan plates."

"It did. Maybe it wasn't his car. Or maybe he used to live in Michigan and recently moved to Ohio. We'll know when we get there."

"We're going there?"

"Yup. I talked Trev into letting us check it out. The kennel is in a small town between the Michigan border and Toledo. Tomorrow, we'll fly to Toledo, rent a car and stop at the kennel on our way home."

"What about the real estate agent?"

"We'll pick up his report on the way out of town. And stop at the sheriff's office to say good-bye. Our flight doesn't leave until three o'clock, so we should have plenty of time."

"You already booked a flight?"

"As soon as I was off the phone with Trev."

"Thanks for including me in the decision."

"I thought you'd be excited."

"I am. I just like to be included." Kate glanced toward the lounge.

Ray said, "Don't start worrying about Wilkey. He's doing all right by the folks here."

"I know."

Ray carried the luggage to the car. Kate stopped at Wilkey's room. She gave him her book and a hug, and promised to write.

Ray was already in the car. Climbing in, Kate asked, "Did you say good-bye to Josh?"

"Yes. Would you close the door so we can go?"

They passed by the sheriff's office, found only the deputy on duty and left word that they would be in touch.

At the real estate office, Jensen was just opening up. Ray joined him on the porch and explained that they had a plane to catch. He paid the agent and headed back to the car with an envelope in his hand.

"That's that. We're off," said Ray, merging with the local traffic.

"I was beginning to get attached to this town," said Kate.

"It's where Theresa was born and raised." Ray took Center Street to Bolder Road for a last glance at what remained of a kennel and a motel and the dreams of a young family.

They were nearing the Canadian border when Ray said, "Read what Jensen found out."

Kate pulled a crisp sheet of bond paper from the envelope. She read it aloud:

> The Sportsmen Kennel
> -Built in 1909 by Wilmar Bloomfield. Owned by him until 1949.
> -Purchased by a woman with a veterinary license; name: Fay Forester. Upon her death in October of 1951, the property was repossessed by the First National Bank of Northpointe, which owned the mortgage. It was sold in 1959 to a company by the name of Cogitations Inc. It is still in their possession.

The Fredricks checked in for their flight, passed quickly through U.S. Customs, and boarded their plane ten minutes later. They changed planes once and landed in Toledo early on the morning of August seventh. They took a taxi to a motel recommended by the driver, checked in and slept till noon.

Ray showered while Kate did the little packing that needed to be done. In turn, Kate showered while Ray called a rental agency and arranged for a car to be delivered to the motel by two, along with a detailed map of Toledo and the surrounding area. Next, he called the operator and obtained the address and phone number of the Doghouse Kennel.

"I'm starving," called Kate from inside the bathroom.

"So hurry up." Ray set the luggage by the door. He looked

at his watch.

"Why? Are we expected?" Kate came out of the bathroom, drying her hair with a towel.

"How much longer are you going to be?" asked Ray.

"Fifteen minutes. You're the one who was in the shower for a full half-hour."

Ray unzipped his carry-on bag and removed the file on the Hubbard murders. He sat on the unmade bed and began reading.

Kate turned on the hair dryer and seated herself in front of a floor-length mirror.

"Listen to this," shouted Ray above the din.

Kate switched off the dryer.

Ray said, "There's a list of things found in the bedroom where Casey and Phillipa were murdered. Guess what it includes. A receipt from the Sportsmen Kennel for a rabies shot given on August ninth."

"Meaning what?"

"Meaning the same day of the murders, Theresa had been over at the Sportsmen Kennel."

"It could have been the husband who took the dog," said Kate. She switched the dryer back on.

They ate at the motel. By ten to two, they had checked out and were waiting in the lounge. The car rental agent arrived a few minutes early. Ray filled out the required forms and took the keys to a Chevy Caprice.

The Doghouse Kennel sat on the outskirts of a rundown, boarded-up part of town. A landscape of trees and untrimmed shrubs made it inconspicuous to passersby.

Ray parked next to a Ford Escort. He took the key from the ignition.

"How are you going to handle this?" Kate asked.

"Depends on who I talk to. If it's a tall man in his sixties,

I'll ask him for literature and we'll leave. I'm not taking any chances. When we get back to Tanglewood, I'll have his prints from the literature checked against those the sheriff gave me. If we have a match, we'll have to work with the Toledo police to wrap things up."

"And if it's not a tall man in his sixties?"

"I'll decide then. Just follow my lead."

Swatting at a swarm of flies, Ray climbed a short stoop. He pushed open the screen door and followed Kate in. A loud creak announced their arrival.

A woman with a broom in hand gave them a shy glance from the corner of the room. She was in her thirties. She tried to smile but only managed a nervous twitch at the corners of her mouth. Just as Ray was about to speak, she dropped the broom and disappeared behind a door.

They could hear her telling someone that they were in the office.

Ray looked around. The room was neat and clean and furnished with a metal desk and chair, a filing cabinet, and charts on dog anatomy and diseases.

The door opened and a short, obese woman appeared. She was carrying a tiny puppy, feeding it with a bottle. Her gray-streaked hair was pulled tightly back and tied with a yellow ribbon.

"Afternoon," said Ray.

"Afternoon," she answered. "What can I do for you?" She took a seat at the desk and continued feeding the pup.

"I'm looking for someone," said Ray, watching the woman carefully.

She seemed simply to be waiting. She lifted the little creature affectionately to her cheek, and the pup licked her nose.

Ray said, "He drives a green Pontiac."

She stiffened. Her eyes seemed to hunt for a place to rest.

"Does anyone here drive a green Pontiac?" Ray asked.

"Who are you?"

Ray showed her his identification and hoped she wouldn't bother to read the particulars.

She barely glanced at it. Meekly she asked, "What did he do?"

"Where is he?" asked Ray.

"He's not here. I don't know where he is. He's supposed to be here, but he's not."

"When is the last time you saw him?"

"About two weeks ago."

"Did he leave by car?" asked Ray.

She shook her head. Her fingers dug into the puppy's fur. She looked anxious and tired and sad.

"Did he leave by bus? Taxi?" pursued Ray.

"I don't know. He just told me he'd be gone for a couple of days and left."

"Where's the car?"

"Out back in the barn."

"Can I see it?"

"He hit somebody, didn't he? I knew it. That's why he left without it."

"Are you his wife?"

"We live together. Whatever that makes me."

"And your name?"

"Janice Linn."

"And your friend's name?"

She didn't answer. Ray said, "You might as well tell me. It will just take a phone call and the license plate number to find out."

"Richard Hixson."

"Describe him, please?"

"He's about my height. He has a beard." She stood slowly, holding back tears. "The barn's locked. I'll get the key."

"And the car keys, if you don't mind."

She nodded and left. Kate took hold of Ray's arm and whispered, "She thinks he left her."

"I know."

"How long are you going to keep her in the dark?"

"For as long as I need to. And I want you sticking with me when we go to the barn."

"Don't worry, I will."

Janice came back with the keys and without the puppy. She started for the front door, her head bent and her wide shoulders rounded with worry. They headed toward the back of the building. A young man was hosing out the first in a line of fenced dog runs attached to a long narrow building. Swinging doors let the dogs come and go at will. One dog barked and others followed. Some of the inmates poked furry heads through the small doors, and others came hurrying out for a better look. Golden retrievers, spaniels, setters, a bloodhound—all were happy-looking dogs with shiny, combed coats, bright eyes, and attentive ears.

"You have quite an assortment of breeds here," said Ray.

Janice stopped near the fence and stroked a black cocker spaniel through the mesh with her finger.

Ray looked at the unpainted barn at the back of the property. "May I have the keys?"

She handed them to him and continued stroking the dog. Ray and Kate moved on. The closer they got to the barn, the more dilapidated it looked. Ray slipped a key into the old padlock that held the eight-foot doors. The curved shackle slid easily from its metal base. Ray removed the lock. He pulled on one of the doors. It opened slowly and noisily.

Janice approached, hands in the pockets of her shapeless print dress. Ray released the ground latch on the second door and forced it open. Sunlight poured in.

It was there. The green Pontiac. Only it had Ohio plates.

Ray asked, "Have you ever seen Michigan plates on this car?"

"Michigan plates? No."

"Did you and Richard ever live in Michigan?"

"Never." Janice stared at the car. She asked, "Did he kill someone?"

Ray didn't answer. He circled to the front of the vehicle. The left fender and headlight were smashed. Kate was at his elbow. "This is it, isn't it?" she whispered.

"It seems so," he answered.

Ray walked back to where Janice stood waiting and watching and worrying. "Do you mind if I look inside the car and trunk?"

She shook her head.

He opened the driver's door. He leaned in and searched under the seats, looking for a Michigan plate. He opened the trunk. Inside were a toolbox, a spare tire, and a large cardboard container. Ray checked the toolbox first. Then he emptied the cardboard box, taking out a quart of oil, rags, a flashlight and flares, and a bright orange vest and cap. No plates. Ray slammed the trunk.

"I see your friend was a hunter. Where does he keep his gun?"

"Why do you want to know that?"

"If I didn't need to know, I wouldn't ask."

"The gun's not here. He took it with him when he left. He said he was going hunting with his buddy."

"He forgot his hunting outfit," said Ray.

Janice asked, "Is he in real trouble?"

"Can we go back to the house and talk?"

Ray closed the barn doors and locked them. He dropped the keys into his pocket. Janice said nothing. They walked back past the barking queue of dogs. Janice took them through a side door and into a kitchen. "Is here okay?" she asked.

"Here's fine."

Her heavy bosom rose and fell. The younger woman they had seen in the office appeared in the doorway. Janice shooed her away. "Your daughter?" asked Ray, suddenly aware of the resemblance.

"Richard's and mine," she answered.

"What's her name?" asked Kate.

"Sylvia."

"Did you ever make raspberry meringue pie for Richard?" asked Ray.

Looking confused, Janice said no.

"Ms. Linn, do you know anybody by the name of Fay Forester?"

"That's Richard's half sister. What does she have to do with any of this? She died years ago."

"I think it's time I tell you the whole truth," said Ray. "I'm going to show you a snapshot. It's a man who was found dead in a Michigan swamp. I think it's your friend, Richard."

Janice turned her fearful eyes toward Kate. Ray laid the photo on the table. The woman's gaze searched the rest of the kitchen for refuge before settling on the snapshot. Her tears came soundlessly. She struggled up, knocking the chair to the floor. Her breath came like a runner's in hard, tugging intakes of air and long, loud exhalations. She fumbled her way along the counter, past the refrigerator and the stove and out of the kitchen.

Thirty

The Fredricks waited in silence. A minute stretched to five. Suddenly Sylvia appeared. She inched her way into the kitchen and asked, "Is my dad dead?"

Ray nodded.

Sylvia sat down on the chair her mother had vacated. "Is he in heaven?"

Ray looked at Kate, his eyes pleading. She smiled at Sylvia and asked, "Was your dad a good man?"

Sylvia nodded several times.

"Well, we know for sure that that's where all good men go."

"My mom's crying real hard. Maybe she doesn't know that Daddy went to heaven."

"Maybe she doesn't," said Kate.

"I'll go tell her." Sylvia made a brave attempt to smile and abruptly left the room.

"Now what do we do?" asked Kate.

Ray shrugged. "A lot more questions need to be answered."

Shortly, Sylvia came back. She twisted a strand of dark hair around her finger. "Ma says to make you tea." Without another word, she marched importantly to the counter and filled the kettle.

The Fredricks shared tea, bread and cheese, and animal crackers with the daughter of the man who had murdered Theresa. They talked about dogs; Sylvia brought in a brown terrier with black ears and eyes and whiskers. She sat with it on her lap and explained it was her very own, a gift from her father.

Janice Linn returned to the kitchen just as Sylvia was

refilling their cups for the fourth time. Her eyes were red and puffy. She handed her daughter a five-dollar bill and asked her to go to the store and buy some cake for their guests.

Only after the door slammed behind her daughter did Janice speak to the Fredricks. "Was it a hunting accident?"

"No. It's possible that your friend was murdered."

"Was it because he hurt someone with the car?"

"Ms. Linn, we think your friend Richard shot someone. Killed her. After attempting to run her down with his car a few days earlier."

Janice turned in the direction her daughter had taken. "Am I in trouble?"

"Only if you refuse to cooperate," said Ray, in a quiet voice.

"What do you want me to do?"

"I'd like to keep the keys to the barn and Pontiac," said Ray. "Is that all right with you?"

"Yes."

"You don't need the Pontiac to do your shopping or anything?"

"I have a car. It's out front."

"I'd also like to look around the house," said Ray.

Janice pulled herself up and led the visitors out of the kitchen, down a narrow hall. Ray glanced into a small, neat living room. Janice identified the door to the office and the one to the kennels. She took the Fredricks through the bedrooms, allowed Ray to rummage through drawers and closets. Finally she pointed to a closed door. "That's Richard's office. It's locked."

"Do you have a key?"

She went into a bedroom down the hall, came back with a key and opened the door. The room was dark. Janice opened the drapes. The small room was furnished with a desk, chair, sofa and a wall of books dealing mostly with the care, training and breeding of dogs.

Ray started opening the desk drawers. In the first one he

found a stash of a dozen or more boxes of toothpicks. Ray asked, "Did Richard have problems with his teeth?"

"No. Just a habit of chewing toothpicks all day long. He did it as a kind of ritual."

"Ritual? For what?"

"To exorcise the memory of his mother and half sister. He started doing it to keep from thinking about them."

Ray suggested that Janice and Kate sit on the couch. He straddled the desk chair and said, "Tell me about his mother and half sister."

"I don't know much about them except that they were both very mean to Richard."

"In what way?"

"They treated Richard like a freak. They called him all kinds of names. And when they weren't doing that, they ignored him. Once, they even took a dog he'd found and befriended and drowned it in front of him, forcing him to watch. It was his half sister who thought that one up. She was worse than the mother."

"What about the father?"

"His mother was a whore. He never knew his father, other than by the wisecracks his mother would make about him."

"Did you ever meet his mother or half sister?"

"Never. I didn't want to."

"The sister, was she older or younger than Richard?"

"Older. By ten years, I think."

"Where was Richard born?"

"In Cincinnati."

"Did he ever live in the state of Washington?"

"I don't think so."

"How long have you known him?"

"Thirty-two years."

"You met where?"

"In a pet shop where I was working."

"Where was that?"

"Cincinnati."

"Did he ever talk to you about a place called Northpointe?"

Janice shook her head. Her gaze strayed to the window.

"Did you know that his half sister lived in Washington for a number of years?"

"No."

"Is it possible that Richard went there to visit her?"

"He hated his half sister. I don't know why he'd want to visit her."

"Did you know that she was mauled to death by a dog in a kennel she owned?"

Janice rubbed her thigh. She didn't answer.

"Did you know?" repeated Ray.

"I knew she ran a kennel. And I knew she was killed by a dog. Richard told me." Janice hesitated and added, "He also said something about her finally getting what she deserved."

"What else did he say?"

"Nothing. He wouldn't have said that if he hadn't been drunk. I'm not even sure he knew I heard him."

"The toothpicks—were they a regular habit?"

"He always had one in his mouth. He'd break it when something angered or frustrated or worried him."

Ray studied her for a moment. He stood and continued his search of the drawers. In the second drawer from the bottom on the right, he found a copy of the *Saint Luke's Herald,* the issue that carried the picture of Theresa Loomis. Ray lifted it carefully by a corner. He held it up to Janice and asked, "Did you ever see this before?"

"No. Richard never went to church. I can't imagine why he would have that."

"Do you have a large plastic bag you could give me?"

Janice struggled up from the couch. "A clean bag," Ray called after her. She came back with the bag and handed it to

Ray. He thanked her, had Kate hold it open and carefully slipped in the *Herald*.

Janice returned to her seat on the couch.

Ray finished his search of the drawers and again straddled the chair and faced the couch. "Tell me about the trip Richard took with the Pontiac. What brought it on?"

"A phone call."

"From whom?"

"I don't know. He didn't like me asking questions."

"Can you tell me the exact day he left?"

"I think it was around July thirteenth. It was a Sunday."

"And what day did he come back?"

"Two days later. A Tuesday."

"How did he act when he returned?"

"Excited."

"Even though he had damaged the car?"

"That didn't bother him. No, he was real happy. For a while anyway."

"Why only for a while?"

"He got another call. When he hung up, he was mad."

"Let me get this straight. Richard got a call on Sunday and left in his car. He came back two days later with a damaged fender. He got another call, and left again, this time without his car, but with his gun. Is that right?"

Janice nodded.

"He just walked out of here with his gun?"

"It was in a case. And he didn't leave immediately. He moped around the house and kept watching the time."

"How long did this go on?"

"About an hour."

"Do you know who made the second call?"

"I think it was his buddy. He's the only one who could pull Richard's strings like that. Come here, go there. Do this, do that."

"Tell me about this buddy," said Ray.

"There's not much I can tell. He never came here. I never saw him. Richard always got angry when I asked about him."

"How long have they known each other?"

"A long time. From things Richard has said over the years, I think they went to school together."

"And he never mentioned his name?"

"Just called him Buddy. Richard said that they had made a pact that they would never talk to anyone about each other." Janice's eyes narrowed. Her mouth made a small pout. "This buddy of his, he called Richard *Runt*. Told him he should look at his size the way blacks are supposed to look at their color, with pride. Richard even took to calling me *Fatso*. Imagine. I had to threaten to leave him to make him stop."

"You didn't like this Buddy, did you?"

"He used Richard. He had some hold on him. When he called, Richard would drop everything. And when they were going to get together, Richard acted like a kid going to see Santa. It was disgusting."

"Do you know what school Richard went to?"

"No."

"Is there anything else you can tell me about Buddy?"

"He's the one who got Richard in the habit of breaking toothpicks and pretending he was doing it to the one he was mad at. He'd even do it in front of me, anytime I said something he didn't like."

Janice looked Ray in the eyes. She asked, "Do you think his friend killed him?"

"There's a strong possibility. That's why it's so important that I track him down. Is there anything at all you can think of that might help? Did Richard ever phone his buddy from the house?"

"Never. He received calls, but he never phoned out. Not from here. I'd know; I pay the bills."

"Letters? Photos?" pursued Ray.

"There is a picture. Something out of a newspaper. The only picture Richard ever showed any interest in. Except maybe Sylvia's baby pictures."

"A picture of his buddy?"

"I don't know. I only saw it from a distance."

"Do you know where it is?"

Janice looked around the office. "I know he kept it here somewhere."

"Was it in a frame?"

"No."

"Did it look like it had been folded small? Like something he kept in a wallet?"

"I don't think so."

"Can you give me an approximate size?" Ray asked.

"Maybe a little smaller than a magazine page," she answered, measuring with her hands.

Ray stepped to the bookshelf and began methodically riffling through the larger books. He found the clipping in a hardbound volume entitled *You and Your Dog*.

It was yellow with age and showed a double row of boys posing in their basketball uniforms, faces blurred and smiling. Ray looked for something with the name of the school. Nothing. Just numbered shirts and wide grins.

Except for one of the boys, the only one not wearing a uniform or a smile. He was standing to the side of the others, a ladle in his hand, a bucket at his feet. And he was very short.

Ray showed the clipping to Janice. "Anybody there you recognize?" he asked.

She studied the faces. She pointed at the shortest boy. "That's Richard"

"If you don't mind, I'd like to keep this."

Janice shrugged. Ray studied the photo again and wondered if he were there, this Buddy, the man responsible for so much bloodshed.

Thirty-one

They followed I-75 north, crossing the Michigan border with the sun hovering on the horizon. "What do you want to do about supper?" Ray asked.

"Let's pick up a pizza and take it home."

"You sound depressed."

"I'm just thinking about Janice and her daughter."

"They'll be all right. She said the kennel was in her name."

"Do you think you'll find him, this friend?"

"I know I'll keep trying."

"How?"

"For one thing, we'll contact schools in Cincinnati, show them the clipping, identify the team and the players. Alumni lists will supply recent addresses."

"We don't even know for sure if the man we are looking for is in the picture," said Kate.

"Somehow I don't think Hixson kept the clipping because it was a picture of him as a water boy. And besides, even if he's not there, one of the players might know the name of the man who hung out with Hixson."

"Maybe Buddy gave Richard the license plate off his car?"

"I doubt that. He's made it a point to stay in the shadows during all of this. Giving his plates to Richard would be flirting with danger. He's much too careful for that. I'd sooner go with the idea that Hixson stole a Michigan plate on his way to Tanglewood. Ran Theresa down. Thought he'd killed her, and went back home, stopping on the way to remove the Michigan plate and toss it. Then he gets a call telling him that Theresa was only injured. His pal probably arranged to meet

him near the kennel, and bring him back to Tanglewood.
Made sure he brought his gun."

The Fredricks arrived in Tanglewood at dusk. They stopped
and purchased a pizza and a half gallon of ice cream.

The house was like an oven. "At least we don't have to
worry about the pizza getting cold," said Ray. He set the
carton on the kitchen table, slid the patio door open and
stepped out.

"The message light's blinking on the machine," called Kate.

Ray came back in and turned on the machine.

"Fredrick," snapped a harsh voice. "Sitarski here. I'm waiting for a call from you." Two similar messages followed. In his
fourth messrge, Sitarski ordered Ray to report to the station
without delay, and he ended with a threat: "I can't run a
department with a chief of detectives who takes time off to nurse
a damaged ego. Get the hell in here, if you want your job."

"That son of a bitch," spat Ray.

Kate took a couple of beers out of the refrigerator and
handed Ray one. Saying nothing, she gathered up the pizza
and carried it out to the patio, along with a handful of napkins.
She dusted off the chairs and sat down.

Ray followed her out. He folded back the lid of the box,
yanked loose a slice of pizza. "I'd like to stick his fat head in
a meat grinder."

"Come on, Ray. Let's not spoil our first evening home."

Kate took a slice for herself and set it on a napkin. "Are you
going to call Trev tonight?"

"Probably not."

"Should we leave Thumper with Pam until tomorrow?"

"It's all right with me."

"I think tomorrow I'll go see Karl and ask him if he wants
to trade my car for his truck."

"Don't forget, he's working for Lodwick now."

"Oh, that's right. Wait a minute, tomorrow's Saturday. So

he should be at home. Molly too. Meals aren't delivered on weekends. Want to come with me?"

"No, thanks. First thing I need to do is go see that creep of a chief and set him straight about a few things."

Questions came into Kate's eyes. She kept them to herself.

Hugging the Hubbard folder under one arm, Ray passed the empty squad room. He continued down the hall to his office, went in, and found Trev in his chair with his feet on the desk. He was reading a computer printout and eating his usual Mars bar.

Immediately, Trev vacated the seat. "Didn't know you were back," he said.

"We got back last night." Ray sat and swiveled a half circle. "Is the bastard here?"

"Saw him earlier in the john, so he could be." Trev settled in the visitor's chair. "Did you get over to that kennel in Ohio?"

"Yeah. And you were right on the money. Found the green Pontiac hidden in a barn on the property. And I found this in the house." Ray passed Trev the plastic bag with the *Saint Luke's Herald.* "I'm hoping the lab can lift prints to match the ones from the Hubbard bedroom back in fifty-one."

"How do we do that if we don't have those prints?"

"We do." Ray dropped the folder onto the desk. "That's the file on the Hubbard case. The prints are in there."

Ray opened the folder. He laid the old newspaper clipping on the table, and pointed to the boy by the bucket. "That's Richard Hixson. The missing owner of the Doghouse Kennel and Theresa's killer. It's possible that the other man we're after is also in this picture. Have the lab make some copies before the thing disintegrates. Also, individual blow-ups of the players. And see if they can turn up something that might identify the school. I know it's in Cincinnati, but that's all."

"Anything else?"

"Yeah. Call the bakeries around town and find out if any

of them sell raspberry meringue pies. From what I hear, it's not a common menu item."

"The killer's last meal. Good idea. That it?"

"What's the scoop on Keyhoe? Did you find out where he was back in August of fifty-one?"

"Keyhoe was born here, raised here and went to school here. In fifty-one he was still in high school. All confirmed by a birth certificate and school records."

"Well he wasn't in school in August."

"True."

"Anything more on his lawsuit?"

"Not a whisper."

"Well, let's get him out of our hair for good. Send someone to his place for fingerprints."

"You want to stir him up again?"

"Send a policewoman dressed like a coed. Have her sell magazine subscriptions or something. Whatever it takes to get his prints for the lab."

"Anything else you want me to squeeze into my Saturday off?"

"Come back and ask in an hour." Ray smiled.

Trev stood up and leaned forward. "Are you back to stay?"

"For now."

"The guys will be glad." Trev wiped chocolate from the side of his mouth. He gathered the papers and clipping and left, grinning back at Ray before he slammed the door.

Ray crossed to the window. He watched a stiff breeze sweep across the parking lot, watched pedestrians in the distance holding tight to children and packages and hats. He found his reflection in the glass and stared it down like a man out to make his point. He took a deep breath and headed for the door.

Moving quickly and deliberately, Ray passed Records and Administration and approached the office of the chief of police. He knocked.

"Yeah, come in," called Sitarski.

Ray entered, making no effort to close the door quietly.

"It's fucking about time."

"I see you've brought both class and weight to this office, Don. That is another chin I see, isn't it?"

"Is this the way it's going to be, Fredrick? Or are you going to make my day and ask to retire?"

"I'm here to tell you that I'll retire when I'm goddamn good and ready, and not before. And I wouldn't be in too much of a hurry to rush the process, if I were you. Who knows what I might do with all that free time? I might just spend it looking up a certain girl from our past. Let's see. She was sixteen then. She should be in her forties by now. Good age for a person to feel the urge to even scores. Perhaps I could give her a few suggestions on how that might be done. Get her to reconsider what she has to say about that night you and I remember so well. So don't be too eager for me to retire, Don. Not if you really prefer to keep the past out of the present."

Sitarski's face turned as red as the polka dots on his tie. His eyes bulged behind his black-framed glasses.

Ray stepped to the door. He faced Sitarski and said, "Anyone who didn't see what I saw, might think that if something *did* happen, it was an isolated incident. An accident. A mistake. You know, idealists do that to help them cope. Perhaps I'll just ride on their wagon for a while, pretend they could be right. It would be a shame if something made me change my mind, don't you think? So be a good boy, Chief; your guardian angel is watching." Ray stepped quickly out and slammed the door. He opened it again. "Another thing, *Chief*." His voice was low but deadly serious. "No more nasty messages on my answering machine. My wife plays them back, and there's no reason she should *ever* have to deal with your shit." Ray slammed the door again. He listened for an eruption from inside the office. Waited for shouts and the door opening and Sitarski's huge frame spilling into the hall, spitting expletives. Nothing happened. No shouts or movement. Just silence.

He walked slowly back to his own office, wondering what his victory might cost him in the future.

"I don't smell supper," said Ray, ambling into the kitchen and dropping a fat manila folder on the table.

"We're eating late. And what's with you? For as long as we've been married, your first day back on the job has never brought you home happy before."

"I had a run-in with Sitarski."

"That's something to celebrate?"

"I'm celebrating the fact that I had the last word. Why are we eating late?"

"I promised Karl I'd take my old car over tonight so he can have a look. If he decides to buy it, I'll need someone to drive me back."

"Drive the truck back."

"He's keeping the truck." Kate grabbed Ray's arm and propelled him toward the door. He grabbed the folder.

"Why are you bringing that?"

"To occupy me while Karl haggles for a lower price."

Ray began thumbing through the pages in the folder.

"Are those blow-ups of the newspaper clipping?" asked Kate, stopping to lock up.

"Player by player," answered Ray.

"Are you any closer to finding the school?"

"No. But we're closer to identifying Hixson's buddy. Forensics found an excellent set of prints on the church paper we found at the kennel—prints that did not belong to Hixson. And they're a perfect match for the ones from the Hubbard murder scene. Now all we have to do is find the hands they belong to."

"Well, good luck. It's no fun knowing he could be walking

around town."

Kate took the lead in her blue Chevy. She drove to Junction Street to the tenement building shared by Peter Kruger and the Dunns. The rusty pickup was out front at the curb, its windows spanking clean. Kate parked behind it. Ray pulled into a free space further up the street.

A curtain moved in the window of the first-floor apartment. Seconds later Lucy Hammer was on the front stoop, flossing her teeth. An open bottle of beer hung in the pocket of her smock.

The Dunns were next to appear at the door. Karl had the look of a man bent on business. He marched toward the curb. Molly stood near the stoop, the stiff breeze wrapping her dress around her skinny legs.

Ray waved from the curb. He leaned against the car door and started a serious study of the papers in the folder. He could hear Karl critiquing the condition of the Chevy's body and Molly countering him with exclamations on how lucky they were. Ray smiled. He brushed a lock of hair out of his eyes.

With a burst of wind, the folder and its contents went flying like so many paper kites. Ray swore and scurried to gather them up. Lucy bellowed a laugh and settled on the top step, beer in hand, to watch the show.

Kate and Molly and Karl helped Ray recapture the papers: reports from the lab, pictures of basketball players, sheets listing the schools in Cincinnati, grids of fingerprints.

Molly handed Ray the three sheets she'd retrieved. Kate passed him several others and patted his arm. "I keep telling you to leave your work at the office."

Ray glanced about the yard to make sure everything had been recovered. He walked over to Karl, who stood holding the papers he'd collected. "Thanks," Ray said, reaching for the sheets in the old man's hand.

Karl released them. He pointed. "Seen that picture before."

Thirty-two

The sun, a red half-round on the horizon, illuminated the west wall of Saint Luke's church as though it were a movie screen about to tell a story.

The Fredricks pulled in and parked at the back. Ray put the car in park and finished his meal of fries, hamburger and coffee. All the while his attention stayed on the rectory across the lot.

"I hope he's home," he murmured.

Kate squashed her cup and dropped it into the carry-out bag.

"He's going to have a long, sleepless night ahead of him. And then Sunday Mass to say and parishioners all around."

Ray put the lid on his cup. "Are you ready?"

"Is there a chance that you're wrong?"

"The more I think about it, the more certain I am. Let's go." Ray drove the car across the lot and stopped in front of the rectory. The Fredricks mounted the steps and rang the bell. Ray switched the folder from one hand to the other.

Monsignor Becker answered. He was dressed in black slacks and a short-sleeved yellow shirt, unbuttoned at the neck. He surprised Ray by smiling.

"Evening, Monsignor," said Ray, verbally capitalizing the *M*.

The priest nodded. "Can I help you folks?" His diction was a little garbled.

Getting a whiff of liquor, Ray considered asking if they could share his bottle. He said instead, "We'd like to see Father Mike, if he's in. It's rather important."

Monsignor took the visitors into Father Killian's office. Shortly, Mike entered wearing his Roman collar and cassock. "I didn't know you were back from Washington."

"We got back last night," said Ray.

The priest studied their faces. He closed the door and unbuttoned his robe. Hanging it in the closet, he said, "I just got in from a sick call. An older parishioner who likes to see priests in uniform."

Mike pulled out his desk chair and sat down. "Was your trip successful?"

"Very successful," answered Ray.

"You don't look like the news is any too pleasant."

"I'm afraid it isn't."

Mike waited. Ray reached across with the photo of the Hubbards. "That's Theresa and her family in nineteen-fifty."

For a moment, Mike thought he was seeing a picture of Theresa's parents with Theresa herself as a small child. Then the significance of the date set in. "Nineteen-fifty?" he asked.

Ray nodded. Mike studied the snapshot for another long moment. "It wouldn't be like Theresa to abandon a family to enter the convent."

"She didn't," said Ray.

Mike's gaze found Ray's. Again, he waited.

"Her husband and child were murdered right in front of her."

The priest lowered his head into his hands.

"Theresa was left for dead," said Ray.

Mike turned and faced the window, his eyes bright with tears. The remaining daylight made a haze on the horizon.

"That's what was too painful for her to talk about," said Ray.

Mike said, "God gave her back to us for forty more years." He faced the Fredricks, not hiding his pain. "So it's over."

Ray shook his head.

"But the papers said that the police had found her killer."

"Yes. But he was just a flunky. Someone else pulled the strings. The same man who murdered Theresa's family."

"Are you sure?"

"I'm sure, Mike. And I know who he is. I hate to say this, but you introduced me to him."

"I—? Who are you talking about?"

"Simon Lodwick."

Mike gripped a small tray of pencils. "Simon?"

"Simon."

"I can't believe that."

"Think it through with me. Who arranged for the sisters to have a loaner after the accident?"

"He's guilty of murder because he did them a kindness?"

"A calculated act. It gave him some control over their movements after the first attempt on Theresa failed. And remember how quickly they repaired the nuns' car and returned it to them? Who do you think arranged that? And I'd wager the repaired car had an extra piece of equipment. A tracking device."

"You're guessing," said Mike.

"Am I? After the sisters left for the Mother House, I saw their car parked near the convent. The next time I passed, it was gone. What happened to it?"

Mike's brow furrowed; he stared down at the desk and said, "The dealership called to say that a reconditioned part had been used in the repairs. They said the new part had finally arrived and asked if they could pick up the car and install it ."

"Convenient way to remove the bug," said Ray.

"It's still hard for me to believe," countered Mike. "Monsignor and I had him here for dinner. He's had us over to his place. He's at church every Sunday. Contributes substantially to the collection. And," he paused, "he's been invited for lunch tomorrow, after the twelve o'clock Mass."

"So you were in Lodwick's house. Did he happen to take you into his study?"

"Yes. Why?"

"I'm told he has a picture hanging on the den wall. One that shows Lodwick as a high-school boy in a basketball uniform."

"I remember the picture, but I don't understand what you are trying to say."

"Karl Dunn has been in that study as well. Not that he was supposed to be there. He took to wandering around in the house to help pass the time. He saw that same picture."

Ray recounted their trip to the Doghouse Kennel. He talked about the newspaper clipping and how he had ordered individual blowups of the players made. Ray removed a blowup from the folder and set it in front of Mike. "Is this what you saw in Lodwick's den?"

Mike didn't answer.

Ray said, "Doctor it up, have it enlarged, colored..."

"It could be," said Mike. "Yes, it probably is."

"Exactly what Karl said." Ray showed Mike the group picture. He pointed to the boy by the bucket. "That's Theresa's killer."

"Couldn't this all be coincidence?" asked Mike.

"I don't think so. But there is an easy way to find out. I have the prints of the man who murdered Theresa's family. When we compare them to Lodwick's, we'll know. And I was hoping you might have something he has handled, something that might be fairly clean of other prints."

"I have the sketch he made of the ad he wanted placed in the—"

"What is it?" asked Ray.

Mike banged the desk with his fist. "My God."

"What is it, Mike?"

"Theresa's picture. I showed it to Simon. Right here in this office. He was here to discuss a deal between Saint Luke's and the dealership. We talked about advertisement in the *Herald*. I showed him that Sunday's edition. It was the one with the write-up on Theresa and Seraphina. I remember now. I remember him staring at the front page. And asking if he could keep it to study the layout of the other ads. And then he said he had to go. He'd only been here a few minutes. I thought maybe he wasn't feeling well. We finished the negotiations by phone, and he mailed me the sketch of his ad."

Ray said, "That explains a lot of things. Once Lodwick knew Theresa was in the area, he had to go into hiding. That's why he wasn't around when I went to the dealership about Kate's car. They said a tragedy had called him away. They were right about that. The man buys a dealership, sinks his future into the business and finds someone living nearby who could ruin everything."

"That must be where the Michigan plate came from," said Kate.

"You're probably right. I bet they have twenty to thirty cars in for repairs at any given time. There wouldn't be any problem borrowing a set of plates for a day. And even if they were traced back to the dealership, it wouldn't matter. Those cars sit out in the open. Anyone could steal a plate.

"Mike, do you have that sketch Lodwick made?" The priest rose slowly and moved to a file cabinet.

Ray knocked on the door of apartment twelve.

"It's unlocked," shouted Trev from inside.

Ray found his friend sprawled on the living-room sofa, eating chips and watching a rented video.

"Can you turn that thing off?"

Trev aimed the remote. The image on the screen froze.

Ray walked up to the set and switched off the TV and the

VCR. "Finish it tomorrow."

"Why the hell should I? This is Saturday night. I already wasted the day looking for raspberry meringue pies."

"Never mind that." Ray cleared the seat of a chair and sat down. He smiled and said, "I found our man."

"Good. Put him in jail and leave me alone."

"There are some details—"

"Fine. I'll get in early Monday." Trev aimed the remote.

Ray grabbed it. "Trev! This is important. I don't want this guy to get away. Between tonight and Monday, maybe he'll hear something, feel something. He could even be planning a trip to Ohio to make sure there's nothing at a certain kennel that could implicate him."

"Oh, shit. All right. So what's the plan?" Trev sat up and ran a hand over his balding head.

"First, I need to compare some prints against the ones from Northpointe."

"I'm supposed to do that? Hell, just give me a minute or two, and I'll buzz through a crash course in Forensics."

"I want you to call Foler and get him out for a beer. He's more apt to believe you than me. Then you can hijack him to the station."

Trev hauled the phone to his lap. He asked, "Who is he, and how did you find him?"

Ray told him about Karl Dunn and the picture in Lodwick's den. He explained his theory of how Lodwick had located Theresa at Hush Hideaway.

"If I were you, I'd be worried about this Dunn telling Lodwick about your picture."

"I don't think so. He was embarrassed to admit he had been poking around in his employer's house. And tomorrow is Sunday. He won't go back to work till Monday. Another reason why we have to get things moving tonight."

Trev lifted the receiver and punched in Foler's number.

Trev pulled up to the station. Foler bolted from the car and confronted Ray. "I should have known you'd be behind this. Just make sure you're carrying a fat bankroll. This is going to cost you more rounds of drinks than you can count."

Ray grinned and opened the side door. Fred barged ahead, taking the stairs down to the basement at a near run. He slapped on the lights and forged ahead, his small frame pitched forward. He unlocked the doors of the lab and stuck out his hand in Ray's direction. "Just give me the prints. And wait here. I don't like heavy breathing at my back."

Ray handed him Lodwick's ad sketch, and the prints from the Hubbard murder scene. Foler shut the lab door behind him.

Trev felt his pockets. He moseyed on down the hall, purchased coffee and a candy bar from vending machines in a large alcove, and settled at a nearby table. Ray changed a dollar in a machine and did the same.

Trev said, "I never met this Lodwick. What's he like?"

"Smooth. Charming. Likes being a big wheel." Ray took a sip of hot coffee. He said, "Remember that phone call you took on my direct line at the office? I bet it was him, checking up on me. Seeing me drive away from the dealership with the nun's car must have tipped him off."

"No kidding," said Trev. "What is he, a ventriloquist as well? That was a woman who phoned, not a man."

"So he had his secretary call. As far as having my number, I gave it to his salesman. You can be sure it was in the dealership's file. Probably found the directions to Hush Hideaway there too. They delivered Kate's car to the lake earlier in the week."

"So why would he need a homing transmitter, if he did use one?"

"Because it was the only way he could be absolutely sure

of locating the nuns. Everything else was conjecture."

A bark from down the hall brought them to their feet. Abandoning their snacks, the two detectives trotted off in the direction of the lab. Foler waited impatiently.

"Well?" snapped Ray.

"They match. No doubt whatsoever."

"Great. Let's get a warrant and go get him." Ray pulled away.

"Are you planning on extraditing him to Washington?" called Foler.

Ray stopped and turned back. "Hell, no. He's ours."

"He's theirs. His prints tie him to an out-of-state crime, not to the Loomis murder. Everything else you have is circumstantial."

"Shit, you're right." Ray leaned against the wall.

"Damn right. And that will cost you an extra round."

"Give me a rain check, will you, Foler? You just gave me more work to do. I don't want this creep going to Washington. Who knows what will happen there? I want him right here behind bars."

"Rain check? I already have enough bad rain checks to keep me in toilet paper for years."

"Save 'em. When you get enough to fill a bag the size of Trev's paunch, you can trade them in for one of Kate's dinners."

"Yeah, sure. I'm out of here." Foler locked the lab doors. He headed for the stairs with Trev following.

"Thanks," called Ray.

Foler waved behind him with a middle-finger salute.

Thirty-three

Sunday morning, August ninth. Ray was up early. After a quick shower, he phoned Mike at the rectory and explained in detail his plan.

Kate served breakfast on the patio. Thumper lay sprawled under the table with his nose at Kate's feet and his tail dusting Ray's shoes. Kate took the front section of the Sunday paper and started reading. Ray fiddled with his fork and stared into the distance. Around ten, they went inside. Kate rinsed the dishes and put them in the dishwasher.

"Don't forget to take Thumper back to Pam's," said Ray.

"I won't. And I don't see why I can't come with you."

"Kate, believe me, it's better if you don't go. If there's one thing you don't have, it's a poker face. You'd give it all away."

"I could at least go to Mass with you."

"I'd feel better if you didn't."

"The first time you've been to church in years and I can't even be there for the occasion."

"Fine. I'll go next Sunday. And you can take a picture."

"So, what am I supposed to do about church?"

"Go to Saint George's. Or Saint Helen's."

"Saint George's is Episcopalian and Saint Helen's is in Livingston."

"Go to an earlier Mass at Saint Luke's."

"Right. The last one before the twelve o'clock started five minutes ago."

"Please? You should want this to work as much as I do."

Suddenly Kate smiled. "All right, Ray. But next Sunday we go to Mass at the sister's Mother House."

"You want to drag me to a Mass in Canada?"

"A favor for a favor."

"You can be so stubborn sometimes."

"Do I have a deal?"

"All right."

Father Mike said the twelve o'clock Mass.

Ray remained in his pew at the back during the whole service, sitting and standing and kneeling in sync with the worshippers around him.

He spotted Simon Lodwick at the front of the church. He watched him on and off. Saw him sing, head high, chin out, the hymnal in his hand. Saw him bow when the bells rang and the host was lifted high above the priest's head.

Monsignor Becker and two middle-aged parishioners joined Mike for the distribution of Communion. The four of them descended the altar steps, chalices in hand.

Ray flinched when he saw Simon stand. He lowered his head and prayed Lodwick wouldn't take Communion from Mike. And that if he did, Mike wouldn't do anything to make the man suspicious.

Simon moved into the shorter line where a woman was distributing the Eucharist.

Mass ended at five past one.

Ray remained in his pew. The church emptied. He still sat, keeping an eye on his watch. Women appeared from the side aisles and entered the sanctuary. They started clearing the altar of candles and prayer cards and other priestly paraphernalia.

Ray stood, genuflected halfheartedly, and left through a side door. He walked to the rectory and rang the bell. Mike answered. "Hope I'm not late," Ray said, following the priest down a short hall.

Monsignor and Simon Lodwick were seated across from each other at the dining table. Mike took the seat next to Lodwick and Ray the one across from Mike.

Simon asked to say grace. In a sure, deliberate tone, he gave thanks for the food they were about to receive and for the gifts that day might bring.

Ray said a loud amen in his heart.

The housekeeper entered with platters of homemade stuffed cabbage and parsleyed potatoes and string beans. She returned with hot rolls and a tray of pickles and relishes. She poured hot coffee.

The four men dished up hefty helpings.

Without lifting his eyes, Mike asked, "How was your trip to Washington, Ray?"

For the briefest moment, Lodwick paused with his fork in the air. He took the bite of stuffed cabbage and purred with appreciation. Slicing himself another bite, he asked, "Were you there on vacation?"

"Mostly business. Which doesn't mean I didn't enjoy the view." Ray reached for a roll, buttered it.

"Anyone for wine?" asked Monsignor.

"I'd love some," said Simon.

"I think we could all use some," said Mike.

Ray raised a concerned glance in Mike's direction.

Simon brought his wine glass closer to the center of the table and smiled kindly as Monsignor filled it. He took a sip and smiled again in approval. Turning to address Mike, he asked, "When are the sisters due back?"

"Toward the end of the month."

"It's going to be difficult for them. With all that's happened." Simon wiped his mouth with the linen napkin. "At least they know the killer is no longer walking the streets."

"I'm not so sure of that," said Ray.

Monsignor set the bottle down with a loud clink. "What do you mean?" he asked.

"Sorry. Slip of the tongue. I do that sometimes when I get

keyed up about a case."

Mike said, "Are you going to leave us dangling, after making a statement like that?"

Ray looked chagrined. He glanced around the table. "I suppose I could tell you a little more. As long as I know it will stay right here." He studied the food on his plate and said, "There's a possibility that the killer wasn't working alone. But I won't know for sure till Monday."

"I don't understand," said Mike.

Ray answered, "We've identified the dead man. He ran a kennel out of state. An old clipping I found at his place, plus what I learned in Washington, could prove that there is a second man involved. When I get the evidence to the lab on Monday, I'll know for sure. If I'm right, you'll read all about it in Tuesday's paper."

Simon said, "The man found in the swamp—I've never read anything about his motive for killing the sister. Did I miss it?"

"No. Up till now, we had no idea why he shot Theresa. But if my theory is correct, you'll be reading that in the newspapers soon. But that's all I should say."

Mike said, "Simon and I intend to play eighteen holes if it doesn't rain. Why don't you join us, Ray?"

"Wish I could. But the wife's got us going to some relative's wedding upstate."

"Join us for nine holes," said Simon.

"What time are you playing?" asked Ray.

"Five. But we could make it earlier."

"You'd have to make it a lot earlier. The wedding's at eight. And it will take us two hours to get there. And to be truthful, I'm still a little tired from my trip to Washington. So if you don't mind, I'll pass."

At exactly six o'clock, Ray backed the Olds out of the

garage and stopped halfway down the drive.

Kate came out the front door, locked it and cut across the grass. She wore a red silk dress, heels and a pearl necklace. She was carrying a box wrapped in silver paper and decorated with a big blue bow.

Ray shoved open the passenger door. Kate set the gift on the back seat and got in. She turned up the air-conditioning.

They followed Willow Avenue to Fifth Street and made a left. Minutes later, they were on I-75 heading north.

"How far are we going to go?" asked Kate.

"However far an hour takes us."

"I would have thought you'd want to be there when it happens."

"He's not going to try anything before dark."

"Why are you so sure he'll show?"

"How else is he going to get a look at the 'evidence'?"

"Why wouldn't he just run for it?"

"And leave everything behind—dealership, house, everything—without knowing for sure that the evidence would implicate him?"

"I just hope he doesn't set the place on fire to get rid of your imaginary evidence."

"He won't. Not with Trev and Sam there."

At seven, Ray left the freeway, then got back on, going south. They reached Tanglewood around eight and drove to Trev's apartment. They entered with the key Trev had given them.

Ray picked up the phone and dialed their home number. After one ring, he hung up. He dialed again. Trev answered. Ray said, "Anything happening?"

"Nothing. And how come there's no beer in the fridge?"

"You're on a stakeout, not at a party."

"Well, get over here or you'll miss both."

"You left the patio door open?"

"Yeah."

"I'll come in from Pam's yard."

"You know, Sam and I can do this without you."

"The hell you will. This is my baby. I want that son of a bitch bad." Ray hung up. "Sorry," he said to Kate.

"Why? He is a son of a bitch."

"You know how I hate to hear you swear."

"And I hate to think of that guy in our house."

"Me too. But this is all I could come up with in the time we had. Other than tricking him into going out to the Doghouse Kennel, which just happens to be out of my jurisdiction. Besides, that would only put Janice and her daughter in danger."

"I know. We'll fumigate after he's taken away."

"And celebrate."

"And celebrate," said Kate. She put her arms on Ray's shoulders. She eyed his beige suit, white shirt and blue tie with brown stripes. "You're looking very handsome tonight."

"Couldn't let myself be out-dressed by a woman." He touched her pearls. "Too bad I have to change. We could take our celebration to a nightclub."

Kate wrinkled her nose. "I'm more in the mood for an in-home pajama party."

Ray smiled and gave his wife a quick kiss. He grabbed black slacks and a blue shirt from the sofa and headed for the bathroom. A minute later, he came out. Kate handed him a black knit watch cap. "You look perfectly criminal. Don't get stopped on the way, or mistaken for Lodwick."

Ray said, "Sorry you can't come."

"I didn't want to, anyway. It's bad enough knowing he's going to be in our house without seeing him there. Besides, ever since I saw this mess of a place Trev calls home, I've been itching to get at it."

"In your good dress?"

Kate pointed to the wrapped gift. "My change is in there."

"Maybe Trev won't like you messing with his place."

"Messing with his place? Interesting phrase in this setting. Besides, I'm not going to sit all evening in a pigsty. Now get out of here. We both have to do what we have to do."

Ray drove past his house and pulled up the drive two doors down. It was after nine. Pam smiled and Thumper wagged at him from behind the side-door screen. Ray waved but didn't stop. He moved quickly to the back of the house next door. He put on his cap, and pulled the collar of his shirt up around his neck. He could hear the sound of popcorn popping in the neighbor's kitchen, heard his neighbor ask for the salt. He moved on, reached the corner, inched his way to his own patio, and slid open the glass door.

Trev stepped out from the cover of the refrigerator. Ray said, "Where's Sam?"

"Upstairs. Watching the rear of the house from your bedroom. Moon's due up in an hour. Ought to help out."

"You take the front door," whispered Ray.

"I'd rather stay here."

"Would you get going?"

Time passed slowly. A hall clock chimed ten. It chimed eleven. When it chimed twelve, Ray swore loudly enough for the neighbors to hear.

Trev barged into the kitchen with his revolver in hand.

"Put it away," said Ray.

"What's with you?"

"He's not coming."

"How do you figure that?"

"He knew we had a two hour drive there and back. Say we stayed only two hours. We'd be back by midnight."

"I always thought it was a lousy idea," said Trev.

"You always do, when they don't work," snapped Ray. Again he swore.

"Now what?"

"I bet the creep decided to leave town. Get Sam down here."

Ray switched on the counter light. He picked up the phone, dialed, and prayed for the right priest to answer. "Mike. Thank God it's you. Sorry about the hour. But this is important. Did Lodwick play golf today?"

"Yes."

"Did he say or do anything different, strange?"

"He kept asking about you."

"Like what?"

"Like how long you've been on the force. Things like that. Nothing to do with Theresa or the case."

I bet, thought Ray. "Anything else?"

"Yes. We were heading for the tenth tee when he said he was feeling a little tired. So we stopped. He drove me home."

"What time was this?"

"Between seven-thirty and eight. What's happening, Ray?"

"We'll talk tomorrow." Ray hung up.

Trev and Sam came into the kitchen. Ray said, "I bet that clever bastard read our charade. Either that or Mike said something he shouldn't have. I should have made him cancel that golf game."

"What we should have done is pick him up," said Trev.

"Damn, damn, damn." Ray leaned heavily against the counter.

"We could drive over to the airport," said Trev.

Ray said, "Sam, get one of the uniforms to go with you. Check all the flights out since eight. Look for someone paying cash. Tall, mustache, balding. Bags under the eyes. In his sixties. A little on the heavy side."

Sam left.

Ray switched off the light and headed for the front of the house.

Trev lumbered behind. He asked, "Where are we going?"

"Lodwick's. If he's home, we're picking him up."

"Without a warrant?"

Ray pulled a folded paper from his pocket. "I had it ready, just in case this didn't work. Only it means he goes to Washington when we get him."

Ray forced himself to keep to the speed limit. They followed Grand River Avenue to the east end of town and pulled into a subdivision of expensive homes.

"How come you're so sure of where you're going?" asked Trev.

"Once I realized he was our man, I looked up his address and drove over to get a look. Let's just hope the creep's home."

"How do you propose to be sure if he's there or not?"

"Call him from the car phone. See if a light goes on."

"What if it does? Could be the maid or some bimbo he picked up."

"One of us will check out his garage. See if his car is there."

"And if it isn't? Then what?"

"Then it's your turn to come up with an idea."

They found the house. A two-story brick and wood building on a well-landscaped half-acre. Ray parked across the street. He took the car phone and punched in Lodwick's number. The house remained dark. Ray started counting the rings. When they reached twenty, he handed the phone to Trev. "If he answers, hang up. I'm going over to have a peek in his garage."

Trev snatched up the watch cap and handed it to Ray. "With your silver mane and the moon up, Lodwick won't be in jail tonight, we will."

Ray waited for a cloud to pass in front of the moon. He lunged across the street. He darted from tree to bush to tree, thanking each for the cover.

Trev was still holding the phone a few inches from his ear when Ray slipped back behind the wheel. "Hang up. There's no car in the garage."

"Great." Trev slapped the phone onto its cradle. A light went on in the house on their left. "Let's get out of here, Ray."

Ray started the engine and pulled slowly away. Trev watched the lit window and saw a man's face between the curtains. "You better do some evasive driving. Our curious neighbor over there is probably on the phone calling the station."

Ray increased his speed. Back on Grand River, he said, "I could kick myself."

"Get in line."

"Goddammit. Where is he?"

Trev said, "Let's hope he's at the airport and Sam spots him."

"The man's going to need cash," said Ray. "He won't be able to use a credit card or bank funds for a long time."

"And he won't find a bank open in the middle of the night," added Trev.

"He probably kept lots of cash in a safe at home."

"Figures," said Trev.

Suddenly, Ray laughed and slammed his foot down on the accelerator.

Trev barely saved himself from a hard crack on the head. "Good. Get us killed."

"How much do you want to bet he's at the dealership. He's probably filling a van with car parts, anything he can hock, and emptying the safe while he's at it."

They turned onto Church Street. Ray killed the headlights.

The dealership was well lit, inside and out. Ray turned in. He drove slowly across the lot and up to the service entrance. Nothing seemed amiss.

"What kind of a car does he drive?" asked Trev.

"I don't know. Never saw it. Probably a Cadillac."

"Yeah, well, there are only about a hundred around."

"If he's here, he'd have parked close to the building."

"If he's here."

Ray stopped near a line of cars in for service. He whispered, "Let's start feeling hoods. If we find a warm one, he's here."

Ray switched off the dome light. The two men climbed out and quietly closed their doors. Ray headed for one line of cars, and Trev for another. Suddenly Trev jumped as a stone hit close to where he stood. He spun around to find Ray gesturing to him.

The hood of the burgundy Sedan de Ville was warm. Barely, but enough to show that it had been driven recently. Ray squinted in through the windows. The passenger seat and back seat were packed with suitcases and boxes. "You can figure the trunk's full, too," whispered Ray.

"I suggest we get out of sight," said Trev. They moved to the row of cars behind Lodwick's. Trev sat on a rear bumper facing away from the dealership. He said, "I'll watch our rear."

"What the hell for?" whispered Ray.

"So I can sit."

"We'll rotate the sitting," said Ray. He crouched low and fixed his eyes on the service door of the dealership.

The moon appeared for a moment, then vanished behind more clouds. Time dragged. Trev whispered, "Why don't I walk across the street and get us some coffee."

"Get serious."

"I am."

"He's not going to be in there any longer than he has to, Trev."

Several minutes passed. Trev said, "I could have been back by now."

"What the hell is he doing in there?" fumed Ray. "It doesn't take that long to empty a safe. His car is already full. He can't be collecting things to hock."

The answer came in a flash. Ray said, "Oh, shit. I know what he's doing. He's on the damn computer, transferring funds."

"So? He's not going anywhere when he comes out."

Ray stood up. "We have to stop him."

"We will."

"I mean now. If he makes bail in Washington, he'll skip the country and live like a king on the money he's putting in a Swiss account *right now*."

Trev stood. "Okay. But it means breaking in."

"No it doesn't." Ray pointed at some wires overhead. He darted from the line of cars and over to the building. Trev followed. Ray pointed to where the wires fed into a gray box. He yanked his .38 from its holster, braced himself for a good shot, and fired.

There was a flash, sparks, then total darkness.

"Now we wait," said Ray, a smile stretching across his tired features.

They heard the click of a lock, a door opening.

Trev drew his gun.

The steps were hurried. Coming closer.

Ray touched Trev and signaled, *Now*. They sprang out from the cover of the wall, guns raised.

"Hello, Simon," said Ray.

Thirty-four

The Fredricks flew to Ontario on the Friday following the capture and incarceration of Simon Lodwick. They traveled from the airport to Small Falls by taxi, and checked into a local, family-run motel in the middle of town.

Kate set about unpacking the few things they needed for the night. Ray switched on the TV, picked up the remote. He asked, "Are we going to eat out?"

"Let's order room service. You do it. Surprise me."

Ray picked up the receiver. When he'd finished, she said, "Yesterday I asked Molly about their Social Security checks. They get their checks, all right. The money's directly deposited into their bank account. But Molly was hospitalized for her heart condition a while back, and they've set up automatic withdrawals for the whole amount to pay off the hospital bill." Kate shook her head. "Taking obligations seriously is a good thing, but I think Karl's pride helped make their situation worse. I was thinking maybe Homer would like us to settle the hospital account."

"We'll look into it when we get back," said Ray. "And by the way, I found out where Hixson got his raspberry meringue pie. His buddy Lodwick bought such a pie at the church bake sale, which is held once a month after the twelve o'clock Mass. Obviously served him a piece, along with the rest of his last meal and enough booze to get him drunk and ready for his last ride."

"Lodwick was certainly buttering up the parish, wasn't he?" said Kate.

"A real calculating charmer. So charming that the woman who sold it to him has no problem remembering who bought it. A fact that will help us with our case, if and when we get Lodwick back."

"When will he be extradited to Washington?"

"Probably next week. By the way, I got a message to Les Bailey. He called last night after you had gone to bed. I filled him in. If it weren't for the distance, I think he'd have hugged me."

"There's no chance Lodwick could beat both charges, is there, Ray?"

"No. And the more we dig, the more we find. In Lodwick's backyard, near the barbecue, we found toothpicks with traces of Hixson's saliva. Even found dog hairs in Lodwick's car that were identical to some of those found on Hixson's clothes. Plus there was a receiver in the car, and a small transmitting device. Some of the glue he used to fasten it to the nun's car stayed stuck to the undercarriage. And besides all that, the Livingston police have a witness who saw Lodwick near the spot where Hixson's body was found.

"That's another charge he'll have to face. Hixson's murder."

Kate sat on the side of the bed. "So why did he do it?"

"Once Hixson killed Theresa, Lodwick had no more use for him. And Hixson could have been a threat."

"I mean, why did he go after Theresa in Northpointe?"

"He's a sociopath. He has no feelings for people. He saw a woman he felt like having, and set out to take her. I've seen too many of his kind through the years."

"Why was he in Northpointe in the first place?"

"The best we can figure, he and Hixson went there to murder Hixson's half sister. They were probably out of sight at the kennel when Theresa brought her dog in for its rabies shot. No doubt Lodwick decided his own pleasure took priority over eliminating a woman who meant nothing to him.

"Then when things went sour, they took off. They saved the business with the half sister for another time.

"My guess is that Hixson came back on his own a few

months later, and brought a trained attack dog with him. He staged the killing to look like one of the dogs at the kennel had turned on her."

Kate asked, "Why didn't Lodwick go after Theresa himself?"

"Simon Lodwick? Put himself in danger when he could snap his fingers and get his flunky to do it? Besides, if Hixson was with Lodwick at the Hubbards, or simply knew what was happening there, he was an accomplice to the crimes. So Theresa was as much a danger to him as she was to Lodwick."

"Still, you'd have to have a strong hold over a person to get them to kill," said Kate.

"You heard what Janice said. It's my guess that the only constructive attention Hixson ever got growing up was from Lodwick. For lack of anything better to compare it with, it probably seemed to him like love. People do all they can to keep that feeling. It makes the world go around and the world go awry."

"My poet." Kate crossed to where Ray sat and messed his hair. She said, "It's interesting, isn't it? Simon, tripped up by his pride. If he hadn't taken that picture of himself, enlarged and colored and framed it, he would never have been caught."

"You're right." Ray brushed at his hair with his fingers. He said, "You might pick up one of those pies for us next time there's a bake sale."

"You do it, since you're going back to church."

"I only go for special occasions."

"Yes, I know. When it helps you solve a mystery. Well, just think of church as a place that offers some good clues on the mystery of existence."

"My priestess," said Ray. He aimed the remote and changed channels.

Saturday morning, the Fredricks rented a car. Insisting he

knew the way, Ray drove off without asking directions. A half-hour later, they were still on the road. Kate started humming.

"All right. All right. I'm lost."

"Fine with me," said Kate. "I'm enjoying the scenery. And I have no objection to staying an extra day."

"I'm not *that* lost."

Coming down the road from the opposite direction was a man driving a tractor. Ray stopped abreast of the machine, shouted a greeting, and asked if he could direct them to the Mother House of the Sisters of Saint Joseph.

The man turned his head and spat, turned back and pointed in the direction they'd come. "Get yourselves back to the last junction, make a right. Shouldn't be more than a kilometer."

Ray made a U-turn. They both waved as they passed the tractor. The directions were exact. Within minutes they caught sight of the complex. As they drove through the front gate, they found themselves glad to be back.

Ray drove to the building where Mother Jean's office was. Kate said, "She's going to be surprised."

"In more ways than one," said Ray.

"Don't forget what we discussed."

"I know. They're not children. They don't need to have the big bad truth kept from them. I hope you remembered to bring the Hubbard photo."

"I brought several," said Kate. "Mother Jean may want to give one to Sister Charles or Seraphina or one of the others."

They mounted the broad stone steps at the entrance. The double doors were locked. Kate rang. An elderly nun buzzed them in from her seat behind a desk in a large marble lobby. Next to the desk was a walker.

Kate told the nun that they were there to see Mother Jean.

The old nun busily went about pushing buttons on a phone. "We have visitors here for Mother," she said into the receiver.

Almost immediately, they could hear the *click click* of quick steps. Sister Ann greeted the Fredricks by name.

"Mother Jean never mentioned you were coming," she said.

"We thought we'd surprise her," said Kate.

"You'll do that for sure. Only she went out for a walk. Let me send someone to fetch her."

"You don't need to do that. Just point us. We'll find her."

Sister Ann walked with them out the door and around to the rear of the building. In the distance, close to the cemetery, a small figure sat on a bench.

The Fredricks started down the long path.

Mother Jean's back was to them, her head bowed. The bench where she sat was on a patch of grass just outside the circle of gravestones.

Kate cleared her throat as they neared. Mother Jean turned. A warm smile brightened her tired eyes. She made a movement to stand. Kate hurried forward, telling her not to bother.

"What a surprise," she said, clasping Kate's hand warmly.

On the nun's lap lay an open notebook.

"I hope we're not disturbing you," said Kate.

"Never." The old nun brought the pages of the book together and set it aside.

Ray said, "That looks familiar."

Mother passed a hand over the faded black cover. "It belonged to Theresa. Yavonne thinks we should publish it."

"Is it a diary?" asked Ray, regarding the book with his detective's eye.

"No. Just thoughts and ideas she collected over the years. Some verses. Much of it is very revealing. I had no idea Theresa was so tormented in her early years."

Ray and Kate exchanged glances.

"Maybe what we came to say will explain why," said Ray.

Mother Jean's humped shoulders rose and fell in a sigh.

Ray said, "It's all right, if you'd rather we didn't tell you."

"No. It's not that. It's..." The nun's gaze moved to a freshly dug grave next to one nearly as recent. She said, "Sister Charles died. We buried her yesterday."

Kate sat next to Mother Jean. "I'm sorry."

"It was time. But it's still a loss." The nun smiled through tear-filled eyes. "The day before Charles died, I went to see her and she said, 'You keep wearing yourself out with visiting me, I'll be the one going to your funeral. And that would make me very angry.' The next day I didn't go. That night she died."

Tears ran down the old nun's cheeks. She took out a handkerchief and wiped them away.

Kate said, "We can talk about this tomorrow. We thought we'd come for Mass anyway, if that's all right."

"That would be wonderful. I'll tell Gabbie. She'll want to make you a special breakfast." Mother Jean straightened. She slid to the end of the bench, made Ray take a seat next to her, and said, "Whatever it is you found out, I'd rather you tell me now."

Ray spoke for over a quarter of an hour. He told of their trip to Northpointe, of the Hubbards and the tragedy that befell the family. He told her of Janice and her daughter, and of Lodwick and his capture. He spoke quietly and quickly, not lingering on any one point.

Mother Jean listened with her eyes closed. She was leaning forward, one hand on her cane, the other holding tightly the notebook on her lap.

Ray finished. The three of them sat in silence. From the distance they could hear the faint hum of a plane. Nearby, ducks quacked and splashed.

Mother Jean leaned her cane against the edge of the bench. She reached down and plucked a tiny wildflower hidden in the grass. She regarded it with affection, turning it gently between her fingers. "In her notebook, Theresa wrote that flowers reminded her of beauty and order. And that perhaps that was their work here on earth. To bring hearts back to that which is healing."

A smile played over her wrinkled features. She opened the notebook. "May I read you something Theresa wrote around the time she went to Tanglewood?"

The Fredricks waited.

The nun's thin, bony fingers turned the pages one by one. She leaned close to the handwritten script and spoke clearly:

> Sing for me, said the Master.
> I can't, said the man, I'm too sad.
>> Then the Master touched the man's elbow
>> And laughter came alive.
> Now can you sing? asked the Master.
> No, for I'm bored, said the man.
>> And the Master touched his home
>> And color was born.
> And when the man said he was troubled
> The Master made beauty.
>> Or cold or hot
>> And the sun and breeze took shape.
>
> Then the man looked up at the Master.
> For my weakness, what can you do? he asked.
>> The Master smiled.
>> He laid his hand on the man's heart
>> And made him a friend.
>> And man sang his first song.

The old nun slipped the flower between the pages of the book. She took Kate's hand, then Ray's. "You've been good friends," she said. "To Theresa and to all of us. May you never lose the song that you've helped to bring to us."